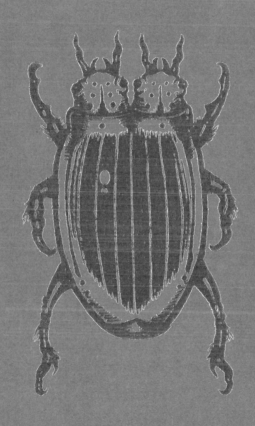

Día

de

los Muertos

Also by Kent Harrington

Dark Ride (1996)

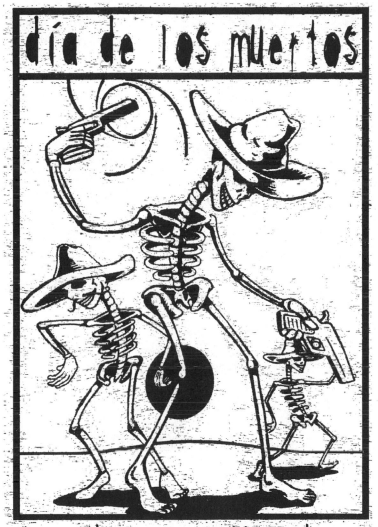

día de los muertos

kent harrington

19 97

FIRST EDITION
Published December 1997

Dustjacket and interior artwork
by Scott Musgrove

ISBN 0-939767-30-9

Dennis McMillan Publications
1581 N. Debra Sue Place
Tucson, Arizona 85715
http://www.booksellers.com/dmp

For my friends:
Shelly MacArthur
Maggie Griffin
Patrick Millikin

Día de los Muertos

And whoever walks a mile full of false sympathy
walks to the funeral of the human race.

— D.H. Lawrence

Volver Volver (Mexican folk song)

Éste amor apasionado
anda todo alborotado
por volver

Voy camino a la locura
y aunque todo me tortura
sé querer

Nos dejamos hace tiempo
pero se llego el momento de perder

Tú tenías mucho razón
me hago caso al corazón
y me muero por volver

ONE
Tijuana, Mexico / November 1 — 2:00 P.M.

It was Tijuana's knack at getting back at you that worried Calhoun. Looking like a sun-savvy reptile in his chic, wraparound dark glasses, Vincent Calhoun stepped off the curb into the traffic that circled the central plaza; immediately, car horns began to blare and brakes slammed. Calhoun shot his hands up, signaling halt. The drivers saw a big American in a foreign legion-style hat and white summer suit. Calhoun crossed in front of them, ignoring the barrage of ugly looks from the drivers. Somehow, the drivers knew they didn't want to fuck with him. There were people in Tijuana you just didn't want to fool with. The ones who looked like Calhoun—the players, the reptiles from the desert—you stayed away from.

Once inside the cool ring of shade that bordered the plaza, Calhoun heard the offers for the city's most popular products from its front line businessmen. "Pussy, pot or pills . . . Got some *young* pussy, brother . . . She'll suck your dick till you think you're dead," a kid sitting on a bench, the shade darkening his face, said to him. Calhoun left the offer behind him, crossing into the open stretch of plaza, the no-man's land of pavers and sunlight. The heat was penetrating, alive, walking next to him like a madman. It radiated off the stark white concrete. He could feel it through his shoes, as if he were barefoot on a beach. He realized for the first time that there was something absolutely cruel and quintessentially Indian

1

about the plaza, the sheer enormity of the space cut from the heart of the city, ceremonial. It conjured up human sacrifice. *Maybe the city was really still Toltec,* he thought. Workmen were hanging bunting and lights on the plaza's bandstand in preparation for the upcoming holiday.

At the other side of the plaza Calhoun stopped at a kiosk on the corner and bought the *Diario de la Sierra,* which gave race schedules and odds at Caliente. The paper's front page shouted **Police Search City For Frank Guzman** in a banner headline.

"When were you born?" Calhoun asked the newspaper vendor, peering at him inside the messy interior of the kiosk. The man looked at him from his shell of clapboard, the only bit of shade on the noisy street. The vendor saw the big white man looking at him. A spotless white cotton suit. The ball of sun caught in the yellow tint of his dark glasses.

"*¿Cómo . . . ?*" The man's face was framed by girlie magazines, girls in short shorts with big asses. A municipal bus roared by the kiosk, leaving the street behind it showered with black exhaust.

"Amigo . . . what day were you born?" Calhoun repeated the question over the grinding of the bus engine. He tried to smile but it was hard. "I need a lucky number," he explained. "For the races."

"On the day they ripped Jesus Christ down from his cross to get at his wallet," the man said and laughed. He pounded the counter for emphasis, thinking it was funny.

Calhoun made his way down the sidewalk toward the Playa Azul. He knew suddenly that Tijuana had won. That nothing he could do would restore his luck. He'd exhausted his *suerte*—his good fortune. It was obvious. It was over. Everyone gets so much *suerte* and that's it. His was finished, used up.

In the restaurant Playa Azul he took a clean handkerchief out of his suit pocket and wiped down his face. Today the heavy canvas havelock he wore hadn't been enough protection from the heat. Even through the clean starched handkerchief his face felt wet and dirty. He pulled it away. It was soaked and he was worried. *Nothing wrong,* he told himself. *Nothing wrong at all. No past, only future.*

. . .

"It's time to pay up." Slaughter smiled at him in a friendly way. The young Englishman had a Stars and Bars do-rag tied around his head like an already-dated grunge band singer. He pushed his hair off his unctuous face. There was something in the Englishman's countenance that was evil, the cold, psychotic variety of evil that is shockingly pedestrian in Tijuana.

The restaurant was crowded. The air conditioning made it almost cold. Brightly colored *gallardetes,* paper pennants, hung in rows from the ceiling. You could hear them rustling, blown by the air conditioning. Calhoun had chosen the Playa Azul because it was the only restaurant that he could stand to be in during the heat. It was like a refrigerator. Calhoun kept his sunglasses on and everything was tinted yellow by his Vuarnets—the Englishman's face, the blue linoleum floor, the murals of idyllic *jalapas* on a beach painted on the wall. The restaurant was full of tradespeople, no tourists, just businessmen, talking against the white, clean walls.

"I want a steak and French-fried potatoes. Can you do that for me, dear? No cilantro," Slaughter told the waitress. The rich golden tones of his middle class English voice were commanding and superior. He'd been to Oxford.

"It's a fish place," Calhoun said. He didn't know why he'd said it. Slaughter turned to look at him, pushed the do-rag

3

higher on his forehead. He wore a soiled yellow *guayabara* shirt. Without realizing it, Slaughter had gone to seed. All the money he was making in the rackets didn't seem to matter—it was as if Tijuana was infecting him and he couldn't stop it. He'd gone completely native in that peculiar English way.

"Is it really?" Slaughter said. "There's no such thing in Mexico. It's either frijoles and meat or frijoles and chicken." He laughed at his own joke. Like most of the foreigners in the city who had gone native, he relished hating things Mexican.

"And for you, *Señor?*" the waitress asked. Calhoun looked at the assorted bottles of condiments on the table. He saw there was a fly in the sugar container. For a moment, with the fever, he seemed to see every conceivable detail: the thickness of the glass, the particles of sugar, the colors of the dead fly. He wondered how the fly could have possibly managed to get inside the jar. He picked it up and handed it to the girl.

"A mineral water," Calhoun said.

"How much money?" Calhoun asked. Slaughter dragged out his Day Planner, lifted the cover and thumbed through its well-worn pages. Calhoun picked up the glass of ice water and put it to his forehead. There was the sweet smell of tortillas and hot grease in the air. Slaughter stopped, found the page he was looking for and stabbed it with his index finger.

"Two hundred twenty-eight thousand pesos. I want it by tomorrow," Slaughter said. He closed the book.

"How about next week?" Calhoun touched the sweating glass to his cheeks, first one, then the other. It felt wonderful. The waitress came back with his mineral water. She put it down and, with it, a fresh sugar dispenser.

"I don't know how they get in the bottles," the girl said in Spanish apologetically. "We do everything we can and they still get in." Calhoun nodded.

"Forget it," Calhoun said. *"Olvídalo."*

"I have an offer . . . a job offer," Slaughter said when she left. "Do it and I will cancel your debt. The whole thing."

Calhoun lifted the mineral water and drank, emptying it in several swallows. Some of it ran down his chin. With the fever, no amount of liquid seemed to be enough. Calhoun put down the empty bottle and wiped his face with a paper napkin. He tried to act like there was nothing wrong. That he wasn't sick.

"What did you say . . . ?" Calhoun looked at the Englishman. He was suddenly seeing two faces, two do-rags, two sets of blue eyes, two sets of girlish Jagger-style lips. Someone fed the juke box behind them. *Volver, Volver* came on loud, adding another layer to the cacophony and hubbub in the room. Calhoun glanced at the street outside. The world looked cockeyed, as if it were bent.

"Say that again," Calhoun said. He tried to get control of himself.

"I said I will forgive your debt, old boy," Slaughter said. Calhoun put one of his big hands on the table and forced himself to focus.

"Why would you do that? You're an asshole."

"Because there's something I want you to do for me." Slaughter ignored the insult.

"What? Tell your mother what an asshole you are?"

"I want you to cross Frank Guzman. He's in Tijuana and he needs to get across the wire. I think you are the only coyote that can do it," Slaughter said. Calhoun was gaining on the spinning world, it was slowing. He laid another palm on the table and it all suddenly stopped.

5

"Frank Guzman? You want me to kill Frank Guzman?" Calhoun said.

"No . . . *cross* Guzman."

"Cross Frank Guzman? You *are* an asshole."

"If you do that, you can forget what you owe me," Slaughter said. Calhoun smiled. "I thought you would like that." Slaughter reached over and slapped Calhoun on the shoulder. He hit the forty-five under Calhoun's jacket.

"That's suicide," Calhoun said. "Only a prick would ask someone to do that."

"That's the deal. As you Yanks put it, take it or leave it."

"That's like the deal you guys gave the Fuzzy-Wuzzies."

"What?"

"The Fuzzy-Wuzzies, you stupid prick," Calhoun said. He saluted in the English manner palm out. "The battle of Omdurman? . . . Kitchener? . . . Suicide, asshole!" He was in control again. That was the way the fever attacked, suddenly, and then left you just as suddenly.

"What the hell are you talking about?" Slaughter asked. "Are you out of your fucking mind?" Calhoun ignored him.

"Anyway . . . no problem about the money. I'll have it all for you tomorrow," Calhoun said. It was a bald-faced lie and he enjoyed it. *If you're going to lie, tell big ones,* he thought. Calhoun stood up. "Enjoy the steak. But you should have ordered fish here."

"Just get me the bloody money by tomorrow then," Slaughter said.

Calhoun walked to the back of the restaurant and closed the thin door to the men's room. He looked at himself in the mirror. It was warmer here. He took his havelock off and wet his face in the dirty sink, then the back of his neck. He let the water drip down under his collar. When he looked up there was a bathroom attendant, a man his age, sitting on a bench

6

in the back staring at him. Calhoun smiled. It was something about Mexico he never got used to: bathroom attendants.

"He thinks I'm a fucking Zulu," Calhoun said looking into the mirror, his face dripping wet. The attendant stared back at him and then smiled, thinking Calhoun was drunk. Calhoun dropped ten pesos in the box and left.

On the way out Calhoun heard his name called. He looked across the restaurant. A Mexican was waving to him from one of the tables, Miguel Cienfuegos, a dog trainer he knew from Caliente. Calhoun went to his table and sat down. Cienfuegos was a short brown bullet of a man, very dark. He always seemed to be hiding from someone, or at least looked that way. Even when he was eating.

"I have something for you," Miguel said. "I told you I'd have something for you one day. I've been looking for you." Calhoun nodded. "Today is your lucky day, amigo," the trainer said. He leaned forward conspiratorially. "Tomorrow at Caliente. Everything you can get your hands on. I want you to put it on 99 in the second race. Vincente—*99 cannot lose, I promise you.*"

"You're sure?"

"Vincente. I owe you a favor. I wouldn't fuck with you." Calhoun started to laugh. In part it was the fever that had him a little off and in part it was the sudden rush of excitement. "What's so funny?" Miguel said. He looked closely at the big white man with the havelock and dark sunglasses, his spotless white Tommy Hilfiger suit, just a white T-shirt underneath. He didn't seem well. The way he was laughing, there was something wrong with it. Calhoun's handsome face glistened with sweat and water.

"I thought I'd run out of luck," Calhoun said, trying to explain. He stopped laughing and leaned in across the table, pushing beer bottles out of his way. Cienfuegos thought how big he was then. Huge. "But you see, every time I think that . . . *every goddamn time*–I'm always wrong. Now that's good fucking *suerte,*" Calhoun said.

• • •

The theater's new marquee advertised Jane Austen's *Sense and Sensibility.* Calhoun thought it was a good joke because both were so lacking in Tijuana. The truth was it didn't matter to Calhoun what was playing. (He'd told the taxi driver to find the closest movie theater with air conditioning.) In fact, the most banal Mexican movies were sometimes the best, the most relaxing. Calhoun simply hated the city's endless stifling afternoons. Once he was seated in the dark of the theater, things became oddly quiet despite the noise of "entertainment." It was a perfect place to hide. The perfect place for surcease. The perfect place to be still and let darkness rescue him. He could hear his heartbeat, or at least feel it. Feel the ignorant life in him–beat after beat. *I'm alive . . . I'm alive . . . I'm alive.*

Calhoun watched the English countryside unfold on the screen, watched Emma Thompson's huge pleasing face and bosomy décolletage. His uncomfortable sense of being too alive was gradually forgotten and finally swept away by the well-metered voices of the actors who had never smelled Mexico or broken the law or fired a shot in anger.

An hour into the movie Calhoun's cell phone rang and, reluctantly, he took the call in the dark. He listened to the voice on the other end. He agreed to meet the caller later at the Escondido and hung up. For a few minutes he was actually happy and emotionally empty. Happy because he knew that, outside, what he dreaded the most, the raw afternoon, was being killed off, its energy drained. He knew that when he returned to the streets it would be safe. It was as if the afternoon was a Titan monster walking the streets looking just for him.

At 5 P.M. Calhoun left the theater. He was pleased with the movie's unreal ending. The familiar Austen claptrap went down well. Like everyone else, he wanted to believe in miracles and beautiful endings. The air in the new shopping mall was cold and artificially clean. It smelled slightly of Lysol and popcorn. Middle class Mexican families seemed happy with their Kmart purchases and their frozen yogurts, their brief vacation from the grim streets. Calhoun pushed open the double doors of the ersatz America and joined the countless people on the sidewalk.

On the Avenida Dolores, the air was dirty and warm, and Calhoun felt as if a filthy rag had been thrown in his face. An ugly crepuscular light turned everyone on the street into either a devil or moron. The red light seemed to capture everything miserable and missed the human. Disappointed, Calhoun realized that the afternoon wasn't dead. It hung on. Like an old man, it kept breathing, grasping at the corners of buildings, on roof tops, afraid to let go and die.

The peso had crashed two months before. Money and wealth had been vaporized. All the cities along the border were hysterical and on the verge of bankruptcy. It was that very male hysteria that nations and middle managers get in crisis. They get very quiet and brutish just before they explode with testosterone and blood, and mindless things happen, none of them good. But that afternoon it was still quiet on the eve of the holiday, *Dia de los Muertos,* Mexico's second biggest and the most celebrated of its pagan holidays. A day when everything Spanish and everything Indian fight for control one more time.

At the corner of Benito Juarez and Revolución, Calhoun stopped in front of a shop window. There was a Frida Kahlo print he'd admired for days, a cheap reproduction of *Henry Ford Hospital.* Even behind warm dirty glass it was startling, no matter how many times he'd seen it; a self-portrait with medical tubes. Like the woman in the painting, Calhoun felt as if he, too, had tubes and rubber hoses coming out of him. Tubes taking his humanity and exchanging it for something else, pumping diesel exhaust and cold blood back into him.

Inside the shop tourists glided by the painting, pausing for a moment on the verge of trying to understand Kahlo, then giving up and moving on. His shorts-wearing countrymen, Calhoun knew, had a taste for simpler mementos: the awful German helmets made of plaster, black with "cool" little hand-painted white swastikas. (What was it they liked *exactly*–the Nazis or their regalia?) The helmets were popular. On the spur of the moment, Calhoun went into the shop and bought the poster. He had no proper place to hang it. No one to send it to. He had had no wife or children, no real friends. (Perhaps *they* could have cured his fear of afternoons. But he knew without consciously thinking it, that his days for that kind of friendship were over. He was in too much trouble, after all.) Once it was wrapped and tied, Calhoun took the poster back out onto the busy street.

Calhoun walked on toward the plaza Tijuana, the light changing every moment, a dismantling of daylight. He reached inside his jacket and checked his shoulder harness, lifting it for a moment off his shoulders as he walked, feeling the weight of the forty-five, and the wetness it made on his T-shirt. His illness was making him sweat and the harness felt uncomfortable and tight-fitting. He stopped and tried to adjust it. Music poured out from a bar. *You wanted it all, You wanted it all . . . And there's nothing at all . . . Nothing at all.* He looked at himself caught in the reflection of the window for a moment—*we aren't what we tell ourselves,* he thought, looking, then went on.

After going to the moon and producing Adolph Hitler and the drive-in liquor store, the Smart Bomb, Infomercials and the Hollywood Freeway, the Working Poor, Infibulation, and her final masterpiece, the Folksy Billionaire, the Twentieth Century was tired. She found a city that was equally exhausted, equally worn out and tired of promises of any kind. Home of the desperate and the weak. This was it: the end of the line. The US-Mexican border. The great scrabble of progress was ending here, Calhoun thought, despite himself. He caught a glimpse of the plaza below: *Liberté, Égalité, Fraternité, my ass.* It was finally getting dark. He was thankful for that at least.

TWO
Tijuana, Mexico / November 1 — 5:30 P.M.

The lights strung in the trees made the plaza seem lush and Mediterranean and special that night. In the daylight it was strictly a border town plaza—very ugly and too big, full of bums and cripples. The plaza was the old Tijuana, something left of the desert town it had once been. A mariachi band was playing on the bandstand—the music traditional, a lot of bullfight music and *rancheras*. The celebration of the holiday had started in earnest now. The poor who could afford nothing else came to the plaza to celebrate with the free music and bottles of cheap *aguardiente*.

There was a group of *milicias* in the crowd, maybe ten or fifteen men. The PFN—*Partido Fascista Nacional*. The men wore cowboy hats and armbands with the party symbol: clustered arrows and a yoke. The letters PFN had sprung up on walls all over the city since the collapse of the peso. What had been an obscure party was growing. They were in the plaza looking for converts. The PFN hated foreigners, they blamed foreigners and Jews and gangsters like Calhoun for the collapse of the peso and everything else that was wrong with the country. They were the analog of the American militias. Calhoun made a point of walking by them on the way across the plaza. He stopped in front of the gang and lit a cigarette, then he smiled at them for the fun of it.

"How you fellows doing tonight?" Calhoun said. The men glared at him. "No chance I could join, is there?"

"*Cabrón*," one of them said and spit on the ground.

13

• • •

"How'd you do?" Calhoun asked over the music. Miguel Castro was a tall, well-built man in a bicycle racer's uniform sitting at one of the roped-off sidewalk cafe tables at the Bar Escondido across from the plaza. The short brim of Castro's racing cap was turned up rakishly. The bright colors of his racing uniform, yellow and red, were the colors of the police team. Castro had ridden that day in the annual Ensenada-Tijuana race, part of the holiday festivities.

"Fourth . . . Fourth place." Castro was drinking a Tecate. A waiter trotted up to the table. Calhoun was a regular at the Escondido and got good service because of it. He ordered a Bohemia. The bar's terrace was full, the crowd much more elegant than the one in the plaza.

"There was wind all the fucking way past La Bufadora. I'm getting too old for racing," Castro said. "The younger riders take more chances."

"You came in fourth . . . that's good. Are you going to the track with us?" Calhoun asked.

"No." Calhoun saw El Moro inside the bar and nodded his head. The bullfighter motioned them to come in. "El Moro is drunk," Castro said turning around and waving back. "I have a busy day for us tomorrow. Two crossings, maybe three. Slaughter's Chinese in the morning . . . "

"That's crazy," Calhoun said. "Three crossings is too much."

"Vincente, stop worrying." Castro's tone was insouciant. He was a captain in the *judicales* and they were used to getting away with murder.

"It's too much," Calhoun said. "That's too many crossings in one day."

"It's Day of the Dead tomorrow, amigo. The U.S. side will be busy with tourists. The U.S. Customs people will put more people up on the freeways," Castro said. "We should do as much business as we can tomorrow."

Calhoun's beer came. The waiter nodded, put it down in front of him, said it was already paid for by someone inside. Calhoun poured the beer into his glass. The music across the plaza changed again to a Selena tune played over the loud speakers; they had switched to recorded music.

"I love Selena," Castro said. "I would have liked to have seen her live . . . Breen is in the bar, too," Castro said. "He's looking strange. He asked for you. I heard him ask the bartender if you had been around. He doesn't act like a policeman."

"He's a homosexual," Calhoun said. He didn't know why he said it that way. He didn't hold it against his partner. But he'd just found out and it had surprised him.

"In Mexico that's like saying someone died," Castro said.

"He's a good partner," Calhoun said. "A good policeman."

"He isn't crooked like you, though," Castro said. He finished the rest of the beer. "I have a date . . . Miss *Día de los Muertos.*"

"There's a Miss Day of the Dead?"

"Of course," Castro said. "Her father owns every *tortillerría* in the city. I want to marry her." Castro winked and got up. "Tomorrow morning then."

"You got us too much for tomorrow, Miguel." A chill went through Calhoun's body from the fever. He smiled as it went through him.

"Stop worrying, amigo. You sound like an old lady. *Hasta mañana.*"

"What time?" Calhoun said.

"Six A.M. tomorrow, at the station." He grabbed the seat of his bicycle, an expensive blue Cannondale, and steered it around their table. The click of the gears was pleasant sounding. "I'm riding to her house and changing there," Castro said. "I want her to see my ass in these pants."

Calhoun laughed.

"It's irresistible, I know," Castro said. Castro picked up the bike and swung it onto the sidewalk, then onto the Avenida Revolución. He pushed off into the traffic, his long legs making short work of it. Breen had been waiting for him to leave. Calhoun's partner stepped out of the bar's double doors and came over to the table on the sidewalk.

"Who was that?"

"I don't know. Some bicycle racer," Calhoun lied. "He said he just won a race. They had some kind of race today."

"You haven't been in the office in two days. I can't keep covering for you . . . I'm running out of excuses . . . "

"I've been sick," Calhoun said. He drank the rest of his beer in a few swallows, hoping that Breen would get the message that he wasn't interested in working or talking.

"Listen, Vincent, the DEA already has a bad reputation here. If we . . . "

"Max . . . I've been sick. And fuck the DEA, okay? We're partners, right?"

"Right."

"We're working in a foreign country where half the government is selling drugs to the other half and no one gives a shit, right?"

"Right."

"Well then, let's take advantage of it. *Nobody gives a shit what we do here*," he said, putting his hands on the table. "That includes Washington."

" . . . I'm thinking of leaving . . . quitting," Breen said. Calhoun looked at him, not really surprised. Breen was very thin. He was wearing blue jeans and a T-shirt and could have been a tourist. He looked straight. Nothing swishy about him.

16

But there were temptations. *Anyone would have succumbed here, in this town, of all places,* Calhoun thought. It was sexually corrosive. You could buy anything for a dollar and a half three blocks from where they sat. *Anything.*

"Look, Max, the country is falling apart. Look . . . look at them. Everyone is broke. Everyone is getting drunk. I suggest we not take it too seriously. What you should do is consider this as a kind of vacation."

"You didn't hear what I said," Breen said. Calhoun understood for the first time that Breen was an honest man, *that he cared despite everything.*

"Yes, I heard . . . You can't leave because then I wouldn't have a partner. They'll give me some gung-ho kid with a crew cut and then what? I'd have to actually do something."

Breen looked out at the crowds on the plaza. The music had changed again. There was something going on inside Breen. Calhoun watched him. You could tell when Breen was upset, his face got slightly pinched. He liked Breen, but they were too different to really understand each other. When Calhoun heard that he was a homosexual, he'd pulled away. They were friends still, but not pals now. Calhoun had a prejudice, he didn't like it, but it was a fact. He'd been brought up that way. He'd been taught to think that homosexuals were dirty faggots, period, end of story.

"What's happened to you?" Breen asked, looking at him. He had clear blue eyes. He was younger than Calhoun, only twenty-eight or so. He rolled a wet beer between his hands.

"Nothing's happened to me," Calhoun said. "Maybe I got smart."

Breen looked away again. "It's a dirty town . . . Everyone is dirty. I don't like anything about it. I don't like the food. I don't like any of it. It makes me sick," Breen said. *Mira como ando me amor . . . Tu solo tu.* The Selena tune broke through the noise of the crowds.

For a moment Calhoun said nothing. He looked away. The silence built. He wanted to make it clear that he couldn't answer. He wanted it clear that Breen's personal problems were of no interest to him. It was the only way he knew of doing it.

"Want to come to the track with us?" Calhoun asked finally.

"No, thanks." Breen turned around and looked into the bright yellow lights of the Escondido. Calhoun's friends were waiting for him. He stood up. Nothing was working between them, not even conversation now.

"I'll see you later then," Breen said.

"Yeah," Calhoun answered. "Later." He watched Breen work through the tables and called to him suddenly.

"Max."

"Yeah," Breen turned around.

"Max, for fuck sake, take it easy, will you?"

• • •

Calhoun's party, all Mexicans except Calhoun, were on their way out to the dog races at Caliente. Nobody was feeling any pain. There were two bullfighters and two millionaires and Calhoun—a DEA agent and smuggler of human beings for money. All of them were gamblers.

The Escondido was one of their places and the men acted like they owned it. They spoke in loud voices; they had their orders for *tapas* and drinks filled quickly, the bill chalked on their table, by the waiter. The men always got the same table, one of the best, closest to the door with a view of the plaza. Tourists who came in were ushered to the back by the restroom and got bad service or were ignored completely. In the evenings the front tables were reserved for the city's high rollers: bullfighters, Mexican movie people, gangsters, and the business elite.

"Come here," El Moro said to a girl.

El Moro told the Yaqui girl he wanted her to read Calhoun's future. The young girl looked at the men and nodded, glad to get away from the tourists who were afraid of her because she wasn't wearing shoes. El Moro pushed Calhoun toward her and made a joke about him needing to change his luck and soon. Calhoun bumped up against her. He could feel her strong girlness through her dress.

She wore what passed for glamorous among the poor in Tijuana—a black cotton beach dress with big white orchids. The dress was meant as a beach wrap for tourist girls. It was wrapped tight. She wasn't wearing a bra and she had a good figure. Her eyes were big and dark and serious. Like most Yaqui girls, she was slender in the hips and wore her hair long; she wore no make-up and didn't bathe, so that she smelled slightly of the day's heat, which had been considerable. Her hair looked like a dark wet midnight in March. He imagined what she might look like without the beach dress. El Moro came up behind him and said something about how you hadn't made love unless you'd done it with a Yaqui girl out in the desert. Calhoun could feel the bullfighter's heavy brandy-smelling breath, his overbearingness, his friendship, his disorder, all of it. All the things that made him capable of throwing himself at the bull. Calhoun thought he was probably right. He looked at the girl's bare feet. Unlike the tourists, he was intrigued.

"The gringo needs your help," El Moro said. The girl asked Calhoun his name in Spanish.

19

"Vincent Calhoun," he told her, saying it like he was a movie star and bowing slightly. There was laughter from the other men.

"Come on, tell us his fortune," El Moro said.

The girl began to lay down her tarot cards. The men got quiet and you could hear the tarot cards go down one after another, with a plastic slap, one after the other on the dark, drink-wet table top. She put them down quickly and in a line. There was something about Mexico in the Escondido then, in the air itself that smelled of diesel and border scent. Something that went way back and was combustible and dangerous.

When she had fourteen cards out the girl looked at Calhoun. She reached for the first card and began to turn it over. El Moro nudged Calhoun. *"Sólo toros y mujers y espadas,"* he said in his deep voice. *"Sólo toros y mujeres y espadas,"* he said again, *only bulls and women and swords,* as if that were the answer to all men's problems.

The girl reached for the first card. No one said a word because the first card, the Mexicans say, is the most important. It is your destiny card. The first card came up and stopped her. It was the death card. Even for a street girl, she seemed surprised. His companions hooted because they loved the death card. El Moro slapped Calhoun on the back as if he'd won a prize. It was the macho card, and for bullfighters good luck . . . but Calhoun wasn't a bullfighter.

The girl crossed herself twice quickly. Calhoun laughed, spilling some of his drink on his T-shirt as he did. He felt the alcohol on his skin. He looked at the girl again, then at the card.

El Moro told the girl that was enough. One of the millionaires took out a ten thousand peso note and laid it over the card. Then someone else did the same and another and another. It was customary when the death card came up to hide it with cash money. In a moment the men had covered all the cards in dirty peso notes until you couldn't see them any more. Then El Moro took a switchblade out and planted it an inch into the table through the pile of cards and money, and they left.

THREE
The Border / November 1 — 11:00 P.M.

Tijuana is worse at night, sinister. Paloma Vasco liked the tawdry, salacious feel. Going back into Tijuana was like putting on crotchless panties. The sight of the foreign town across the bridge made her feel like doing nasty things, not giving a shit about anything. She was kind of a sexual vacuum cleaner and right now the motor was on. She was like a fat man looking forward to that next big meal. Her lover was in for a workout. She started walking more quickly just thinking about it. Tall and very young, a Latin Vargas girl, the lights on the skywalk caught her perfectly, how tall she was. Even under the shiny black raincoat, you saw she was all thighs and calves and that her ass would make men see stars and give up their wives. She didn't need a push-up bra.

Vasco was in a hurry. She passed by U.S. Customs and started across the skywalk that led into Mexico. People's faces coming the other way were distorted by the bright halogen lights that lit the bridge. There was a raucous, gritty feel to the crowd. Her black plastic raincoat reflected the light like a black mirror. She stood out taller than most of the men. There was a carnival atmosphere as if they were all going to a circus instead of a different country. Every face she passed, brown or white, was garish, compelling, illuminant, greasy-looking, its ethnicity magnified and slightly bent somehow, like faces in a fun house mirror. She loved crossing at night. She loved catching those locked-up looks she got from the men. She was very aware of her effect on them.

23

At the middle of the bridge, Indian women begged, dark little sirens, sloe-eyed and wretched. They caught Vasco by her coat, held her and begged for money, imploring. Vasco laughed and pulled away unafraid. There was a moment when her beautiful midriff was exposed. She threw a handful of change over her shoulder, the coins rolling under the feet of the crowd.

At the end of the bridge she descended the long series of steps. She was pushing past the slower pedestrians now, her knees exposed, pumping, moving quickly. Her boots made noise on the concrete stairs. The crowd and she entered the *chiaroscuro* of portals and ominous shadows and ugly smells as you come off the bridge. She could hear the sound of hundreds of footsteps. Then, just as suddenly, at the bottom, everything changed and she was thrust into Mexico. A fleet of waxy yellow taxis shone in the night light, scores of them, like metallic beetles. The first impression, the one the first-timers in the crowd never forgot, was that of a riveting chaos, as if the population of Mexico was still fleeing the conquest and had all taken taxis to the border. She headed for a taxi.

Vasco told the driver to take her to the Hotel Española. They pulled through the taxi stand, which was lit like daylight at midnight. The driver looked at her several times in the mirror; something about Vasco's face told her story. Something about where she'd come from and what she'd been doing still clung to her. When you'd seen the things she had, you play them back on your face without meaning to. The taxi driver saw a rich Latin girl. Maybe it was the black cherry lipstick, or the almost savage quality in her green eyes. The driver looked up into the mirror and for a moment he thought the *Malinche*—a female evil spirit—had climbed into his cab.

"What's going on?" she asked him in Spanish. Vasco was looking out at the crowds on the streets. There was a party atmosphere she hadn't seen before in Tijuana. *"¿Qué pasa?"*

"Fiesta mañana," the driver said. He looked at the girl again. Her dark, full lips, the black shiny raincoat catching all the lights as they drove down the Avenida Benito Juarez.

"Fiesta. Yeah? . . . Cool," she said in English.

Vasco lit a cigarette. Her coat had come open. The taxi driver took the opportunity to stare at the girl's exposed skin, the brown marble of her waist. She was wearing black stretch pants and a black workout halter top. There was something inside of her that was screaming. It was on her fresh face, the excitement that rages in some young women, the ones with too much sexual energy for their own good.

"What's it about?" Vasco asked. She was Chilean and Mexico was foreign to her.

"Día de los Muertos," the driver said.

"Day of the Dead," she said in English.

"For many it's good luck," the driver added.

"And for the other bastards?" Vasco asked.

FOUR
Sunrise — Day of the Dead

ay of the Dead, Calhoun told himself. *So what.* Calhoun unwrapped the traditional holiday candy he'd bought the night before at the race track. A black licorice figure with its skeleton superimposed in white. He threw the candy into his mouth and bit it in two. *So what,* he thought. *Another day, another peso.*

It had rained hard the night before. The violence of the storm had been translated into frustrated, noisy sex at a place in the city he didn't want to remember. All the time he was fucking, he relived his night at the track: heard the noises as he kissed a tit, saw the people in the stands as he stripped. He saw the bright lights when she turned over in the dark, heard the dithyramb of cheers for the dogs and their chase as they started screwing. The girl's face under him when he stopped, finally broken, had the look of a dog at the end of a race it had lost. *"Tormenta,"* she said looking up at him, round-faced, and only then had he heard the thundering rain.

The storm had blown up from Mazatlán and had vanished by sunrise. Only a strange wet tension and few bits of scud were left behind now. The air was slightly electric, muggy and close-fitting. *Typical of the desert,* Calhoun thought. *A few hours of downpour and then it's gone.* The rain, he knew, would make their work more difficult. Some of the jeep tracks they used would be flooded and impassable. He looked out on the Plaza Tijuana from his table at the cafe. It had been swept clean by the storm. The brilliant stone pavers glistened bone

27

white. Dark puddles, shallow lagoons of watery tension, gave faultless reflections of the breaking dawn sky.

Calhoun knocked down one of the two Tio Pepes he'd ordered. The cold sherry was mouth cleansing, alcoholic. He was careful to wipe his mouth after the first. He waited for the liquor-calm. He knew the rest of the day would be dangerous, hot and unpredictable.

Three pigeons burst from under a parked taxi, spooked by a passerby. He let the candy and alcohol burn his lips as he watched the race. The inside of his mouth held the juicy mixture, mixing it with his own saliva that was squirting: alcohol, burn, saliva, sugar, lips smacking slightly. He finally allowed himself to say it. *Lost everything.* He didn't understand what had happened to him, to his *suerte.* He was mystified by his bad luck. His eyes followed the pigeons until they disappeared, like his money, into the big nothingness of the city. He'd lost everything he had. *Not even enough now to take up Cienfuegos on his sure thing.*

The glass in Calhoun's hand suddenly burst. For a moment there was no blood, only the shard imbedded in his wet palm just below his thumb. He stared at the sliver of thick glass protruding from his hand. The blood began to ooze out around the glass, the red liquid soapy looking. It dripped onto the metal table. He touched the edge of the green, thin wedge of glass. The pain raced across him, a wonderful relief from the tension, like a cool hand on his forehead. The Mexican businessmen at the adjacent table had stopped eating and were looking at him. It wasn't everyday they saw a man squeeze a glass to death. Calhoun looked up, saw them staring at him with the big faces of the wealthy. He smiled at them. It was a smile that none of the men looking at him thought they'd ever seen before.

"I guess they don't make 'em like they used to," Calhoun said to them fatuously. He pulled the bent sliver out of his skin. He took out his handkerchief and wrapped it around his palm, threw four greasy thousand peso notes on the table and went into the bar.

"I need the jeep this morning. It's in the parking lot of the Arizona." The bartender nodded and called the kid they kept around the place for errands. The bartender put a cognac in front of Calhoun and told the kid when he came in the bar to go get Don Calhoun's jeep at the Hotel Arizona. The bartender threw the boy the keys.

The boy, only fourteen or so, nodded hello to Calhoun. The kid was one of the dark little street urchins that wear plastic shoes and look like they could eat for a week; the city had hundreds of them, maybe thousands. The waiters at the Escondido had adopted this one. The kid had woken up one day to find his family had moved on across the wire without him. Calhoun motioned the kid closer to the bar and handed him a twenty dollar bill. The bartender noticed the tip and rolled his eyes, walked away shaking his head. Twenty dollars in Tijuana was a big deal.

"Don't spend it in one place, *compadre*," Calhoun said, turning back around.

"*Gracias, compadre.* I wash, too?" The kid touched Calhoun on the back.

"No, no time to wash," Calhoun said, not looking at him. There was something filial in the way the boy had touched him. "I have to go to work." He felt the kid staring at his back but wouldn't turn around. The kid left at a trot for the hotel a few blocks away.

"He can barely reach the pedals," Calhoun said turning to the bartender, an older Mexican, who looked like he'd been

29

behind the bar his whole life. The bartender wore a red jacket with gold epaulets and a spotless white shirt. The uniform, old-fashioned in the states, was still *de rigueur* in Mexico's classy bars. "How did he learn to drive?" Calhoun asked.

"Mexicans never learn how to drive," the bartender said. They both laughed. "We're born to it," the bartender said.

"He's a good kid . . . Why would his folks leave him?"

"Many are left behind at the wire," the bartender answered. "His parents caught the fever."

"What fever?"

"Greenback fever," the bartender said.

"That's not funny." Calhoun said.

"I wasn't joking, greenback fever. What else do you think makes people risk so much?"

It was still very early and there was nothing for him to do but watch the traffic on the square and smoke. The sun started to splash against the trees. They would all be under the power of the sun soon, he knew, sweating like pigs, breathing the bad air. He put the cigarette out and looked at his watch.

The bus from the prison at Rio Sangre stopped in front of the plaza, as it did every morning to let out the newly released prisoners. Like the others at the bar, Calhoun watched the prisoners get out. It was their first act as free men and women and it was always interesting to Calhoun to see what they did with freedom. How they acted, where they went. Who picked them up. The kisses exchanged with loved ones, the ones with no one. The way some would wait in the plaza sometimes for hours wondering what to do next, like lost dogs, like human tablets dissolving in the sunshine.

Calhoun watched the driver open the bus doors. An armed guard led each prisoner down to the sidewalk, their plastic handcuffs were cut, and a paper signed. Calhoun wondered what the paper said. *The state of Baja California releases you and wishes you luck, please come again.*

He was about to ask the bartender where the hell the kid was when he saw her. At first he wasn't sure. Calhoun watched the girl as the driver brought her down then went back for her things. She was older of course, thinner, but it was her. He was sure of it, Celeste Stone.

She had the white plastic handcuffs in front of her and was bending her elbows up looking around, her red hair unkempt and long, her denims dirty, her skin porcelain white, a blue prison issue shirt with *Propiedad de Cárcel* stenciled on the back of it when she turned around. The girl looked toward the cafe as the guard sawed off her plastic manacle. Calhoun saw the look on her face—indifferent, phlegmatic. Her hands suddenly free, she brought them to her sides, then rubbed her wrists. The bartender looked too, as did most of the men sitting at the bar now.

"Well, son of a bitch," Calhoun said out loud.

"You can say that again," the executive next to him said. "Look at the ass on that broad."

Calhoun called to the bartender and ordered two espressos, ignoring the man's remark.

"Dos? Señor Vincente?"

"Yeah. One for me and one for the young lady." He put his cigarette in the glass ashtray, crushed it and looked again. Stone was signing her release paper. She dropped the pen into the guard's hand. Calhoun looked for a boyfriend or family, but there was no one waiting for her. The guard came back out of the bus with a backpack and put it down at her feet. Calhoun noticed she was wearing tattered, filthy, blue espadrilles, which were pathetic looking.

"When pretty young girls are in prison, it goes very badly for them," the bartender said in Spanish. He looked across the street over his shoulder while he spoke, the coffee machine hissing; he knocked the grounds out with a violent bang.

"I heard about the American girl. She was there without money. I heard from one of the jailers who lives near me," the bartender said. The machine started to sputter out coffee. The bartender poured the coffee with his back to Calhoun. "The guards took advantage at first because she didn't have any money. Then there was another girl . . . " But Calhoun wasn't listening now, he was looking at her very carefully, the way you might a gem you just bought.

"Then the warden took her over, as they say. He would go into the prison, you know, the courtyard at Rio Sangre. He would have her there in her cell." The bartender turned around, put the coffees down in front of Calhoun. Calhoun turned and looked back out the spotless window at Stone, remembering so many things at once.

"What was she there for? I mean in prison. Do you know?" Calhoun asked. He took a sip of the bitter coffee and looked at her. She bent over and picked up her backpack. He saw her heart-shaped ass and swallowed.

The waiter shrugged his shoulders, giving Calhoun the standard Latin shrug that was used to explain everything from hysterical dictators to bad water in Latin countries. *"¿Quién sabe?"* he said.

Calhoun had been at the prison once. He'd seen the courtyard at noon, the masses of men and women lining up at the big tubs of food put out like swill in red plastic garbage cans. The sun, the noise, the chaos. The filthy sheen of people's faces from the greasy food. The sound of the corrugated metal roof that thundered when it rained, a frantic watery hysteria as he sat in the warden's office. The colonnade where gangs of men in dirty T-shirts stared out at the courtyard, where wives cooked for their husbands. The prisons in Mexico were so different from back in the states. The prisons in Mexico were more like little towns. Calhoun got up from the bar and walked out into the street. She hadn't moved from the spot. The bus was pulling away. Stone was looking at the clock on the plaza, her possessions at her feet.

"That clock is always wrong, Celeste," Calhoun said. "As long as I've been here." He felt a chill go through him. He wasn't sure if it was seeing her again or the illness, but a big one went through him as he stood there looking at her.

The American girl, about twenty-five, looked up at him. She gave him an indifferent look, not recognizing him at first because of his hat and the sunglasses. Her face was red from the sun. She looked dirty but beautiful at the same time, efflorescent. The long torso and legs he remembered. Her eyes, bits of sapphirine crystal–those hadn't changed. That was what you always remembered about her, those bright eyes in that exotic Irish-girl face. A face with a mouth that was very full and terribly sexual. There was something in her eyes that you had to contend with, something supremely feminine and powerful that grabbed you. It was a kind of super femininity–the ultimate *yin,* the passivity in her eyes like exotic blue flowers constantly blooming sexuality. Calhoun found *it,* the yin, immediately attractive, compelling, despite everything that had happened between them.

"It's me," he said. "Vince . . . " He took his sunglasses and havelock off.

"Vince?" Calhoun nodded. The girl shook her head for a moment in disbelief, the red curls moving on the blue tattered prison shirt.

"I see you've just left the hospitality of the State of Baja California," Calhoun said, trying to make a joke of it.

33

She scratched her arm and looked at him carefully now. He could see there were flea bites from the bus ride on her pretty, thin arms.

"I can't believe it's you. How did you know?"

"I didn't. I was sitting in the place across the street." She looked across the street. He noticed the cup of her breast, the narrow waist, the push of her skin against the jeans, and felt the pull of her. He rubbed his face and realized he hadn't shaved. It seemed as if the space between them was being reduced, as if he were sliding into her, like a planet sucked into an orbit.

"My lucky day," she said, the tone of her voice deeper than you would have expected.

"I thought you could use some coffee. I've ordered you some." He nodded back toward the bar. "Why don't you join me?" Stone pulled her hair back from her face. She stared at him for a moment, gave him a fey look.

"You're kidding?" she said.

"No."

"You must be a fucking angel."

"I guess so," he said. He put his sunglasses back on. She dropped behind the yellow tint of his Vuarnets.

"You haven't changed much," he said. She smiled at him. It was a dreary, secret smile, things-maybe-you-didn't-want-to-know moving across her face, a string of unsaid things/events/acts/ turned into lips moving slightly, considering her response.

"You have," she said finally. "Which way's the border?" She picked up her bundle and swung the backpack onto one shoulder. "Maybe another time. When I'm not so busy."

"About four blocks that way," Calhoun pointed north. He was disappointed and didn't want her to go away. He wanted

34

her to come to the bar with him. He wanted to talk to her, to sit next to her.

A new Ford sedan pulled up to the curb behind them, with a gold *State of Baja California* insignia on the white door. A man in his fifties, dark-skinned, with patches of white in his jet black hair, got out of the back seat. He said something to the driver who was in uniform. The man who got out was very dark and low to the ground. He walked up to them.

"Come with me," the man said to her, ignoring Calhoun. Calhoun recognized the warden, Zamora, from his visit to the prison when he and Breen had interviewed an informant in the warden's office. The warden glanced at Calhoun but didn't recognize him.

"Move on, amigo." Zamora said it rudely and angrily. His jacket was open and he was strapped. A big automatic swung under his arm.

"Celeste, I want you to come back with me . . . " Zamora said turning back toward her. "Please. I have a place for you here in Tijuana." Zamora reached for her cardboard box. She stood there looking at the men. Zamora snatched the parcel out of her hand. Calhoun waited for her to do something but she didn't.

"Please, Celeste. *Por favor.* I love you . . . *por favor,*" Zamora said. She looked at Zamora. It was a look Calhoun had never seen before: ambivalence taken to some kind of new level. Zamora turned and looked at Calhoun, thinking he might be responsible for her not obeying. Calhoun put his arm around the warden's shoulder. The warden looked into his eyes.

"You remember me now, don't you?" Calhoun said. He was holding his DEA credential out away from the girl. Zamora glanced at it. Calhoun felt him physically change.

"Yes." Calhoun walked him back towards his car.

"She's ours," Calhoun said when they'd gotten a few steps away from her. "If you don't leave her the fuck alone, we will assume you have something to do with the trouble she's in." The warden looked back at the girl. He thought for a moment whether she was worth having the DEA on his ass and decided his obsession with American girls had its limits. He got back in the car and they drove off.

Calhoun turned around and walked back to her. She'd always been trouble, even back then in Palmdale, he warned himself. The only thing that had changed, from what he could see, was that she'd gotten prettier and the trouble was nastier.

"He'll leave you alone," Calhoun said. He wanted to get closer but didn't. She was looking at him the same way she'd looked at the warden.

"Thanks."

"How about that coffee?"

"No, I think I'll just go." She picked up her things. "Thanks Vince. He's been a *real* drag." They looked at each other. She smiled. "I mean, he *owns* that place . . . " He watched her pick up the box.

"Well, good luck then," Calhoun said.

"He's in love," the bartender said when Calhoun came back. "Did you see the way he looked at her? Have you ever seen anything so pathetic in your life?" Calhoun was going to say that he had, once, a long time ago. But he kept his mouth shut. They all watched her walk out across the plaza alone.

"She's going the wrong way," Calhoun said.

The kid pulled up to the front of the Escondido. The jeep had been washed. Calhoun got up and went out on the street. It wasn't six o'clock yet.

"Did you check the gas?" The kid nodded. "Where you going to spend that twenty bucks?" Calhoun asked him in Spanish, climbing into the jeep.

"I'm going into business, *compadre,*" the kid said.

"Yeah?" Calhoun said.

"*Sí,* I'm going into business. *Condones.*" He showed a box of twenty-five French balloons he'd bought with the money Calhoun had given him.

"Good," Calhoun said.

"I'm going to be rich some day, *compadre,*" the kid said, looking at him. "Like you, big car, beautiful girls, just like you," the kid said. "Where you go today, *compadre?*"

"Up the line, *compadre,* up the line," Calhoun said.

"When you come back?"

"When God is finished with me," Calhoun said. Calhoun found the new auxiliary gauge for a back-up gas tank he'd had installed. Both gauges read full. Pleased, he started the engine and pulled out into the traffic. Celeste was standing waiting for him at the first stop light. She walked out into the traffic to his window, not sure of herself.

He was surprised. He hadn't expected to see her again. "The asshole took my passport. I don't know what to do. They won't let me cross, will they?" She tried a smile. It worked. It was the complete opposite of the face she'd given the warden. She did her "beautiful girl" face and it worked.

"What do I do, Vince?"

"I don't know," Calhoun said. "You could probably cross without anything. They'll ask you if you're an American, that's all. Clean up maybe. You look kind of rough," he said, relishing the remark.

Stone shifted the backpack to her other shoulder. There must have not been anything in it, the way it was hanging. Calhoun couldn't keep his eyes off her. They looked at each other again. She was waiting for him to say something. He understood better than anyone why Zamora had fallen in love. Her bust pressed against the dirty prison shirt. She was at that exact age when women have it all going for them, every sexual nuance spine-tingling. She was right there at that moment now, standing in the middle of the street in Tijuana. Dazzling sexuality. You could almost smell it.

Stone put her hand against the door. "I'm broke, Vince . . . on empty."

"Yeah," Calhoun said. "You better get in."

• • •

They'd caught them on a Saturday night. Her father caught them in her room. Her father and his girlfriend had forgotten their tickets to a Padres game and come back to the ranch. They were doing it, nothing really kinky, but she was down on him when they came into the room. The old man ran for his gun and held it on Calhoun (never saying a word) until the sheriff came and took him straight to jail.

There was a picture in the paper the next morning of him in an orange jumpsuit. The reporter, whom he'd grown up with, had no mercy at all. None. Never even made it clear that they'd been going out for a year already.

It was a brutal headline: STUDENT TEACHER ACCUSED OF RAPE OF LOCAL HIGH SCHOOL GIRL. Nobody ever lives that down. It was over then, everything he'd worked for. He'd wanted to be a teacher and it was gone. Just like that. No questions. No chance to explain. Nothing. Just gone. Everything he worked for blown off the table because he couldn't stay out of Stone's pants. The judge had offered the Marine Corps, and he'd taken it. Every day he asked himself if it had been worth it. He'd seen bad things as a result, war and death. Every day

38

since, he'd told himself yes, even that night in Panama when men were screaming for their mamas, he thought it was worth it. Every last goddamn red cunt hair he'd spit on the floor of that room was worth it.

FIVE
Amigo Motel — 6:15 A.M.

Celeste followed him into his room at the Amigo Motel, still not knowing exactly what to expect from him. They hadn't talked much in the jeep. Calhoun could tell she was disappointed by the place but tried not to show it. He explained he kept his things here, not offering any more of an explanation than that.

"You can clean up here." Celeste looked around the motel room. The blinds were drawn, the bed unmade. It was dark inside and seemed always to be that way. She went to the window and opened the shade. A courtyard full of busted-up old cars sprang into view. She closed the shade again.

"I'll be back later." Calhoun opened his wallet and put fifty dollars on the dresser. She turned around. "There's some money if you need anything. I suggest you buy some new clothes. I've got to go. I'm late." He watched her slide the backpack off onto the floor. Calhoun noticed the detail of her neck, that it was thin and beautiful and tanned from the sun.

"Why are you doing this? Why don't you hate me? You have every reason to," Stone said.

"I like to do good deeds for old friends. You know, good Samaritan."

"Are we friends?" she said. "I mean, after what I did, I wouldn't expect you to . . . I'm sorry I acted stupid back there. It was a shock seeing you like that . . . "

"Forget it. Yeah, we are." He smiled at her. He wasn't sure why he had brought her here, all he knew was that he wanted

41

to look at her. He wanted to see her broken like this, be superior to her, give her money. She pushed the hair out of her face again. He half meant what he'd said. "I let bygones be bygones." The phone rang. Calhoun looked at it and let it ring. They both watched the phone.

"Can you do me a favor?" Calhoun said.

"Sure."

"Pick it up and tell whoever it is I've left."

"Whoever it is. What if it's your girlfriend?"

"That's right, whoever it is." Stone picked it up. She stretched out on the bed. Calhoun saw her stomach, the shirt pulled up over the flat white hardness of her stomach. Something got bolted to his groin then and he let it sink in.

"Hello . . . no. He's not here. Sure. Me . . . ? Jane Doe," She said. She looked up at him and smiled. "That's right—Mrs. Jane Doe." Stone put the phone down on the cradle.

"It's someone called Breen. He says he has to talk to you. To come by the office as soon as you can. He sounded disappointed."

"Well, I'll let you get cleaned up. I've got a business meeting—maybe we could have lunch later."

"What do you do?" she asked.

Calhoun laughed. It seemed a stupid question for some reason, and he realized he was angry, that he'd gotten angry the moment he'd seen her climb out of the bus, and that he wasn't sure why he wanted her here in his room, but he did. He knew that. He wanted her here when he got back because he wasn't finished with her. He wanted to do something to her, he didn't know what. He wanted to fuck her, he was sure of that, but something else, something to pay her back for what she'd done to him.

"Computers . . . I sell computers."

"Oh . . . " she said " . . . right." Stone looked at him, narrowing her eyes. "Somehow you don't look like a computer salesman, Vince. What happened to the Marine Corps?"

"I got tired of the uniform. Who was your friend in the plaza?" Celeste sat on the end of the bed and looked around, avoiding Calhoun's eyes, as if the scene on the plaza were just another event in a long series of events: men, bedrooms, and houses and parties she shouldn't have gone to.

"The warden at Rio Sangre."

"He seemed to be upset about something."

"I'd like to forget the last six months, Vince." She leaned back on the bed. "Sometimes a girl's got to do what a girl's got to do," she said. She moved her legs like a kid, leaning back, elbows on the bed. She let him look at her that way.

"Are you going to tell me what you really do? Or is that going to be a secret?"

"I've got to go out."

"Okay . . . go out." There had been a slight shift in power. He was losing his control and she was sopping it up.

He watched her walk to the bathroom and close the door. He waited a minute, then opened the drawer. He had two guns in the drawer and his extra harness. Something told him he shouldn't leave them in the room. He picked up the harness and slipped one of the guns into his coat pocket, then on impulse he took out another hundred dollars and laid it on the bureau. He wanted to give Celeste money. He didn't understand why.

Stone opened the door unexpectedly. She'd taken off her shirt and bra and had a towel around her. Her face was wet, her hair pulled back. She saw the guns and harness in his hands. "Somebody forget to pay for their computer, Vince?"

• • •

Calhoun drove out of the motel parking lot and remembered it all. The whole mess of his past.

Their home town was called Palmdale. It was one of those desert towns you pass through on the way to Calexico and forget immediately. Everything wavers in the sunlight—a strip mall, Mike's Gun Shop, a hardware store, three stoplights, a dozen bars. Rural California, it never changed. Maybe you'd remember the way the river moved, flat and thin-green, toward Tijuana 25 miles away, the way the sun would play silver coins on it at one in the afternoon, a few spindly cottonwood trees along the banks, a desultory breeze moving the air if you were lucky. Palmdale was just another jerk-water border town.

That first morning Calhoun had seen Celeste Stone in the hallway of the high school his whole world had disintegrated and been rebuilt with just two people in it: Vincent Calhoun, a student teacher, and Celeste Stone, high school girl with a body that tore you up. It was a paradigm for temptation.

In his mind the lights dimmed, or seemed to, and they weren't in a high school hallway seeing each other for the first time, they were already doing it. That's how fast it was. Why are words so small in the face of something so big? She had been like one of those flash floods out in the desert—no one believes it, until you hear the roar of the water and it's on you.

It was all there in her eyes. She'd fixed on Calhoun, while she twisted her lock, returning Calhoun's stare from her locker. Something passed between them then. She'd been wearing blue jeans and boots and a felt cowboy hat that was worn. Long red hair spilling out of the hat down to her skinny ass and very white skin. She was a ranch girl—no makeup, nothing about the city.

44

Calhoun waited for her to come to her locker before lunch, and then, armed with a lame excuse, he went out into the hall. He'd asked her if she could help him hang a poster. He didn't wait for an answer, just dropped two tacks into her hand. The horrible thing was he'd thought the whole thing through. How he would get her to hold the poster, how she would have to bend over the counter and spread her arms apart, how she would have to turn around and look at him as he told her how to move it.

"A little higher," he'd said and she'd arched her wide back. A little higher. She turned and looked at him, her butt pointed out, and she knew then what he was doing, and she took the tack she'd stuck in her mouth with the feminine ranch girl power and stuck it in the right corner of the travel poster without waiting for him to say that it was okay. Then she said the first thing she ever said to him.

"What's your name?" It surprised him because of that voice, all its timbre, older than her, and deep and coarse. Like she'd been yelling into the desert wind all her life.

She was looking over her right shoulder, pushing in the tack. He saw how narrow her waist was. She got on her knees and pulled the bottom corners of the poster tight. He looked at the line of her jeans, the way it split her ass, and then at the worn heels of her cowboy boots.

"Vincent."

"Teacher or student?" she said. He couldn't stop then. It was like he'd been pushed down Mt. Everest on skis.

She turned around and studied him. She already knew what effect she had on men. She just let him hang for a moment. Like a side of beef in a slaughter house. Still slightly warm and bloody and steamy.

"Are you a student or a teacher?" she said again. She smiled, disarmed him. The smile was real. The ranch where her father lived was in her voice. The high desert people had that voice that seemed to be hollowed out by the big spaces up above Palmdale, the long arroyos and the strange rock formations stained by the sun and rain. She was part desert, part chicken farmer's daughter, part 4H beauty. What he didn't know was that she was a young girl who had just fallen in love. Calhoun smiled. He was twenty-five; there was no question he was a teacher.

"Why?"

"Because you look like a student." She smiled again. "You look too young for the job," she said. He noticed her lips then, how full they were.

"I'm a student teacher."

"What do you teach?" Calhoun looked around the room for an explanation.

"Spanish . . . " Calhoun felt his mouth getting dry. He was suddenly sorry he'd asked her into the room. He felt horribly guilty. Why didn't he just stop it . . . thank her. Nothing had happened yet. Nothing. She was a nice girl. *But god, look at her, look at her.* He turned and made sure the door to the classroom was still open. It was open, but not all the way. He went toward the door . . .

"You were looking at my *behind.* Weren't you," she said behind him. Calhoun froze, stunned. He put his hand on the door knob. And then he did it, he turned the corner that he would never forget. The corner that would get him fired, arrested, and sent to join the Marine Corps or go to jail. He closed the door and leaned against it, felt his shoulders on the cool wood. They were alone now. He saw how raw she was, something raw about her, and yet innocent. She had something that he wanted more than anything he'd ever wanted before.

"Yeah, I was," he said. "And it's real nice."

Two weeks later he'd driven her home. It was as if they understood what was going to happen the moment she got in his car. She'd taken him out to one of the chicken sheds her father kept. The chickens, thousands of them, Buff Rocks, White Leghorns, Brahmas, making a strange sound, the automatic feeder machines buzzing and dispensing, the desert outside the long, low, clap-trap chicken houses dirty and boiling red at sunset. He'd never been in a place like it, the air filled with feathers, like a pillow had been broken, snowing inside, motes of glittering dust, the smell of feed. Calhoun could see her father outside through the slats of the coop, leaning over the front of a tractor, his big greasy overalls in the air a hundred yards away . . . and Celeste looking at him. The chickens wandering all over the floor, scurrying in a white blur toward the feeders, the vivid red wattles under their pecking tools.

"We can do it here," she said. "If you want to. He won't come in here now. Not until after dinner." She was wearing a jean jacket and her jeans, worn at the knees, and western boots. He watched her take the jacket off and throw it down like a gauntlet and they kissed. And while she led his hand to her tit he looked out through the slats of the chicken house and saw, through the snow of feathers, feeling then the warm tit and her groping him, her old man's ass in the air, big elbows, rusted tractor, the desert around them turning sienna crush and then red, and then the old man pushing himself off the tractor in a sloppy oafish way and going across the yard toward the ranch house. By then they were half naked and he saw her in her panties and bra. And it was the best thing he'd ever seen. He picked her up off the floor, the chickens milling under them as he made for a wall.

He remembered now, barely seeing the streets of Tijuana, the way the coop walls bent out and gave when he leaned her naked shoulders against them. How pliable it all seemed. How white her skin was against the dirty walls of the coop. The look of the feeder above her head, metallic hoses gurgling power. Her reaching up for the machinery to hang off of it as they fucked. How good it felt. He would never forget that, the way she hung from the feeder, her shoulders bouncing against the dirty boards, the rhythm of the machinery feeding the chickens and them feeding desire.

He'd never come so hard in his life, scattering the chickens when he moaned. They'd slid to the floor. He was looking at that white ass in his hands, one boot under her leg. And he'd never felt so alive. There was no excuse for it and no escape. It was wild like the desert. And he had never forgotten it. Ever.

SIX
Wang's Rancho — 7:15 A.M.

Driving into Wang's rancho, Calhoun had glanced at Castro. He was his one true friend. In Tijuana, that was saying a lot. There was something about Castro that made you know he liked you. The way he looked at you. Castro was talking about a movie they'd both seen one night while they'd been stuck with cargo in the Hotel Arizona.

"You remind me of Jaffe in *Asphalt Jungle.* Do you remember that picture? They're all captured in the end. Everybody has a . . . what do you gringos call it?"

"Foible," Calhoun said. He smiled. He remembered the picture. "Yes, I remember him. He stopped to look at some young girl in a roadhouse and the cops catch him."

"We all have weak spots, don't we. Mine are women and movies. And we already know what yours is," Castro said. "You don't listen to anyone."

There was a mirage on the road in front of them, silver water that seemed like human emotion, always changing, mercurial–a trick of light and asphalt that stayed just in front of the jeep. They could see Wang's rancho and the grove of cool cottonwood trees around up on the left. There was nothing else out there except the desert, which, at this time of the morning, was white with glare. They'd made this trip so many times that the danger seemed almost negligible. They saw the Cessna that was bringing the cargo fly overhead, dip its wings, then start to land. There was a dirt runway behind the rancho.

Castro had turned his body toward him, his cowboy shirt unbuttoned so you could see the sea of coarse black hair and the automatic and the gold cowboy belt buckle. All his handsome, dark Latin features were in sync now with that smile, the desert scenes going past his face in the window of the jeep. Castro was a *judicial.* The Judicial Police were all the worst, the bottom of a corrupt barrel, vicious, opportunistic, but the fact was Calhoun liked him despite everything. He was the only one in Tijuana Calhoun could really trust.

"You're ill, you know that," Miguel said. He said it almost casually. "I decided you have to see a doctor. I've been meaning to talk to you about it. I'll give you the name of someone on the plaza."

"You know, amigo, someday I'm going to have to shoot you for not minding your own business," Calhoun said.

Calhoun looked at the Mexican's face, the dark eyes, the spotless white cowboy shirt wet and stained dark under the arms. He looked very fit. There was something about Castro, about his big jaw and dark wavy hair and the way his face spread out big that reminded you of one of those old movie stars. It was a big face for a Mexican. *Gilbert Roland,* Calhoun thought.

Calhoun pulled off the main dirt road and onto a track that went up to Wang's rancho. The dust from the dirt road to the rancho had billowed up so they were riding with just a little narrow opening in front of them.

"Amigo, you know what's wrong with you? No one ever knows when you're joking and when you're serious . . . That is . . . " Castro searched for the right words. "That is a serious character flaw."

"What time is it?" Calhoun asked. He put both hands on the wheel again.

50

"Almost seven-twenty," Castro said. "We should be back in town by eight."

"Let's load this cargo," Calhoun said. Castro looked at him, but didn't say anything.

• • •

Calhoun's cool detachment of half an hour ago was destroyed. Kneeling in the sun, he was trying to shovel sand with his bare hands. Suddenly it felt as if he'd been hit in the back with a rock. It was the first bad pain he'd gotten from the fever. He stopped working for a moment. Castro was watching him in the mirror. Calhoun tried to speak but the pain was suddenly over-powering, as if his spine had been broken. He let his face fall in the sand. The wave of pain crashed, then flowed away. In a moment he raised his head. His face glittered with bits of sand. He went back to work, slowly trying to clear the jeep's front axle. It seemed hopeless.

Calhoun had been driving and it was his fault. He grabbed a handful of sand and squeezed it till it hurt. The axle was caught on a rock and the rock had the whole front end of the jeep off the ground. Castro was gunning the engine. Calhoun watched the rear wheels dig deeper into the soft sugary sand. They were axle deep in the rear and going nowhere, just sloshing sand and rock, making it worse. Calhoun stood up, threw the door open and looked at Miguel Castro behind the wheel.

"We'll have to rock it off. All of us." Castro stopped gunning the engine. It got quiet suddenly. The noise of the engine and tires stopped. Calhoun turned around and looked across the desert toward Wang's rancho and beyond the jeep track to the highway that led to Tijuana.

51

"Hey, amigo. I think now we have a big problem," Castro said. *"La patrulla rata."*

Calhoun looked up. It was the worst thing that could happen. They'd been spotted by one of the rat patrols that scouted the desert for people to rob. With the jeep stuck they were vulnerable.

"La patrulla rata," Castro said again. "Look."

A car, a half mile below on the highway, had stopped. Four men were standing around the shimmering, burning blue metal of a Ford Taurus. The outline of their car was phantasmic, not clear, from where Calhoun stood.

"I thought you were supposed to stop this kind of shit. You're a cop, aren't you? Mexican federal fucking police." Calhoun felt his soaked shirt sticking to his skin. He was sick again. The fever he thought he'd lost had come back.

"They're my own men," Castro said. *"Judiciales.* I can tell."

"Well that's fucking great," Calhoun said.

"Welcome to Mexico," Castro said, joking. He was trying to pretend things weren't that bad. But Calhoun knew they were. It was that bad and it was only a little before eight in the morning.

"Well, why don't you go down there and tell them we'll pay them off?" Calhoun said.

"It won't work. Not with that sort. They know I'll kill them as soon as I can. That's the way it works here."

"Great. Anyway, they need a four wheel drive to get up here," Calhoun said.

"Maybe," Castro said. He got the binoculars out of the jeep and focused on the patrol. "I know all of them . . . *Judiciales,"* he said again.

"Maybe we don't have to worry," Calhoun said. He wiped the sand off his face. His shirt had turned gray with sweat. "Maybe they don't mean to bother us."

"I don't think you understand," Castro said, lowering the glasses. "You could say that they are 'off duty'."

"Well, maybe they'll show you a professional courtesy," Calhoun said, trying to joke about it.

"Yes, they will tear my asshole out after I'm dead," he said. He wasn't smiling.

Calhoun looked at the newly loaded cargo sitting in the back seat. Four Chinese girls, all teenagers, none of whom spoke any English. They didn't have a clue about what was happening. But they knew it wasn't good and were scared.

"Get the fuck out!" Calhoun said. He held the door open. They didn't move. Wang had told them to stay in the car until they got to the hotel in Tijuana. They weren't going to do anything else but sit there.

"Get out and help, for Christ sake!" Calhoun said. It was useless. They didn't understand a word he said. He let a round off from the automatic in the air. They froze. Calhoun reached inside and pulled one of the girls out roughly. Another girl climbed out on the other end, happy to get away from him.

Calhoun shook the gun at the other two and they piled out, terrified, thinking he wanted to shoot them. He took them to the back of the jeep and put his hands on the bumper and made an exaggerated motion of pulling up. The girls understood now and nodded and tried their best. Calhoun got a few rocks and dumped them in front of the jeep's back wheels but he could see it was useless, the front end was too hung up. He was hit by another muscle cramp and slumped to his knees. *It's a nightmare*, he thought. *I'll wake up. I know it's a nightmare.* He heard Miguel's voice asking him what was wrong with him.

"Hey, amigo, look."

Calhoun turned around and looked behind them down the arroyo. A new, white Land Rover, the kind that the Mexican

53

highway patrol use, a big Land Rover, had stopped by the men in the Taurus.

"Give me the binoculars." Castro pulled them off the seat. He took a look, then handed them to Calhoun. Two hundred yards below there were four federal police standing around a new Ford Taurus with an official government seal on the door. They all had automatic weapons. They were talking to the men in the Land Rover. They seemed to have all the time in the world, their dark faces mean-looking.

"They'll take that Land Rover and come now," Castro said. Calhoun had thrown his coat into the sand. His shirt was open. You could see his white Mylar vest and the shoulder harness and the extra clips, the harness soaked with sweat. His sunglasses reflected back the yellow hell of morning.

"We'll tip it over," Calhoun said suddenly.

"What?"

"Tip the mother fucker over. Maybe it will go right."

"You're crazy. It's too heavy." Calhoun was getting the jack out from under the passenger seat. "It will roll down the fucking hill," Castro said.

"Am I? Look . . . for yourself," Calhoun said, looking up. "We've got about five minutes to do something. Then it's my guess we're going to be in a hell of a predicamento." The Chinese girls had gone to a scrap of shade from a rock outcropping. They looked exhausted and dazed by the heat now. They were talking in Chinese. They were dirty from the sand and dust from the back tires. Calhoun motioned to them to come back toward the jeep. He tried to show them what he wanted them to do. They didn't understand. He got the jack under the passenger door and moved it up so that the uphill tires were lifted off the ground. He kept the jack going. He got on the high side of the jeep and pulled on the running board. It barely budged.

Castro came immediately and helped. They counted to three and tried again. One of the girls stepped forward and got next to Calhoun and they lifted again; this time the whole jeep rocked. The girl told the others to help and they stepped out of the shade. This time with six people lifting and Calhoun using the jack with one hand the jeep tilted, then started to go. Calhoun counted the revolutions; it was like watching dice. The jeep rolled once, rolled again, all of them watching. It came up on the tires and stopped.

It was too late to cross over to Palmdale. Calhoun drove back to Wang's rancho. He knew they couldn't outrun the Land Rover, knew the police would radio ahead if they tried to get on the main road. Calhoun stopped the jeep, looked at the stand of cottonwoods and then at the rancho's white walls sparkling in the sun. Calhoun calculated the size of the rancho's one room in his mind's eye, then threw the jeep forward, drove to the back of the rancho and backed up, trying to maneuver the front of the jeep into position.

"Now what the fuck are you doing, amigo?" Castro said.

"Hold on."

Calhoun backed up ten feet, then floored it and sent them crashing through the rancho's back wall. The wall broke apart like an old clay pot. Calhoun ran the jeep inside the empty room right up to the other wall, slamming on the brakes, trying to stop before they went through the other side, big chunks of wall on the hood.

It was dark inside. Calhoun could see out one of the rancho's narrow windows right in front of them. There were some old yellow curtains over the window. They could hear the Land Rover coming up the hill, its powerful engine growling, and then saw the top of the Rover break the crest of the hill. Calhoun counted five men in the Land Rover and swore under his breath.

The Land Rover slowed, swung around and stopped right in front of the rancho, pointed toward the cottonwood trees. Calhoun waited for them to spot the jeep, but they didn't because the sun was in their eyes. They were looking toward the cottonwood trees and not the rancho. They were only a few feet away. He could tell the men thought they'd hidden down in the arroyo behind the trees. Calhoun pulled his forty-five from the harness. Castro turned to him and shook his head and smiled. They watched the men in the car talking, one was pointing toward the arroyo. Calhoun saw one of the men glance right at them and laugh. Two men got out of the Rover, unslung their machine pistols and walked toward the trees. Calhoun heard the girls whispering; he turned around and told them to shut up. The two men, one of them very fat, came back toward the Land Rover, shaking their heads. The other two got out of the Rover. They were all standing in front of the rancho just on the other side of the wall in front of them. It would only be a moment or so before one of them would get the bright idea to look in the window, Calhoun figured.

"Now what?" Castro whispered. Castro's face was covered with fine red dust from the adobe.

Calhoun turned around. The girls were holding each other. The dust from the adobe wall covered their faces, making them look like Mexican girls. Calhoun realized he was covered with it too, his white suit brown now. The side windows on both sides had popped out when the jeep rolled and let in everything from the wall.

"I'll go around back. When you hear me yell, you drive through the wall, hit the Rover, try to take it out. Try to run somebody over on the way," Calhoun said. "I'll have to back up now a little." Castro smiled and crossed himself. He glanced at the men. They were on the radio.

"They'll hear when you move the . . . ." he said. Dirt fell into Castro's mouth when he spoke and he had to stop. Calhoun shrugged his shoulders. There wasn't much choice, they needed ramming room. He moved the shift lever to R. The jeep started to back up. The noise sounded extra loud inside the rancho. Castro lifted both his automatics up, still spitting sand, and pointed them toward the Rover. They crept back slowly, then stopped, the back end of the jeep sticking outside of the building now.

"When you hear me yell, go for it," Calhoun whispered. Calhoun opened the door on his side and stepped out into the rancho. His leg got tangled in a chair and he almost shot himself. It was cool and dusty in the room. He got the girls out the other door and led them outside into the sun. He made them sit on the ground against the back wall. Calhoun stopped for a moment and looked out at the empty runway behind him and at the makeshift windsock lying against its pole. There was no breeze at all. *I've been in a jam before,* he thought. For a moment, he was frightened. He popped his clip out and looked at it, shoved it home and undid the snaps on his backup ammo. He took an extra clip out and held it in his left hand. He saw the tailpipe of the jeep and the flow of the exhaust, heavy and clear. He could hear the putter of the engine. He glanced at the little slice of shade the girls had crouched in. He heard the voices of the *judiciales,* a car door open, a few words of Spanish.

There was silence. He heard their car doors slam. He walked around to the front of the building and exposed himself. "Hey you guys, let's make a deal!" Calhoun yelled. He saw the men. They were all standing by the window, leaning against it, smiling, two of them looking in. One of them was flipping Castro off and laughing. They'd just spotted the jeep.

"Give us the girls," one of them said. He turned toward Calhoun and fired. Calhoun stepped back around the corner. Hunks of adobe were blown off the corner of the building in front of him. Calhoun heard the unmistakable racking of automatic weapons.

Calhoun held his breath. He heard the jeep's engine gunned. Castro drove straight through the wall in front of him. The whole wall pushed out toward the Rover. The jeep climbed up over the debris and slammed one of the *judiciales* into the Rover, crushing him. The other four backed away, falling over themselves. Two got tangled up with each other and fell down on the sand, chunks of wall falling on top of them.

Calhoun stepped around the corner and shot as they tried to recover; one of them was trying to get his machine gun swung around. Calhoun shot him in the head at almost point blank range, rushing him. The other one fell into Calhoun and bounced off him, the man's machine pistol knocked out of his hands. He got up and ran toward the cottonwoods. It was like a dream, the slow motion of the man making for the tiny hope of bright trees. Calhoun saw how hard he was pumping his fat legs, the sound his boots made on the ground. Calhoun lifted his forty-five and waited a moment, then shot him in the back at ten feet. His cowboy hat flew in the air, the impact from the forty-five knocking the runner face down like he'd been clubbed.

They were back in Tijuana in less than an hour.

SEVEN
Hotel Cuauhtémoc — 8:25 A.M.

The Hotel Cuauhtémoc's wide arcade shaded the rooms against a savage morning sun. The hotel was from another era, when Tijuana was a small desert town. Across the dirt street were the last few hovels in Tijuana's worst neighborhood, *La Cumbre,* and beyond that, a thousand miles of empty Sonoran desert. One of the many lizards that lived in the lobby started to move. Like a windup toy, it crossed the red and white tile floor making a horrible, sentient, dragging sound. Oblivious to people, it crept over Calhoun's shoe while he was talking to the desk clerk, its tail slipping back and forth, knocking him in the ankle.

The night clerk had never asked what went on in room twelve. He wasn't going to ask why Calhoun's suit was stained red, either. He pretended there was nothing wrong. Calhoun had his gun out at his side. They used the Cuauhtémoc as a safe house. The clerk would clean the room himself as soon as they left, and it would be ready again in a few hours if they needed it. The clerk had taken to keeping the key in his pocket. He hadn't told his wife about the hundred dollar bills he'd been collecting all summer. She'd asked once who the men were who came from downtown, and he'd said they were old amigos and left it at that.

"Just like always?" the man said. His greasy hair, done in the pompadour style older Mexican men love, was combed back like the young Elvis. He wore a gold crucifix, the cross held tight up against his Adam's apple.

"No, we'll be leaving soon. Just waiting for a call," Calhoun said. "I want you to call the room if you see any strange men parking out in the street." Calhoun handed the night clerk a hundred dollar bill.

"Today, fiesta," he said, smiling at Calhoun and fondling the bill. "Today, second of November. *Día de los Muertos.*" The man turned around and nodded to the religious calendar on the wall, a picture of the baby Jesus. "Day of the Dead," he said again for emphasis in case Calhoun hadn't understood the Spanish.

"Day of the Dead. *Fiesta alegre! Fiesta alegre!*" He himself planned to go up the street and get laid after the day clerk came in. He fanned himself with the hundred dollar bill Calhoun had just given him. He described the pleasures of the flesh, such as they were, that one could purchase up the street for just ten dollars. Concrete cubicles, one bidet for twenty girls in bad electric light, but pleasure nonetheless.

Calhoun listened to the desk clerk's description. He already knew what day it was. He turned toward the doorway that led out to the dirt road in front of the hotel. He stopped in the doorway and turned back to look at the clerk. He thought about death, what the Yaqui had said to him at the Escondido the night before. *She was wrong—I'm not going to die.* He nodded to the night clerk, then slipped his havelock on, which made him look like an officer in the Legion going out into the Casbah. *Day of the Dead. So what? So what?* Another lizard crept by him, its head up, moving quickly, greenish gills going like a matron at a fancy ball. The lizard dropped onto the road with a pronounced thud in front of him and moved to a puddle of water from the heavy rain of the night before.

"Fiesta alegre," the clerk said again behind him. *"Fiesta alegre."* The phone on the desk rang. The night clerk picked it up, listened, then cupped the receiver and called to Calhoun out

60

in the street. *"Es para usted, señor."* Calhoun turned around and came back into the lobby and took the phone.

"It's Breen. I've got to talk to you . . . " There was a pause while he waited for an answer from Calhoun.

"I'm kind of busy today," Calhoun said. "Can you handle it?"

"Customs just arrested someone called Wang. He says you know all about smuggling people."

"I don't know what you're talking about," Calhoun said.

"You better come into the office. People here are starting to wonder what the fuck is going on."

"How did you know where I was?"

"Wang was nice enough to give me the number."

"All right, I'll come . . . it's almost nine . . . I'll be there in an hour or so."

Calhoun walked out from the slip of shade into the sun, to the front of the motel. He found a garden hose attached to a fifty gallon water barrel which had been set up for guests to serve themselves potable water. He turned the welded spigot and soaked his hat, cleaned his face off. He watched the water, silvery and unreal, darken the hat. He slapped it back on his head, heavy and wet, and immediately felt relief from the heat. He rubbed his dirty face and wiped it off with the back of his hand. He stood up and looked at the jeep parked in front of the blue door to room twelve. The back window had popped out; otherwise it was beat-up but all right.

He fished for a cigarette. It was too hot to smoke but he lit up anyway, tasted it, then threw it onto the empty parking lot that radiated heat and fumes. He looked at his watch again. They were waiting for a call from Miguel's contact who would tell him if it was safe to go further into town. He turned around and looked at the low-lying motel with its primary blue doors. It seemed like he'd already put in a full day's work.

"Wash up, we won't be here long. *Wash!*" Calhoun pretended to rub his face. He looked at the pretty one and made a motion with his hand. "We are just waiting for a call." He held an imaginary phone to his head. "Want to make sure it's okay to go on. No more trouble, I promise." He looked at the girls. They looked at him. Still frightened, they didn't move from the bed.

"What do you expect?" Castro said behind him. "They're still in shock."

"I got a call from Breen . . . He knew I was here," Calhoun said.

Castro had been leaning back in his chair half asleep with his feet up on a table, his white cowboy hat slid back on his head. It was the only thing that was clean—he'd left it here at the Cuauhtémoc on the table the day before. There was a wedge of oiled black hair showing from under the hat. The lieutenant brought his feet down.

There was a short, banging ring, then another from the phone next to him. Calhoun stared at the phone while it rang. Each ring seemed to be louder than the one before.

Castro finally picked it up. He held the phone and listened, looking at Calhoun. "Where? They don't even have any luggage," Castro said. He put down the phone.

"We're the last to know, my friend."

"Know what?"

"That the little darlings are full of heroin. We've been had."

"I'm going to kill him," Calhoun said. "I'm going to kill Slaughter. If we live through this."

"How much do you think it's worth?" Castro said.

"There's four of them. I don't know . . . enough to kill you for," Calhoun said.

They could hear the rumble of a municipal water truck out on the street and the sound of the cow bell that let people know it was passing. Calhoun tasted something in his mouth. He went to the bathroom and spit into the sink. A dark bit of adobe had gotten in his mouth. Someone from the hotel banged on the door and asked it they needed water from the truck. Calhoun went to the door and said no. He saw two late model cars parked on the street. He shut the door and told Castro.

"Friends," Castro said. They heard the bell from the water truck again. "We could just leave them. Wash our hands of it." Calhoun looked at the girls. He took his hat off and wiped his face. It was starting to get warm in the room. His big body was sweating from the heat, suffering from the lack of air.

"No. If people know about the heroin, they'll turn Tijuana inside out to find them. And when they do, they'll rip it out of them," Calhoun said.

"I suppose you're right."

"Of course I'm right. We have to cross them or they won't get out of here alive."

"It would be better at the Arizona then, safer," Castro said. The phone rang again. Castro went to the table and picked it up.

"*¿Quién habla?* . . . Yes, we have them. It's all right. Of course. We're booked up this afternoon. We'll do it tonight. I'm sorry. They'll have to stay at the Arizona in the meantime." Castro held the phone again. "It's Slaughter, he wants them to cross right away."

"Fuck him." Calhoun moved toward the phone angrily. Miguel pushed him away. He spoke with Slaughter and put down the phone.

"Where do you think she'll end up?" Castro said. The pretty one had come out of the bathroom. She had washed her face. She was standing in the doorway of the bathroom. Her face was wet. She had taken down her hair and was putting it up again. She didn't look like she was carrying anything inside her. Calhoun turned around and looked at her, then turned away.

"Did you know? Tell me the truth, Miguel."

"No."

"Fucking Wang . . . They swallowed it at the rancho," Calhoun said.

"Yes, I suppose so . . . "

Calhoun went to the window. He heard the water running in the bathroom. One of the other girls had decided to wash up.

"I said I'd never do drugs," Calhoun said.

"It will be our secret. Where do you think she'll end up?" Castro said again.

"That looks like a rich man's wife to me," Calhoun said. The girls started talking to one another in Chinese. Another girl got off the bed and went to the bathroom.

"She's better looking than that Chinese movie star . . . you know. That's who she looks like. I can't think of her name, it's too hot," Castro said. The phone started to ring again. Calhoun went to the table by the bed and picked it up, then immediately put it back on its cradle and collapsed.

"I told you, you were sick." Castro said. Calhoun tried to answer. He saw Castro talking to him from a corner of the room but he was seeing several Castros. "It's all right. You'll be all right. There's a doctor on the plaza I want you to see," Castro said, picking him up.

"Call Slaughter back and tell him we want more money. Tell him we know," Calhoun said from his knees.

When Castro got off the phone Calhoun was still on his knees, his whole body shaking. His friend looked down at him.

"Well . . . don't look so fucking happy," Calhoun said. They both started to laugh.

"Hey, amigo, you look like shit," Castro said.

"This is what I get for sleeping with your sister," Calhoun said.

EIGHT
Plaza Tijuana — 9:00 A.M.

Calhoun turned back to the doctor. The sign on his office door said *Dr. Kevin Hughes/ Physician/ Cancer Specialist/ Growth Hormones Available/ No Appointment Needed.* Calhoun knew what kind of doctor Hughes was. Tijuana was full of sent-down doctors of his type. The type whose credentials had been pulled up north after amputating the wrong foot or getting too friendly with some of the patients. They came to Tijuana and opened "clinics" of various kinds: sex change, longevity, cancer, bio-feedback. This one sold steroids to American high school kids. Hughes was a notorious pederast, even by Tijuana's low standards. The doctor had one of those big open smiles in a fleshy baby face wrapped under a mess of thinning black hair. It was the kind of smile that people put on when they have a lot to hide.

They were in a second story walkup in a very old building above the Plaza Tijuana. Calhoun was sitting on an examination table from another era. The ancient table's dark leather was creased. You could hear the cars and street traffic on the plaza through the old-style bay windows. The room's three windows had been stenciled with the English words *La Clínica Hughes* in large black letters that looked very impressive from the plaza.

There was a gray pigeon preening itself on the ledge as the doctor spoke. The bay windows were dirty, streaked with grit spewed from the *maquiladoras* that ran night and day outside of town. The view outside was of tiles and roof tops lit by the morning sun. Drab, half-completed buildings stood against the skyline and looked slightly smudged, as if they'd been rendered in red charcoal. Everything looked unfinished, which was the hallmark of Mexico these days. The frantic building that had gripped Tijuana before the devaluation had suddenly stopped, just as quickly as it had begun.

"Dengue . . . that's what you have," Hughes said enthusiastically. "Breakbone fever, the old-timers call it." The doctor turned toward a small white porcelain sink stained with rust marks and began to wash up, his back to Calhoun. The doctor's pants were shiny and worn out and the same charcoal color as his thinning hair. "All of a sudden you will be hit with a colossal pain that shakes you . . . right?"

"Right," Calhoun said.

"A nasty virus . . . mosquitoes, of course, are the vector, as we call it. The tiger mosquito." The doctor bent over the sink slightly in a green paper smock, the half-length type that doctors use in Mexico—the thing made an odd rustling noise. Hughes glanced back over his shoulder at Calhoun. He'd been very careful not to look at Calhoun while he slid his pants on.

"There're two types—hemorrhagic and another. Couldn't say which of the two you have. Need tests for that. I *could* order them . . . "

Calhoun buckled his pants. He heard the rip of the paper towels, the clang of the dispenser, the running water, the rubbery sound hands make while they wash each other. Slightly sexual, the sound was. Calhoun finished dressing, trying to take in the diagnosis.

"If you start bleeding from the ears and gums, well . . . I'm afraid it's a turn for the worse," Hughes said, brightly talking over the water. He turned around and turned the tap off. "But you look strong. About thirty-five, aren't you? I'm sure you'll give the old virus a good run for its money," he said, slapping his wet hands together. "I think it's harder on the dark races," Hughes said, warming to the subject. "Just my opinion of course . . . But it seems to drop these little Mexicans like flies. Especially their women." He snapped one of his still-wet fingers but it wouldn't pop. He clapped his hands together instead.

Calhoun finished buttoning his shirt. His face was warm, as if he were standing in front of an open fire. It could suddenly alternate between Turkish bath and Alaskan glacier. He'd worn his gun in a sling holster. The doctor had looked at it but not commented when Calhoun had taken his jacket off. Calhoun picked the holster off the peg on the wall now and put it on. Hughes pretended he didn't see it, but watched. The forty-five was heavy-looking, the harness worn and wet like something you'd expect to see on a horse that had been run hard.

The doctor made more noise behind him: the ripping of paper towels, the closing of the garbage can lid. He turned around and faced Calhoun again. He seemed pleased with himself.

"What's the prognosis?" Calhoun asked, trying to keep his tone bland, as if he were talking abut a third person. Calhoun looked down at the floor; the linoleum hadn't been mopped in god knew how long. There were bits of blue paper towel and small red caps from the steroid syringes on the floor. Calhoun imagined that Hughes gave out free samples to his "patients," probably telling them the injection must be given in "the large muscles of the buttocks."

"It means you're in for a bad patch, I'm afraid. Your body will fight off the virus or it won't. It's quite simple, really. We don't have much of a bead on dengue. The profession's at a complete loss. Too bad it's not the clap. I'd have you right as rain in a day if it were the clap. Those were the days.

69

Completely in the dark, now, though . . . with this . . . ." Hughes said again. "A lot of nasty things out there. It's the damn five-gallon buckets all over the hills." Hughes stepped on the pedal of the fancy aluminum garbage can. The lid popped up and he threw in the blue paper towel he'd wiped his hands with. "They fill with rain water and breed the vectors." The doctor's words were suddenly modulated, intended to communicate that the consultation was over.

" . . . I take cash. That's the way it is here. Cash and carry," Hughes said. He pulled off the paper smock and laid it by the sink so he could reuse it. It seemed as if everything in the office had been used up and then used again.

"What can you give me for the fever?" Calhoun asked. "I need something for that. And to, ah . . . keep going."

"I've seen you at Caliente a couple of times. Who sent you?" Hughes asked, changing the subject.

"A friend." Calhoun tucked in his shirt and reattached the shoulder harness to a strap of Velcro at his side. The gun seemed to weigh more. He checked to make sure his cell phone was tucked into its holster.

"A friend. I see. Well, Tijuana is full of helpful sorts, isn't it?" Hughes said. "That'll be fifty dollars. You can give it to the girl outside."

"What about a prescription? Something to keep me going?" Calhoun finished adjusting his harness, pulled his white cotton suit coat off the wooden hanger and put it on.

"I can give you something to make you *feel* better, and for . . . strength, if you want. There's nothing for the fever except aspirin. If the symptoms persist, you may have to go to the hospital. I suggest you go to an American one. If it develops into full blown hemorrhagic fever, you won't want to be fooling around in Tijuana. You'll want to get into a good *American* hospital. But you look healthy. I wouldn't worry."

70

The doctor wrote out a prescription for dexedrine and handed it over. Calhoun saw that the doctor's hands were shaking slightly. He noticed a school ring with a green gemstone. Hughes shook his hand. Even the handshake was indifferent and purposefully weak-kneed and unctuous.

"Best of luck . . . By the way, we don't accept pesos. You understand . . . Their currency isn't worth a *damn* lately. The filthy stuff isn't good for anything but flossing a pig's behind." Hughes chortled at his own joke.

Calhoun took the narrow, poorly-lit stairs back down to street level. The stairs were steep and shabby. He passed a young boy, maybe fourteen, on the way up. The boy smiled. It was the smile of a catamite. Very soft and luxurious. He had his arms folded tight like a woman while he stepped. Calhoun stopped at the bottom of the stairs, took out his dark glasses and waited a moment, trying to put Hughes and his handshake behind him. Then he stepped outside into the city. *Hate shaking hands,* he thought. *But then, people still expect it, don't they. One of our niceties. Pederast or president, everyone wants to shake your fucking hand.*

"Where are you going?" Slaughter said. A new red Buick had pulled to the curb. The Englishman was sitting on the passenger's side. One of the kids from his crew was driving. There was a thin, pale white man sitting alone in the back seat. The man tried to get Calhoun's attention. "Get in the car. We'll give you a lift," Slaughter said. Calhoun went to the rear door and slid in. "What good luck, just talking about you," Slaughter said. He turned around and looked at Calhoun. "Where to?"

"The office," Calhoun said.

"I'm afraid I have one for the dumps," Slaughter said. "He's in arrears." Calhoun turned and looked again at the man next to him. He was frightened and looking to Calhoun for help. "I'd like to get out," the man said. He made a move for the door handle, and Slaughter reached over and slapped him hard, knocking him back into the seat.

The kid punched the accelerator. A bus honked at them. The driver of the Buick whipped the wheel, avoided the crash, and they were off into the welter of midmorning traffic.

"I think they're going to kill me," the man said, looking at Calhoun. Slaughter laughed and turned around. The Englishman put his hand on the driver's shoulder.

"Stop the car," Calhoun said. He'd begun to sweat again. "I don't want anything to do with this. Let me out."

"Don't be silly. You don't look well, old boy. Heard about the bad luck this morning. Jolly good show. My girls would have been toast. Sorry, had to keep the little secret from you." Slaughter turned around and smiled. Calhoun gave up. They were only a few blocks from his office. It wasn't worth the argument.

"I suppose you must put in an appearance . . . on occasion, I imagine." Slaughter told the kid to take Calhoun to his office on Avenida Marie de Leon.

"You remember me? I met you once at the Escondido . . . Harry Cohn," the man said. Cohn wiped his mouth. He reached over and tapped Calhoun on the arm. Like Calhoun, he was sweating and seemed to be trying to think of what he could say. His hands were locked one on the other.

"Mr. Cohn has run out of time," Slaughter said. "We never think about it until we run out." Calhoun noticed how dirty the windows of the car were. *The rain,* he thought, *the rain washes down with soot in it. Funny how much it's rained.* "Do we, Mr. Cohn. I mean, you had acres of time to pay me. I was very liberal with you," Slaughter said. The Englishman had worked for some record company in L.A. until he found his true métier, working Tijuana's underworld.

"Jesus Christ, let me out," Calhoun said. *"Pare el coche,"* Calhoun said to the driver. The kid didn't pay any attention.

"Mr. Cohn, I want you to meet my confrere, Mr. Calhoun. He owes me a great deal of money, too. But he's very useful," Slaughter said.

"I owe him exactly forty-three thousand dollars," Cohn said quietly. "I have been losing lately . . . You wouldn't understand . . . Are you a gambler? Otherwise, you wouldn't understand . . . I can get the money." Cohn was looking at Calhoun, his eyes big in his head. He had very short black hair and he was rubbing it with one hand. "I told him that my wife's family has the money, but he won't listen to me. If he would just let me go back to Los Angeles . . . I would get the money and come straight back here. I swear to God," Cohn said. Calhoun looked at the man.

"Oh, but Mr. Cohn . . . You've left out the best part of the story. Why would you do that?" Slaughter said. The car turned onto the Avenida Juarez, the wheels burning rubber. The kid driving liked to speed, it was a big joke. Calhoun saw a body louse crawl out from the kid's shirt collar and move up toward his hairline. He turned away and looked out the window.

"Listen, mister. Please. I don't know who you are but, please, I have kids, I got a wife . . . they need me. This can't happen to me."

"Tell him the rest, Mr. Cohn. It isn't fair if you don't tell him the rest," Slaughter said. Cohn buried his face in his hands and started to cry. It was loathsome. Calhoun looked into the mirror of the Buick. The kid driving smiled. He made a gesture with his free hand, bringing it up to his head and pulling the trigger of an imaginary gun.

73

"I told Mr. Cohn I would employ him in our little enterprise and he agreed. Then he let us down. Didn't you, Mr. Cohn? You let us down. I had cargo that needed moving and you missed your date." Slaughter had been talking facing front. Now he turned around and looked into the back seat. Miguel said he'd been certified psychotic up in L.A. Calhoun could believe it now when Slaughter turned around. There was a murderous look on the young Englishman's face. *"You fucked with my hustle. Didn't you, Mr. Cohn? I would have let you work it off. The entire amount."* Slaughter pulled on his do-rag, adjusting it while he spoke, completely out of control.

"Slaughter, let me out. This isn't any of my business. I don't want to get involved."

"Mister, please . . . Please . . . You have to help me." Cohn took his wallet out and opened it. A plastic accordion full of his life fell out. "Look . . . Please. Help me." Calhoun felt a chill go through his body. He looked at Cohn. He looked like just another American tourist, nothing special about him except the fear. The car seemed to be getting smaller. He smelled something and realized Cohn had wet himself. He looked at Slaughter. He was saying something but Calhoun couldn't hear it for a moment. The Englishman had broken into a blurred image. The car seemed to have shrunk, too, like a tunnel.

"You had no business coming to Tijuana," Calhoun said, turning to Cohn. "No business at all. Now you're in this. . . " He pulled his coat off. He suddenly felt very hot. His pistol exposed, Cohn looked at him not sure now that he'd been talking to the right man, that maybe it was Calhoun who would kill him. "You should have stayed on the other side, but you didn't, you came here. Now you're in this," Calhoun said.

"I don't want to die."

"No one wants to die, Mr. Cohn, no one. Believe me, you are not alone. But it's the right day for it, isn't it, Calhoun? Tell our friend what day it is." They came to a stop in front of the American consulate in Tijuana. Calhoun opened the car door. He was looking into the eyes of a dead man.

"Día de los Muertos," the kid said for him. He turned around, he must have been only fourteen or so. He was smiling.

"What's that mean?" Cohn asked. *"What's it mean?!"*

"How much does he owe you?" Calhoun asked

"A lot," Slaughter said.

"All right. You lied to us about what the girls were carrying. Let him go. That's what the lie will cost you," Calhoun said. "You don't let him go . . . we don't cross them. Period."

"Fine," Slaughter said quickly. "Fine. I admire you, Calhoun. You're a gentleman. And I owe you for rescuing the cargo."

"Get out, asshole," Calhoun said. He grabbed Cohn by the shirt and yanked him out of the car. "Get the fuck out and go home. If I see you again, I'll shoot you myself." He threw him against the car. Cohn ran into the traffic and was almost killed. Slaughter thought it was funny.

NINE
DEA Tijuana — 9:45 A.M.

DEA shared the building with the U.S. consulate staff in Tijuana. Outside, the Avenida Marie de Leon was noisy, buses spewing exhaust, ripping the air with a hellish racket on their way up the hill to the slum neighborhoods of El Cumbre or out to the freeway south to Ensenada and the beaches.

Calhoun watched Breen cross the street through the big plate glass doors. He'd left the cafe where the office staff went at midmorning. Breen was order in chaos, very buttoned-down that morning, slender-looking in the mass of unwashed, thicker Mexicans on the sidewalk.

Calhoun got up from his desk. He hadn't been to the office in days, and it was a mess, piled with unopened mail. The air conditioning was down and it was starting to get warm. A secretary had brought an old-fashioned electric fan up from the basement. Calhoun found the switch and turned it up. The papers on his desk started to flap softly. He could smell the sweet, heavy ambrosia smell of perfume from the women in the office. Breen came through the double glass doors at the entrance; the cacophony of the street slipped in with him, then went quiet when the door closed. They were alone. The staff was still across the street for coffee. Breen had been watching for him.

"So you made it," Breen said. He sounded tired.

77

"I've been working the Slaughter case," Calhoun said right away. "That's why Wang had the number. I gave it to him."

"You're lying," Breen said. Breen scanned the office. He seemed to be searching for something amongst the metal desks, coat stands and potted plants. Breen turned his head toward Calhoun and pushed the bangs off his high forehead. There was something in his eyes that day that was different. Something new, as if Calhoun were seeing them for the first time. A certain openness in his gaze.

"They know. They know about everything. I have it upstairs. It came this morning from Washington. I don't think you have much time. I really don't know how you've managed this long . . . to keep it from them, I mean."

"I'm sorry, I don't understand," Calhoun said. He'd been lying about so much for months that lying now was easy. Breen smiled back at him.

"I took it from Hull's desk. He's gone this week. You don't have to lie to me." Then Breen told him what the Internal Affairs report said about him. They had everything that Calhoun had done since he'd been posted to Tijuana. They knew about Slaughter, about the cargo, Castro, everything— his gambling, all the details of his other life. "Slaughter is a class one offender . . . Did you know that? He's into every-thing—pornography, cargo, drugs, murder . . . everything," Breen said.

"I don't know what you're talking about," Calhoun said. But the sound of his voice made the lie seem ridiculous.

"Class one is as bad as it gets. You know that better than I do . . . U.S. Customs is going to put a stop to it as soon as you cross the next bunch. They don't want to arrest you here on the Mexican side because they know it will look bad—'U.S Drug Enforcement Agency officer arrested . . . in the pay of foreigners.' They're very anxious for things to look good here," Breen said. "Especially now, after NAFTA. They'll be in Palmdale tomorrow waiting for you. For some reason they think you'll be there tomorrow."

"This is some kind of joke," Calhoun said.

"Listen, Vince. I wouldn't try that tack. Your friend's name, the guy I saw last night, that's Miguel Castro, isn't it? He's a captain in the *judiciales* here in Tijuana. You two have been working together . . . They know about Castro. They know about it all." Breen sat down across from Calhoun.

"Why are you telling me this?"

"I'm telling you because . . . we're partners and I like you. It's simple. And I'm quitting the Agency. They're going to make an example of you. I thought that was rather harsh. I mean, why don't they make Salinas a fucking example. Or, I don't know, some Mexican general. God knows they deserve it. But I didn't think you meant to get in this deep. You didn't, did you? The way I read the report, it looks to me that you have a problem with gambling. That you owe these people a great deal of money. Is that it? Were you forced into it?" Breen looked at him quickly, then looked away, afraid that Calhoun wouldn't want to face him.

Calhoun nodded his head. He hadn't expected to, but he was tired and didn't care anymore. It seemed pointless to lie now. "Why are you telling me this? I mean, warning me like this?"

Breen reached across the desk and tried to touch Calhoun's hand. Calhoun pulled it back. *So I've been wrong. He liked me because he was queer. Well, there was nothing I could do about that was there? He liked me that way after all. Nothing I could do about it.*

"What does she look like . . . the girl?" Breen asked. He pulled his hand back. "The one who answered the phone this morning."

"Who?" Calhoun said. Breen watched Calhoun back away from him. It was as if Breen knew he would; that he had expected it–all the while he'd been warning him, he expected it. "Who?" Calhoun didn't know what to do with his hand now. He wanted to punch Breen in the mouth. He knew it wouldn't be right . . . yet he wanted to do it.

"The girl . . . is she pretty?" Breen asked matter-of-factly. "Please tell me that."

"What the fuck are you talking about?" Calhoun said. Breen's face changed. He looked physically pained. He put both hands on his knees and leaned forward. Calhoun looked away toward the street. A pickup truck piled with oranges went by. *What the fuck was he talking about? The fucker is crazy!*

"You're quitting . . . Why?" Calhoun asked. He would have talked about anything except that. He would even confess rather than talk about *that*. He didn't know what else to say. The room seemed to have filled up with a different kind of air now, hostile and thick. Calhoun wanted to get away from him. But he needed to know more. His skin was crawling.

"Because I can't stand it here anymore . . . What are you going to do?" Breen asked. "The Internal Affairs people took Wang to San Diego for more questioning. There's nothing I could do about it. I said you were working the case, that it wouldn't be strange for Wang to think you were somehow involved." Calhoun looked away, onto the street outside, feeling sick.

"What do you mean?"

"I gave them quite a lot of disinformation . . . lies about you . . . I'm good at that," Breen said.

" . . . Thanks." Calhoun had told him about growing up on the border, about Palmdale. He'd even told him what had happened, why he'd had to go into the Marine Corps.

80

There was a long pause and Calhoun and Breen just sat there. Breen was looking at his knees, hands out, screwing something up inside himself, Calhoun thought. *He's doing something to himself.* You could see it. It was like watching a hill give way. You could feel it. He was tearing himself apart internally. "I shouldn't have lied for you . . . but I did. I lied." Breen looked up at him. "Did you hear what I said?" Breen said. "I don't give a shit about much now. Can you understand? When I heard about you, I decided I didn't care what you'd done; you were my friend. That was all I cared about. Can you understand that?"

"I . . . I . . . " *God, man, what does he want me to say?* "Yes. I can understand that," Calhoun said.

Breen went suddenly back to what he had been, a quiet policeman. The other side of him closed up, as if nothing had happened. "Well. I suppose we won't see each other again."

"I guess not," Calhoun said. Breen stood up. "If I can help, I will," he said. "I want to help you. I suppose you're used to people wanting to help you. You *are* going to run away, I hope."

"I don't know. I guess so . . . I should."

"We're trapped, aren't we, you and me . . . Do you love the girl? That might matter. If you love her. Maybe something good could come out of it . . . If you love her," Breen said.

"No. I don't love her," Calhoun said. "Not at all." Calhoun forced himself to look up, to look Breen in the face. He was scared after what Breen told him. He knew that they would catch him, sooner or later now. If they knew so much, it would only be a matter of time, no matter what he did.

"I suppose it wouldn't matter if I told you I'd do anything for you . . . " Breen said. "I disgust you, don't I."

"No. Not at all," Calhoun said. There was another silence.

"I wouldn't stay *here* much longer."

"You said they'll be in Palmdale tomorrow? Not today?" Calhoun asked.

"Yes, tomorrow . . . at the bridge. Well . . . Do you need any money . . . I could give you a few hundred dollars . . . " Breen's voice sounded more ordinary now.

"I'm okay," Calhoun said.

"Yeah . . . you're okay." Breen moved toward his own desk.

Calhoun pulled his coat from the back of the chair and walked out of the office. He could feel Breen looking at him through the double doors of the consulate. He walked by the Chinese restaurant, nodded to some of the secretaries and started down the hill toward the plaza. The secretaries waved at him. *I'll have to tell Miguel.* Then Calhoun stopped and looked back toward the office. Breen had come to the door. He stood watching him.

TEN
Hotel Española — 10:00 A.M.

There are three of us. My daughter, Paloma, and my wife," Heinrich Vasco said. "Shall we have coffee or tea? I prefer tea this time of day. They serve a wonderful tea here," Vasco said. "They even serve Madeleine cake with it. French you know. Leave it to the French to perfect something the English love."

Heinrich Vasco was a gentleman, you could see that. A real Latin American gentleman of the old school, Calhoun thought. He wasn't fifty yet, Calhoun guessed, but he had that grace just in the way he stood. Calhoun had seen it as soon as he came into the lobby of the Hotel Española, the best hotel in Tijuana. Vasco seemed to fit the surroundings, the marble and the greenery and the hush of the lobby. The light was diffused and lush and came from a big, old-fashioned skylight that lit the interior and made everything glow. While Vasco spoke, Calhoun watched shadows and the light come and go. The light painted the marble, making it seem cold and perfect. A coterie of the city's wealthy came for coffee in the lounge at mid-morning. It was the place to do business in Tijuana.

"Sure," Calhoun said. Vasco was wearing a tennis outfit—white V-neck sweater, shorts, white Nikes. He was athletic and slender. He had a towel with him and wiped his face which was sparkling with sweat. Castro had said they had to make the appointment, no matter what had happened that morning. It all started to seem like a dream now. Castro had

83

come and played a game of tennis with Vasco after they'd left Slaughter's cargo at the Arizona with one of Miguel's men.

There was a table waiting for them in the garden room in the corner overlooking the pool and the gardens. You couldn't see any of the city. The hotel was a little walled-off oasis. They could have been anywhere—New York, Santiago, Madrid.

The chairs in the dining room were big and overstuffed. A low table held a tea service and coffee and cake. Miguel and Vasco were speaking in Spanish and Calhoun could follow it well enough, all about their tennis game. Vasco had won and Castro was wondering if he could get his revenge; the Spanish word *venganza* seemed to hang like music in the dining room. Everyone in the place had money except, of course, the waiters, who looked scared of the rich. That is the way it is in Latin countries: the rich scare people, and the poor don't pretend otherwise. A waiter poured the water into the teapot and disappeared.

"I wanted to meet you. We heard, of course, that you are the best," Vasco said. "And well . . . we can afford the best." Calhoun could see that Vasco was measuring him. "I would be entrusting not just myself, but my daughter and wife. My family, in other words." Vasco picked up the lid of the Victorian porcelain teapot and then replaced it absent-mindedly. "Darjeeling . . . You haven't said a word, Mr. Calhoun."

"Sorry. It's been a busy morning," Calhoun said.

"I know what you are thinking: why is a person like me in need of a coyote?"

"The thought crossed my mind," Calhoun said. The waiter came back and poured the tea. Calhoun asked for a brandy and the waiter nodded reverentially and disappeared.

"Don't drink coffee, Mr. Calhoun?" Vasco said, surprised by the order.

"I feel like it's already four o'clock in the afternoon."

"In Chile we have all the best customs from Europe," Vasco changed the subject. "My father was a German. Well, not really. He was Chilean, but my grandfather was a German, a real *Junker,* I'm told." Vasco smiled. "My mother's people were bankers. Since, well, since the Conquest, I think. Tea was always important to us at our house. I miss my mother. Very much. You see, she was a very elegant lady. Anyway, we've had some bad luck since she died . . . at the bank." Calhoun looked at Castro. "Let's just say I want to go to America and that I'd prefer to enter without the need to register. I want to send my daughter to school in the U.S. She's been accepted." Vasco picked up the teacup and looked at Calhoun. "Sometimes fathers do things with only their children's best interests in mind. Do you have children, Mr. Calhoun?"

"No," Calhoun said. He didn't believe any of the dog and pony show. In the silence you could hear the chatter of some Japanese behind them. There were several tables of Japanese from the *maquiladora* plants. Calhoun watched Vasco chew a piece of cake. He had a way of doing it that seemed like not chewing at all.

"I don't want my daughter to know that. I don't want her to know that, well, that what we are doing is technically illegal. I want her to think that it's an adventure. Something unique. She has no idea of our reversal. I've gotten a job in Chicago with some friends. It's very important that she think things are, well, like they used to be."

Calhoun nodded. He glanced down on the garden. A mother and daughter were coming in from the pool. He knew she was his daughter as soon as he saw her because she had the same face as the father. The girl wore a sun hat and a white terry cloth robe pulled around her body. She was tall, very tall and statuesque. Her hair was wet from the pool and made a kind of black rope sculpture around her shoulders. She glanced up and looked at Calhoun and Castro and then her father. Calhoun saw the flat of her stomach, the brown skin, the dark eyes, a Walkman around her neck. She and her mother were holding hands. Calhoun felt his neck tighten the way it did when he saw a beautiful woman. They came by the window and waved. Vasco put his cup down and blew his wife a kiss, then waved them in.

"That, gentlemen, is my family. Sometimes a man can be blessed." Miguel Castro cleared his throat and looked at Calhoun but Calhoun wasn't looking. The beautiful vision was burning into his head, the thin beautiful neck, the elegance and youth. He hardly noticed the mother, who was beautiful herself and probably only forty.

"I have gems and I want to guard them against a very cruel world any way that I can," Vasco said.

"I understand." Calhoun said.

"How much?" Vasco said, putting down his cup.

Calhoun looked at Castro.

"We would have to go alone. I wouldn't want, well, you understand, it would have to be a special trip. Just us. The three of us. And I'd like to leave tonight at, let's say . . . how about ten o'clock?"

"We're the most expensive . . . " Calhoun said. The waiter brought his brandy and put it down in front of him.

Vasco waved his hand. Calhoun noticed the wedding ring fat and gold in the air. Then someone caught it and kissed it. It was her. It was the girl, and from that moment on, Calhoun let Castro do the talking and he listened to them talk, saw all the elegance and all the manners and all the family love; and most of all the daughter, pouring tea and keeping the robe around her lovely body. He saw the expensive sandals, and the wire of the Walkman confused in her hair, the slenderness of her ankles. There was one long moment when their eyes met. She was a big woman. Paloma Vasco had green eyes.

"I want you to meet Mr. Vincent Calhoun. He is taking us on a jeep ride. In fact, we go into the United States tonight," Vasco said.

"Papa, I was just getting used to the hotel."

"My dear Paloma, there is something waiting for you."

Paloma Vasco put her cup down. "But I thought we were . . . "

Her father pulled an envelope out of his pocket with relish. "I didn't want to tell you until I was sure. You have been accepted to my old school. The University of Chicago."

"Papa!" The girl put her arms around him and the robe opened and he saw the brown thighs, the way they were, all the way up. Vasco looked like a man who was still rich and would bounce back from whatever happened to him, Calhoun decided.

"Now, I want you both to meet Mr. Calhoun and Mr. Castro." Calhoun shook the wife's hand and she smiled.

"Mucho gusto, señora," Calhoun said. And then he was looking into Paloma Vasco's pretty face and she was smiling and laughing and shaking his hand. He noticed that she had a powerful grip and shook his hand like a man.

"Mucho gusto, señorita." Calhoun said.

Calhoun and Castro stayed and talked in the lobby; the Vasco family had gone up to their room. Calhoun was looking at the beautiful portico. It was raining slightly. *I have to tell Miguel. I have to tell him that they know.*

" . . . something political is what I heard. The Americans don't want to let him in. Something to do with his bank's failure," Castro said.

"You mean he's running away from something."

"Maybe."

"Why doesn't he just send the mother and daughter on to Chicago?"

"You don't understand Latins. He'd never do that. They go with him. That's my guess. He's the old school. Aristocratic. My guess is that they change the government in Chile again and he'll probably get the bank back. That's the way it is in Latin America," Miguel said. Calhoun nodded. He looked at his friend.

"All right, so we ask for ten thousand dollars."

"All right," Castro said. "Fine. I'll go up and tell him. She's very beautiful. The girl."

"No, she's more than that."

"What did Hughes say?" Castro asked.

"Dengue fever," Castro looked at him. "He said it would go away. I'll be all right, Miguel. I've got to make the two-thirty race at Caliente today," Calhoun said, changing the subject.

Castro looked at his watch. "No problem. I'll meet you at the bus station in half an hour. We'll do this little job for the lawyer and you'll be back here by one-thirty."

"Miguel . . . " *I should tell him. Why don't I tell him that they know? It wouldn't make any difference.* "She's not your type," Calhoun said.

• • •

There was smoke over the valley behind Tijuana where they have the dump. Calhoun drove up in the jeep. Everything

88

was covered with smoke like a fog: the rag pickers and their children, the hulks of cars, the dilapidated cardboard houses, everything partially obscured. Even the road seemed to have disappeared.

We all lie to ourselves. That's part of living. Calhoun was lying to himself as he drove. The people he was going to borrow money from were his enemies and he was lying to himself about that, saying that they were just another source of cash. But he knew it wasn't true. He'd sworn that he would never come out here and borrow money from El Cojo because El Cojo was the lowest thing in Tijuana and, in fact, his enemy, because he ran some of the most vicious rat patrols. *But in Mexico it's easier to lie to yourself than anywhere else in the world. It's just that kind of country,* he told himself.

A priest stood in the smoke and watched Calhoun close the door of the jeep and walk up the short driveway towards El Cojo's house. Calhoun had heard that El Cojo's front man was a priest, but you couldn't tell for sure because they don't let priests wear the collar in Mexico. But they said he was a priest. El Cojo used him because the priest knew the system, and more importantly, he could read. El Cojo had learned one thing in his short life: there was a system bigger than the one he ran out at the dump.

"I have to see El Cojo," Calhoun said. He was wearing a new clean Bill Blass suit, his havelock and sunglasses.

The priest was wearing jeans and a Disneyland T-shirt and was very pale, almost like an albino, so that out there with the smoke he looked unreal–like a doppelganger. His hair was that blond color albinos have, almost white, and thin on a pinkish scalp. The priest, about forty, looked like he was made from smoke and garbage, like the dumps themselves, not quite real. There was a barking Rottweiler. The priest held it by a leather collar.

"I hear El Cojo is loaning money now," Calhoun took his sunglasses off. The priest nodded.

"I run that," the priest said. He kicked the dog. The brute barked once, took it and looked at the priest, then at Calhoun, like he'd like to jump up and tear Calhoun's heart out. "It's 100 percent interest per day," the priest said. He looked him dead in the eye. He'd heard the interest was 70 percent a day.

Calhoun looked around the place while he thought about it. He lied to himself again and said that 100 percent interest a day was no problem. He noticed a gang of teenaged boys sitting on a wall at the side of the house–El Cojo's crew, he imagined. There was an old yellow Toyota Land Cruiser in the driveway. It was what they used out there on the desert. *God damn it, I shouldn't have come here.* More than once they'd chased him. Now he was coming out to borrow money. *I should shoot them,* he thought.

"Okay," Calhoun said. He was desperate and he had a sure thing. Rats or no rats, he needed the money.

"How long you want the money?" the priest asked.

"Let me talk to El Cojo." He wanted better interest and thought he could talk him down to something reasonable.

"Fuck you," the priest said. "Fuck you and go away then."

"All right . . . four hours. Just four hours. So I guess that means that I only have to pay 25 percent of a hundred . . . I need a hundred thousand pesos."

"You pay 100 percent if you only touch the money and give it right back."

They brought it to him in a can. One of the hotshots on the wall, a real small fry with freckles, brown freckles on brown skin, was carrying it with him. He handed the priest the can and the priest counted out one hundred thousand pesos from the roll in the can and handed it over. One of the kids went out to Calhoun's jeep and took down the license number and ran back into the house. That's the surprising thing about Mexico. It seems unsophisticated, but it's not. El Cojo was wired. He even had a radio in the house and he talked to some of the police who worked for him. The license number would go straight down to the police station and be recorded.

Another kid came up and took a Polaroid of Calhoun. The Polaroid that would circulate later that day in Tijuana. It showed Calhoun standing next to a pile of car parts, half a Cadillac and a Pinto. The priest was halfway in the picture.

"God bless," Calhoun said, looking at the priest. He shoved the money into his pocket. But the priest was busy with the dog.

"You don't bring back the money in four hours, we kill you," the priest said, looking up at him. "And don't think we can't find you. We'll go right inside the fucking Escondido and shoot you. I know who you are. *Vaya con díos.*" The priest finally smiled. His teeth were badly rotted.

ELEVEN
Bus Station — 10:45 A.M.

The bus station was crowded. Every day more people from the interior of Mexico were coming north to the border to escape the collapsing peso. *Running in front of a wave that would crash on them here,* Calhoun thought. He had some cargo to pick up, a lawyer and his two sisters. Someone in the states had paid full fare for them and they were going to get the royal treatment. From here on they would be under Calhoun's protection until they were crossed and delivered.

We're better than Federal Express, Calhoun thought, waiting in the cafe for the bus from Chihuahua. Calhoun watched a group of stewardesses walk by. They were in company uniforms, short black dresses and black jackets. He marveled at the womanly asses, then at the crowds of peasants and the noise of the buses as they pulled in from all over the Republic, covered with road dirt and dirty windscreens and the romance of the open Mexican highway. Mazatlán, Calexico, Nayarít, Durango; the buses pulled into their gates, others left for the interior.

Calhoun watched a bus unload. The passengers got off with their possessions in cardboard suitcases and plastic bags. Countless men in cowboy hats with thick arms had that I'm-going-north-don't-fuck-with-me look. Calhoun respected that look. It had taken the human race to the moon. Like the movie said, failure wasn't an option. It would take these dirt farmers across the river, through the gauntlet of helicopters and razor wire.

93

The bus from Chihuahua rolled into the parking lot. Calhoun waited, watching the crowds. Their man got off first and came into the cafe where he was sitting.

"Buenos días."

"Buenos," Calhoun said.

"Where do you want them to go?"

"How many are there? There should be three."

"Yes, three. One of them is a lawyer," the man said, as if it made a difference. He did nothing but complain, the man said. "Do you want to meet them?"

"No, not yet. Take them to the Cuauhtémoc. The desk clerk will handle them. Tell them that we'll leave in an hour. And to be ready. Tell them not to leave their room until we get there. If they leave the hotel, tell them it's not our fault what happens to them," Calhoun said. "Horacio?"

"Yes, *señor.*"

"How much more have you charged them?"

"Nothing," the man said. The young man was a medical student, a cousin of Castro's who rode the bus with clients to make sure nothing happened on the way from Mexico City.

"Don't lie to me. You charge them for this part of the trip, don't you, to the hotel." The young man looked around the bus station cafe. Then at the grimy counter where Calhoun had watched for him. The gringo was *loco.* He really looked *loco* now. Calhoun was sweating again, the beads large on his face, his blue eyes intense.

"Yes."

"How much?"

"Very little, hardly anything."

"Give it back. We're not like the others."

"Give me a hundred dollars. I need the money," the man said. Calhoun peeled off a hundred dollars and put it on the counter.

"Horacio, don't ever fuck with the cargo again. I'll kill you. Do you understand that?"

"Yes, *señor.*"

"No. I mean *I'll kill you,* do you understand that?" Calhoun was sweating and he'd taken off his havelock and put it on the Formica counter. The young man looked at Calhoun, sweating like that, his hair plastered down his handsome face with the cold blue eyes, and was afraid of him. He nodded.

"I understand, *Señor* Vincente."

"I hope you do," Calhoun said, then he waved him away.

Maybe it was the way the Indian nodded. The way he seemed to look after his young wife and the love the couple had. Calhoun watched them. He often sat here in the bus station drinking coffee. He had been doing his finances, what was left of them, on a napkin. There was no more money. He was finished. If he lost today, that was it. He had gambled most of everything away. Today he had a chance to win it back. He assured himself he would win and it would be all right. He decided he would take his winnings and leave, become Mr. Al Smith, address Mexico City. He wondered what he would do there. Maybe from there he would go to Asia. He'd always wanted to go to China, *anywhere but here,* he told himself. *Anywhere but here.*

He noticed the young Indian couple right away, the way they were standing in the lobby, lost lambs, and right away he saw the sharks gathering. One was down by the magazines watching but pretending not to. They were a young couple holding hands, Indians straight from the jungle—Guatemalans, you could tell them right away. It was something about the way she was looking at him, so much in love.

I've never had that . . . someone like that. Somebody who loved me like that. The wife had a scarf covering her head, a round face. *The city will eat them for lunch,* Calhoun thought. All they had was that love. He wondered how far it would go for them. Love. *No se puede vivir sin amar.* He watched the man at the magazine rack nod to someone. The couple picked up their cardboard suitcases and came into the cafe and sat at the counter near Calhoun.

They put their packages behind them, the wrong thing to do. The kid turned to the counter person and tried to get his attention. Calhoun knew the counter person was working with the others. He ignored them for a moment, checked out the scam, then came forward with a big friendly smile and asked the couple what they wanted, making a big show of laying down silverware and water and a basket of crackers. The man from the magazine rack came in and pretended to use the telephone on the wall close to the counter. Another man came into the cafe from the sidewalk. The man on the telephone started to yell. Calhoun got up and walked behind the couple and stood next to their suitcases. The one who was going to steal their suitcases grazed him and kept on going as if nothing had happened. Calhoun pushed the bags closer toward the couple still being chatted up, not understanding what had almost happened to them.

"Hey! You got to watch your bags," Calhoun said in English. The young husband turned around and smiled. He didn't have a clue.

"Bags," Calhoun said. "Your bags. *Tús maletas.*" He nodded to the suitcases on the floor. The husband nodded, but he hadn't understood. Calhoun was going to leave them to their fate, then the wife turned and glanced at him. She was so young, sixteen or so, something he didn't see much in this town—clean, honest. She was still holding her husband's hand. She was scared, and Calhoun stopped. He looked at the man on the telephone. They stared at each other. Calhoun gave him a murderous look and the man put down the phone and disappeared like vapor into the crowds in the station.

I could leave. Why shouldn't I . . . nobody . . . nobody ever . . . He turned around and looked at the couple. They knew practically no Spanish at all and were having trouble ordering.

Calhoun sat down next to the girl and ordered a coffee. He listened to them speak to each other in their soft Indian *Quiché* language. With their language they were able to shut out the outside world. It was the language Cortez heard and later the French, a language from the jungles. Calhoun sat transfixed. He didn't speak until one of the coyotes he knew who hung in the bus station walked up to them and asked them if they wanted to go to the U.S. This coyote was famous for taking you to the river and disappearing you. He was very sweet looking, not well dressed, and looked like a choir boy. That's what the people on the street called him, the choir boy. The husband had turned around.

"Yes, how did you know? Please, how much?" said in bad Spanish. The choir boy sat down next to the husband.

"Many come here to the station looking for help," the choir boy said. He looked at Calhoun. He knew of him but thought nothing of it because Calhoun only did the high-class trade.

"Where are you from?" the choir boy asked.

"Guatemala," the husband said.

"Go away . . . " Calhoun said in English. He picked up the coffee and finished it. The choir boy looked at him. "They're Slaughter's," Calhoun said. The choir boy looked at Calhoun in disbelief and immediately left. The husband looked at Calhoun, confused.

"U.S.?" Calhoun said. *"¿Ustedes quieren ir a los Estados Unidos?"*

"Yes, how much?"

97

Calhoun could have told him that each person paid ten thousand, that they ran the most expensive coyote service in Tijuana, that it was used only by Latin Americans with connections, with family in the states, or by criminals who could afford the price of a ticket.

"Ten dollars American," Calhoun said. "You got ten dollars?" he said in Spanish. The husband translated to his wife. She said something to him.

"Nine-fifty," the husband said. Calhoun laughed. He couldn't remember laughing like that in a long time.

"Okay kid, you drive a hard bargain."

"Juan Martinez." The husband put his hand out. Calhoun shook his hand. "My wife, *señor.*"

"Pleased to meet you, *señora.*" The girl looked at him and giggled. The choir boy would have killed them both. Calhoun turned around and looked again at the grimy counter and at the cook who had chatted them up. He would have let them leave with the choir boy and said nothing.

"Where are you heading?" Calhoun said.

"San Francisco," the husband said. "Is it far? My father is there." He dug something out of his pocket, a letter. "We're to call . . . ?"

"Put it away," Calhoun said, suddenly angry. He wiped his face, felt the cold chills and gripped the counter. The room got smaller, the cook's face seem to recede and his greasy blue T-shirt blurred. The man came towards Calhoun with the coffee pot.

"I said put it away. You'll lose it. Then what? Then what?" He turned and looked at the kid. "What if you lose it? Then what!?"

"Yes, *señor.* I put it away." Calhoun picked up the napkin and touched his mouth. He tried to smile through the chills.

"More coffee, *señor?*" The counter man's face splayed out and there were two counter men offering him their phony smile.

"Get the fuck away from me," Calhoun said. "You fucking cockroach." The three faces started to laugh in stereo, loudly. The coffee spilled in a black shower into the huge cup. Calhoun saw the cup grow as he focused. He looked up again and everything was okay, normal, the sounds of the buses, the cacophony of the cafe, the cook laughing normally.

"Are you all right, *señor?*" The young man had pushed the letter into his pants.

Calhoun turned to him, then to the wife and saw that she was frightened. He tried to smile at her.

"*Vámonos!*" He pushed himself off the stool. They went outside. Calhoun got a taxi driver he knew out in front and sent the couple to the Cuauhtémoc to wait for him.

A white unmarked Ford came down the ramp reserved for buses. It stopped at the guard shack, then sped into the garage. Castro in his police car came through the crowd. Calhoun walked out to the parking lot.

"Where are they?"

"I sent them on to the Cuauhtémoc with your cousin."

"Good." Castro was wearing a black suit coat and black pants and a white cowboy shirt and hat. It was the *judiciales* uniform.

"Amigo, you don't look so good."

"Yeah, I had sex with your sister last night and this happened."

Miguel grimaced at hearing the joke again and pulled out of the parking lot, back up the ramp to the street.

"There's one more . . . a Palestinian. He's very rich. My people are delivering him in person. He paid twenty-five thousand just to come up from the capital. His people are *very* rich," Castro said and did that handshaking thing Latins do when they want to emphasize something.

"And I'm taking two I found in the bus station," Calhoun said. Castro looked at him.

"Two kids from the sticks. They don't have a clue. They would never have gotten out of town. But we're getting paid. I think we're getting nine-fifty but I'm not sure it's American money. It might be Guatemalan money. I forgot to ask."

"You're a romantic. I didn't know that about you," Castro said. "I suspected it though . . . A romantic. I suspected it."

TWELVE
Sonoran Desert —11:20 A.M.

They turned onto Mex. 2, a two-lane asphalt road that ran east toward Mexicali with more potholes than the road to hell. There were six people in the jeep, not counting Calhoun and Castro. The Guatemalan couple Calhoun had rescued, three Salvadorans, the lawyer and his two sisters, and the Palestinian kid who had contracted with Slaughter.

Castro was telling Calhoun that the kid was from some kind of merchant family on the Gaza strip and had come by boat to Veracruz. Castro said the kid's family had big money. Calhoun looked at the boy in the rearview mirror. It suddenly became important to him that he look at each of the faces in the back. He wiped the sweat off his face and adjusted the mirror, picking out the Palestinian kid first. He was in the very back, his feet up on the opposite window, playing a video game, oblivious. He was well dressed, horribly out of style, but expensively.

Calhoun moved the mirror. The three Salvadorans behind Castro were smallish. They had airs from the moment they'd gotten into the jeep—middle class airs. They had paid full price to be smuggled into the U.S. and they resented it. The Guatemalan couple had tried to talk to the Salvadorans but they weren't interested. The lawyer and his sisters smelled peasants and cut them dead. Calhoun moved the mirror to look at the two middle-aged sisters. They were in their forties and they looked mean. Their brother was tonsured, in his fifties and looked soft. He was extremely nervous, as if he

101

expected his throat to be cut at any moment. Calhoun brought the mirror back to its right place. He looked at the Guatemalan couple in the back with the kid. They were holding hands. The boy had shaken Calhoun's hand as he got in the jeep as if maybe the handshake would somehow mean the difference between success and failure.

"What do you want to hear?" Calhoun said, taking his eyes from the back.

"I don't care," Castro said. Castro was looking at his friend very carefully. Calhoun opened the box at his elbow, sweat pouring down his drawn face. He rifled through it till he found the Rolling Stones "Stripped" CD.

"I'm gonna tell you how it's gonna be . . . " Calhoun sang the tune, shoved the CD into the slot. The jeep suddenly started rocking, Keith Richard's guitar at full volume, four speakers grinding against the still late morning desert outside. The Tecate mountains rose to their left, metallic blue and wicked looking. "Hey, you think it's really true . . . Mick Jagger fucked Eric Clapton in the ass?" Calhoun asked.

"I don't know," Castro said. "You're acting strange today, amigo." Calhoun ignored him, waving his hand. *"My love's bigger than a Cadillac . . . "*

The jeep pushed on toward a small chink in the U.S. Border, just east of Palmdale, still ten miles away. The air conditioner blasted over the rock 'n roll music. Tumbleweeds became metallic fire balls. Burning strips of barrel cactus looked iridescent, like biblical fire in Babylon. The tarmac became a viscous silver liquid. Cars that passed were meteors of glaring, roaring chrome, frightening. People's face's were little ugly billboards with teeth and hair. Mick Jagger gave it everything he had. Calhoun's mind started to fill things in, tried to see through the confusion of his dengue fever, make sense of the desert and the tarmac. For long moments the two lanes became blurred and dark. Calhoun tried to see through the sunlight. *That's the desert at noon,* Calhoun thought, *confusion with sunlight.* The brighter it got, the more confusing and dark it was. His hands began to shake and he had to fight the fever's accompanying dyskinesia.

"Are you going to tell them?" Castro asked. He reached over and turned down the music.

"Why should we do that?" Calhoun's voice was loud, as if it too were out of control. Castro knew Calhoun wasn't drunk, the sickness was making his partner erratic and crazy. Not on the surface, but just below it.

"I think it's better that we do. It's always better. You know it's a shock for them as soon as we pull off the road. I don't want a scene," Castro said. "It's not good for business."

"No, I think it makes it worse. They don't look like the type that you would tell. Especially those two." Calhoun nodded to the two older Salvadoran women who were feeding their faces already, holding some kind of *empanadas* wrapped in foil. "They think it's going to be a morning in the fucking country." Calhoun smiled into the mirror and the women smiled back, disarmed by Calhoun's good looks. It was always the same with women and Calhoun. Castro studied the women and seemed to agree that warnings would only make it worse for them. Calhoun grinned at them violently and winked, then turned the music back up.

"I'm gonna to tell you how it's gonna to be. Love is love and I'll fade away. I'm gonna to love you night and day. Don't fade away," Calhoun sang. He began to bang on the steering wheel, moving his right hand in a kind of rocking motion, getting into the music. He seemed oblivious for a moment, lost in the Stones' tune. Castro pushed his cowboy hat back on his head and looked at him.

"The turnoff . . . " Castro said. "Up ahead." Calhoun slammed on the brakes and the jeep skidded for forty feet like they were on a glass table top. They glissaded over the burning rubber and asphalt and came to a stop, smoke coming up around the tires. The women had to grab their jeep straps to stay in their seats. Calhoun smiled and looked into the desert, then turned off onto the dirt track to their left.

"You don't look well," Castro said. "Maybe I should drive." Calhoun turned around and looked at his friend. His face was wet and shiny. His blue eyes wicked-looking. *"I* drive. I *always* drive," Calhoun said. "You know that." He wiped the sweat off his face and smiled at him.

"Maybe this time we should take the long way?"

"Why the fuck should we do that? It's more dangerous," Calhoun said. "What's wrong with you, anyway? I got to get to the track at two-thirty. You know that!"

"Maybe today we should take the long way," Castro said again, repeating himself.

"You mean the jump? We've done it a million times."

"I know . . . but today . . . maybe we should go around. The long way."

"Fuck no. We go around, we're liable to get caught by the rat patrol and get into a fight . . . and I'm not fighting for this bunch." Calhoun reached for his havelock, took it off, and set it next to him on the seat.

"Maybe that would be better today," Castro said again.

"I like the jump. I miss it. Everyone should jump an eight thousand pound jeep once a week over a two hundred foot vertical drop," Calhoun said.

"All right. But you don't look well. You're . . . "

"I feel great," Calhoun said defensively. Castro laughed. He was a brave man and in the end, fatalistic. He prided himself on his fearlessness and didn't want Calhoun to get the wrong idea. He would rather have died than have been suspected of cowardice.

"I'm worried about you, amigo. Seriously, man . . . "

"Worry about yourself," Calhoun said. *He's my one friend,* Calhoun thought. Then they were quiet. There was just the vibration of the big tires on the desert track and the sun blasting everything it touched at eleven-thirty in the morning. Calhoun reached over and turned on the CD again. The Rolling Stones came back on.

"The music will make it worse." Castro had to yell.

"Not for me," Calhoun said. He turned it up. The lawyer made a sign that the music was too loud, covered his ears and squinted his eyes. Calhoun reached forward and turned it down for a moment.

"Ladies and gentlemen, I'll be your pilot this morning. We are going to be traveling at speeds that will reach one hundred miles an hour over uneven, dangerous, desert country. On our right you can just make out the Sea of Cortez. There are several gangs in the area that would like nothing better than to kill us for our meager possessions. Do not worry as we are equipped for these eventualities." Calhoun took out one of his forty-fives and waved it in the air. The Salvadorans looked at him like he was mad.

"We should be landing in the USA in approximately forty minutes . . . the weather is clear. Thank you for choosing our carrier services for this leg of your journey. Cabin crew, please take your seats and prepare for open desert."

"Amigo, you are the worst son of a bitch on the fucking planet. Let me tell you that," Castro said. He looked at the lawyer and tried to reassure him.

105

They hit a rough patch of hard pan. The older women were scared. Calhoun was going sixty plus, sometimes swerving the jeep, cutting the sand, holding tension. There was a constant hard bouncing now of the suspension. Castro was used to it. He glanced at the back. The cargo was white-faced, all of them except the Guatemalans. They'd left the jeep track and were in open desert now. There was no road at all.

"Hey! Please slow down," one of the Salvadoran women yelled in Spanish. As if she were talking to a taxi driver in town.

"What did she say?" Calhoun asked. He had the music on, Keith and Mick kicking it up.

The woman leaned forward, the rolls of her stomach against the cheap fabric of a chintz dress, her face greasy with chicken, her gray hair done up with a yellow scarf, a black purse with grease stains on the leather in her lap.

"Mister drive too fast. You slowly down," she said in bad English.

"Shut up. *Silencio!*" Calhoun roared. He said it in Spanish, turning down the music, glancing in the rearview mirror, fixing the woman with his sick blue eyes that were fever-wide. She looked at him quickly in the mirror, saw Calhoun's strange eyes. Intimidated, she leaned back into the seat.

" . . . And charming, too," Castro said. He made a noise and rubbed his nose.

"Next thing is she'll want to drive," Calhoun said.

"You have a real way with the ladies," Castro said. "You're no good. Look at you." He turned away and looked at the desert. The clouds of reddish dust trailing behind them poured into the pale morning sky. Calhoun liked to feel the desert under the jeep, the roughness of it, the way it threw them around. *You feel yourself less out here,* he thought. *You feel less of everything. You're swallowed up in it. The impossible emptiness of it.* There was just the beautiful sexual pull of the engine and the tunnel of dust and cactus. And then there was the jump. It took a half hour off the trip. But that wasn't why he liked it; it was the going off the edge of the canyon across a divide of twenty feet over a rocky red abyss. The shadow of the jeep traveling along the canyon wall. The screams of the passengers when they were airborne. It was having the shit scared out of him that he loved. The fact was, he liked to cheat death.

"Amigo, you know what's wrong with you . . . no one ever knows when you're joking and when you're serious. That is a bad character flaw," Castro said, trying to engage him.

"I never joke," Calhoun said.

"No! the problem is that you are *always* joking and no one takes you seriously. That's what I mean. Who can take you seriously? You are completely crazy."

"No one takes Mexicans seriously, either," Calhoun said. "At least not where I come from."

There was a large outcropping of rocks, an entrance to a maze of arroyos and washes that marked a change in the desert here, the beginning of the broken ground with washouts, canyons, and spiked hills like big, red, rocky thorns. It was here the trail was the worst, and for the passengers, the most frightening. Calhoun down-shifted and slowed. He looked around for a way through, shifted up, and they climbed on a rock table still going thirty miles an hour. Boulders the size of houses went by the windows. The jeep descended into a long narrow canyon.

"Look at my Guatemalan!" Calhoun nodded to the back. "He's got balls. I bet he doesn't say a word. He'd rather die first." Castro turned around and looked at the young man. If he was scared, you couldn't tell it from his face. The Salvadoran women were holding each other, their brother was saying something but it was so soft you couldn't hear it. The lawyer leaned forward and looked at Castro and said something in Spanish. Castro explained that the driver was very experienced and turned around.

"You're right, he'd rather die than act like that one," Castro said. "I hate cowardice in a man. I hate it more than anything."

"I bet you a hundred dollars I'll make the lawyer break water," Calhoun said. Castro turned around and looked at the little Salvadoran, then at the Palestinian kid who seemed completely at ease, enjoying the ride like it were Disneyland.

The lawyer leaned forward. "I beg you to slow down. Think of the women," he said. The lawyer was wearing a blue *guayabara*. Calhoun sank his foot into the gas and threw the man back against the seat.

"Don't talk to the driver," Calhoun said over the music.

"What are you doing, amigo?" Castro turned and looked at his friend. The canyon here was wet from the rain, the sand darker, the traction secure. You could hear the tires hit the water some moments, hydroplane and lift. Then rumble again. Castro saw that Calhoun's shirt was drenched and that he wasn't well at all. And it hit Castro for the first time that they might, in fact, crash.

"I don't like him," Calhoun said. "Why doesn't he just say he's scared." He put his foot into it again. They descended into a narrow lane that ran between solid rock walls twenty feet high. The engine roared, the Stones doing "Let It Bleed," Richards' guitar raunchy, the man's eyes terrified. One of the women started to scream. The Guatemalan kid looked at his wife and took her hand stoically. They were scared now but determined.

"Guatemalans are tough people," Calhoun said, looking into the mirror, enjoying it. *"Look* at them . . . look at the kids. They're beautiful," Calhoun said over the roar of the engine, *"look at 'em!"* He shifted violently and sloppily. The jeep seemed to stall, then start again in the narrow alley of red rock, the water more frequent here. Castro had gotten quiet. He took his cowboy hat off and set it on his lap. He was sweating, too, now. He knew that there was something wrong with Calhoun, that he was sick, not right in the head. He'd been fine earlier but now wasn't. He tried to be calm. They were going too fast now, much faster than they'd ever gone in this stretch. If he tried to grab the wheel, they would all be dead.

"You're right . . . of course they know something about life . . . back there it's tough. They are tough people . . . admirable." He tried to think of the right thing to say that would work. He had put his hands on his lap and watched the narrow passage seem to shrink with speed. They descended again so that the desert floor was thirty feet above them. The shadows were big here. Then, just as suddenly, the canyon started to open up so that the canyon walls were fifty yards apart, then sixty. They crossed a rill, then a creek, but the water was deeper—a foot or so deep—so that the tires were barely able to hit the sand underneath.

"Look at his woman, look at her eyes. That's *generations* of guts and suffering. Right there, right now, look at it, Miguel, look at her now! Every battle the Mayans ever fought is in her eyes right now. She won't break, I know it. Not like that chicken-eating fuck next to her. Backbone like a fucking *bridge post."* He slammed his hand on the wheel. His hair was wet with sweat.

"Of course," Castro said. He put his hat back on, raised it off his head, thinking now that they weren't going to get out of the canyon. He felt the wobble of the tires, barely any traction left. He tried to look ahead to see if the creek would widen. Again he heard the throttle and the engine respond. They plowed into the deepest parts of the water, sheets of dirty water washed against the jeep's windshield. For a moment they were completely blind, a kind of chocolate mud obscuring everything.

The lawyer covered his face. The women screamed. Calhoun began to laugh and hit the windshield wipers; big thick cake-batter mud was pushed off. There was a sharp turn coming up, the wall of the canyon very red in the sun in front of them. Castro watched the windshield clear. He reached over and turned down the music.

"Look at the piece of shit. Look at him. He's a lawyer but he'll get on welfare as soon as he gets across the line and the liberals will cry for him and . . . " Castro stopped listening. The canyon wall was rushing up, its reddish tone closer and closer, the engine louder against it. "I say make him break water . . . that's what I say!" Calhoun shifted up, the engine noise rough, the speedometer going through sixty. *"My love's bigger than a Cadillac . . . "*

"Vincent . . . ?" Castro stopped talking and looked ahead at the red rock wall that marked a sharp turn in front of them, then at Calhoun's crazed face, his hands on the steering wheel tapping to the music still playing in his head.

Castro suddenly reached over and turned the ignition off. The whole Jeep lurched against the flywheel. The dead weight of the steel and tires and people flew into a pool and slowed, the wall coming at them. Almost as if he'd come out of a dream, Calhoun went to work controlling the slide through the water, bringing the front of the jeep under control. He flipped the key to on. They started again on compression, just making the turn, the wall close enough to see the grasses in its cracks. Everyone was silent. The canyon widened after the turn.

"Sorry," Calhoun said, slowing down. "I saw something beautiful in those eyes, that's all. Sorry. The other one spoiled it . . . sorry, Miguel."

"Don't worry, amigo," Castro said. "Things like that cleanse the blood. They're good for you. I am sure of it. They'll remember it the rest of their lives." The canyon started to diminish, the walls coming down. The water diverted to their right now. They climbed back up to the desert floor.

They were going forty now. Barrel cactus started to crop up again. Calhoun slalomed around them, down shifting and climbing off the floor of the desert, taking a series of switch-backs.

"Are you all right now?" Castro asked. Calhoun nodded. He could tell it was over and the fever had let go some. Calhoun's eyes were more normal now.

"Yes, all right. No past, only future," Calhoun joked. They were suddenly out on top of a mesa and racing along its rocky edge, the whole Sonoran desert below them, the late morning sun on their left. There was a terrific sense of freedom and life. Calhoun reached over and turned up the music, the harmonica blowing. To their left was a hundred feet of nothing, to the right the vast desert plain, all the way to the gulf, shimmering and breaking up. Here and there patches of darker sand from the rains remained. The Palestinian kid figured it out first, what was going to happen. Castro tilted his cowboy hat back on his forehead and watched the edge of the canyon come racing up.

"Don't be careful," Castro said. Then they were airborne, just the noise of the wind against the flying mass of green steel, Calhoun's big hands on the steering wheel, just empty blue sky and sunlight.

THIRTEEN
Palmdale — 12:30 P.M.

Calhoun drove the jeep up to the last gate. Castro slid out of the jeep. They'd crossed the border at the Hittleman's cattle ranch. Hittleman got five hundred dollars a week to keep his mouth shut. Castro walked across the metal cattle guard, opened the gate with a key and waved Calhoun through. The gate marked the end of the Hittleman ranch. Calhoun nosed the jeep over the metal cattle guards and it was over. Calhoun pulled out onto the shoulder of the highway. He glanced into the mirror.

"Well . . . " the lawyer said, "Where's the coyote who takes us to Los Angeles?"

"Up the road a little," Calhoun said. The lawyer looked suspicious, still worried that they were going to kill them. Castro closed the gate and trotted across the empty highway and got back into the jeep. The Guatemalan kids and the Palestinian were asleep; the last hour on the Hittleman ranch had been uneventful as the desert flattened after they plowed through the river that separated Mexico and the U.S.

"Okay," Castro said, closing the door. "I want to buy a pair of sunglasses while we're here. At the Kmart. It will only take a minute."

"Thank god we're here," one of the lawyer's sisters said. She crossed herself. "Thank god we are in the United States." A yellow school bus passed them, and behind that, a green border patrol sport utility, the back windows blacked out.

113

"Well, that's it. We can turn them in now," Calhoun said. The lawyer looked like he was going to die. Calhoun pulled up on the highway and followed the border patrol.

"Is it money you want?" the lawyer said. "I'll pay you more. I knew you were liars and cheats! I knew it."

A half mile up the road the border patrol car pulled into a substation. Calhoun drove on by. Castro burst out laughing.

He'd passed through Palmdale dozens of times in the last few months, but now as he saw it again, he was forced to look and remember. It hadn't changed since the day he'd met Celeste—the low brick buildings, the camphor trees. He remembered the gray linoleum floors of the high school and the way his father had taken him around and introduced him to the other teachers.

They'd delivered the cargo in the parking lot of the truck stop. It was one of those truck stops that was busy night and day. There had been no time for good-byes. The cargo was hustled out and transferred into a silver van and they were gone.

All the time he was drinking coffee at the truck stop, it bothered him. It was a physical feeling. *Why do I care?* he kept thinking. *Why did I want to give her money? Why do I care if she's there when I get back? Why do I want to go back there?* He didn't try to explain to Castro where he was going. He dropped Castro off at the Kmart and said he'd be back.

The red newspaper box nailed to the fence post was still there, the narrow serpentine road winding into the desert hills. Calhoun stopped for a moment at the turnoff to the Stone ranch. It was as if it were that first day he'd brought her home. Calhoun looked at the empty seat next to him. For months now everything had been going by so fast. He'd made so many stupid decisions without thinking. He saw them all now. Today when he saw her again, it was as if he had suddenly come to a stop. He looked around him and realized how stupid he'd been.

Fuck it, he thought. *I have to tell him.*

Calhoun closed the door to the jeep and waited for the dogs to come out of the ranch house the way they used to, but there was nothing, just the sound that the desert makes in late morning, that crackling sound, as if the ground were drying up under your feet. He glanced at the ramshackle ranch house. One corner of the roof sagged. He remembered Celeste's bedroom. There'd been a naked light in the closet. He saw her coming out of it that night before he was arrested. She'd been laughing. He turned and looked at the path toward the chicken houses. He saw how they seemed to be nestled perfectly into the landscape, brown and windblown, like they were made out of rock and not wood. Calhoun stood for a moment, held by the past. Then, looking at the chicken coops, he remembered the charge: *statutory rape, his father's lawyer asking him if it was true.*

"Mr. Stone." Calhoun called it first loud, then again louder. *"Mr. Stone!"* He waited for Celeste's father to answer. He wanted to see him. He wanted to apologize. He wanted to go back to that night and explain that it wasn't what her father thought. He turned from the coops and walked toward the ranch house. It had a tin roof, and the roof looked like pure phlogiston in the sun. Under the porch was a smear of shade. *I want to speak to him one more time before I take her away.* It was then he knew why he'd brought her back to the Amigo. He had no intention of letting Celeste go now. He would have as soon died.

"Mr. Stone!" His shoes kicked up the dust of the yard. A few things had changed. The barn door was open and Calhoun

saw the tractor. It was a new, green International Harvester with a hay cutting rig on the back. He walked up on the porch and knocked. There was a turned upside-down horse shoe over the door. The screen door was new; the front door had been left open.

"Mr. Stone! It's Vincent Calhoun." He braced himself and knocked again on the screen door. He saw a pile of *Readers' Digests* and a kerosene storm lamp on the dining room table, a red and white checkered oil cloth.

"Mr. Stone!" No, it hadn't been like they'd all said, that he'd wanted her for her body, that it was just the sex. He put his hand on the door. *I could go in and . . . but that* was *it. It* was *the sex and it* was *her nakedness, and the, yes, it was the look of her ass and her tits and that was all I wanted, wasn't it . . . my face in that pussy. Wasn't it. And it was wrong because I was a teacher and supposed to be better than that, but I wasn't.* He let the door-knob go, the truth pouring into him. All this time he'd lied to himself. He remembered now how he'd looked at her that first time and what he'd thought. *I want that. I want a piece of that.* He turned around and saw the emptiness of the sun-blasted yard and remembered how he'd looked at her in the car that day. *And it was still the same.* It was an odd desire. But now it was something else, something he had to hold onto. It was bigger than desire now.

He heard the rattle of a truck, the chains on the back. Calhoun saw an old Ford pickup coming down the road, the dust up behind it, the sun burning the windshield. Calhoun opened his coat, ran his hand around his waist nervously. What was he going to say to him? He stepped into the hot sun and waited. The truck got closer, the green rusted Ford coming in and out of the cloud of dust. The truck stopped at the gate. Calhoun looked behind him and regretted having come. He looked toward the coops, and for a moment, he saw her in her jeans, no shirt, the way she used to walk around her room when they were alone. How young she was then. He'd wanted her all the time. Everything about her he'd wanted and nothing had changed. *I'm going back to Tijuana and have her.*

Stone shut off the engine and slid out of the truck. He was older now, maybe fifty. There was a hunting rifle on the gun rack of the Ford. Calhoun walked a few paces forward, his white suit blazing in the sun. He looked out from under the shadow of his havelock.

"Mr. Stone." His voice sounded funny to him. A dog dropped out behind Stone and ran up to Calhoun and sniffed his shoes.

"Calhoun?" Calhoun looked up. Stone grabbed for the rifle and pulled it down from the rack. Calhoun heard the bolt move. He looked into the sun. His sunglasses were perfect for this kind of light. They cut everything down to clear sharp yellows. He saw the rifle against Stone's chest and heard the sound of the bolt going home.

"You son of a bitch. You ruined my little girl," Stone said. Stone moved in front of the Ford's big chrome bumper.

"I came here to say I was sorry." Calhoun heard his own words, and watched Stone lift the rifle. The idea that he was going to shoot him didn't seem to matter. He watched the hardness in Stone's face in the yellow light. You couldn't really read it any more than you could some old desert animal's.

"You're a little late with that, aren't you, boy?"

"Yes, I am . . . I'm taking her away." There was a gunshot. Calhoun flinched at the bit of yard which exploded at his feet. He looked up. "I found her again and I came to say I'm taking her away." Calhoun spoke to the man and the rifle. Neither one of them moved. The dog came back and went

117

and sat, tongue out, at his master's feet. "If you kill me, you'll ruin the only chance she has," Calhoun said.

"Where is she? She here now?"

"No. She's in Tijuana."

"What the hell is she doing there?"

"She's been in a Mexican jail. I found her this morning. I want to help her." Calhoun saw the rifle stock tilt down, the barrel go back on his shoulder.

"The day I saw you, I told her you were no fucking good," Stone said.

"I came here to tell you, you were right about me then. But I can't undo that now."

"She's in Tijuana?"

"Yes . . . " Calhoun said. "I don't have a lot of time here. So I want to know whether you're going to shoot me or not, because I'm going to walk up to you now." Calhoun started walking across the yard toward her father. Stone didn't move. Then he slung the rifle over his shoulder as Calhoun got closer. As he walked up to him Calhoun saw the tufts of white hair coming out of his blue denim work shirt. His face had been etched by the wind. Calhoun was afraid to look him in the face. Then he forced himself to. For a moment, they looked at each other. It wasn't hate Calhoun saw. He had expected hate. He saw pain and hadn't expected it.

"She left not long after you did. Went to L.A. with some *new* asshole," Stone said. "I don't know what she got up to there. She was in a dirty magazine, I know that." His voice was tough and deep and burnt-sounding, pretending he didn't care. But Calhoun saw the look in his squinting, sun-hooded eyes. It was pain. The rest of him was all desert except for the eyes.

"She could come back here. I don't give a damn what she did in any magazine," he said.

118

"You were right about me. I came to tell you that. I was wrong then for what I did," Calhoun said. He felt stupid.

"I keep her things," Stone said. "I got 'em in there, in the house." He nodded toward the ranch house. "Is she all right?"

"I think so." Calhoun said. "I got to go."

"You're going to help her . . . you mean that?"

"Yes, I do." Calhoun turned around and walked toward the jeep.

"There isn't a day goes by I don't miss her," Stone said. Calhoun stopped; it was as if he'd been shot. He realized then that he loved her. That was what this was about. He loved her and he hated her for what *he'd* done. He hadn't let the emotions penetrate, but they had now—both of them. He'd come here to understand it. Both emotions were on his face when he turned around. He'd come here to lie to himself one more time.

"I guess it's been the same for me. Every god damn day," Calhoun said. He watched her father come toward him, the dog following.

"You tell Celeste . . . Tell her I . . . still have her things. You tell her that, then," Stone said. He walked past him into the house.

FOURTEEN
Amigo Motel — 1:30 P.M.

Calhoun hung onto the telephone. He'd placed some bets with his bookie the day before and had forgotten to check in until now. He turned the TV on with the remote control: MTV cut to throbbing pulchritude around a pool, butts and babes, hunks in trunks, grinding it. Calhoun watched the screen as he dialed.

There was a news flash . . . a library in Tijuana had been blown up . . . Something called *Manos Blancos* was claiming responsibility. The local TV station didn't bother to turn down the music, they just ran a news ticker across the screen. The words floated over the smiling face of Daisy Fuentes on the MTV Countdown.

"Press one if you want to place a bet . . . two if you want to speak to someone in Management," the recording said. Calhoun pressed two.

"This is Calhoun. How did I do?"

"Hold please."

"Fuck hold . . . how did . . . ?" There was the sound of rock music suddenly, then a recorded voice giving odds on Wimbledon. Then the Tyson fight in Vegas. Maybe he'd take some action on the Tyson fight, Calhoun thought. *Why not?* He heard a pause, the hum of his bookie's office, a side conversation.

"Well . . . How'd I do?" He was back on hold.

Calhoun's hand clamped down on the phone, moist from where he gripped it. How many times had he been on the

121

phone like this, squeezing the phone like his life depended on it? *Have to have a winner now*, he thought.

"I'll be right with you. This Calhoun? . . . Hold a second," the bookie's voice said.

"Yeah, how did I do?" Calhoun asked. "Well . . . How'd I do, for fuck's sake?" He watched a drop of sweat roll off his nose and fall on the dirty glass top of the night table.

"Checking . . . You really want to know? . . . Zip. The doughnut. Not one out of nine, amigo," the bookie said. "And that's the naked truth." Calhoun lowered the phone. He felt as if someone had hit the elevator button that said *fast-down*. He leaned his back against the wall.

"How about another crack at it?" the voice said. Calhoun put down the phone, didn't bother to answer.

He started with the TV. He pulled it out of the fancy armoire, wrenched it free. Calhoun's huge upper body, veins bulging on his arms, wrestled with the box. The cable cord saved the TV for a few seconds until, finally, Calhoun, grunting like a barnyard animal, got it loose from the wall. He ran toward the bathroom with it, rammed the thing into a corner.

He kicked in the mini-bar door, his expensive shoes cracking through the rattan façade and stopping. He got on his knees and ripped the mini-bar door off the refrigerator, gutted the contents with his big hands, scooping bottles, candies, nuts out onto the carpet. He hurled the bottles through the bathroom doorway and heard them break. The door in his hands, Calhoun backed away, sweating, looking for something else to smash. He saw the painting of three clowns staring at him on the opposite wall and threw the door at it. Missed. The three clowns continued to stare at him, satisfied.

Calhoun went across the room and pulled back the curtain, moved the blinds and looked out on the sun-blasted courtyard of the motel. He knew Celeste was waiting for him. He had said they'd go out to lunch. The idea seemed funny after everything that had happened since he'd seen her that morning at daybreak. Calhoun let his eyes wander the Amigo's courtyard. He stopped when he saw a maid's cart piled with linens and buckets in front of Celeste's room. He'd come back and found a note saying she'd checked into her own room. He wasn't surprised, somehow. *Has it really been ten years?* He'd been so stupid and young. *If she'd just said something, that she'd loved him, that it wasn't the way the prosecutor had said that day. It wasn't the way it had come out in the papers at all, not at all. How could something get so twisted? It wasn't twisted until the newspaper had gotten their lies into it. Until they'd made it the way they'd wanted. But that wasn't the way it had happened at all.*

He watched Celeste come out of her room and walk to the Coke machine at the end of the courtyard. She was older now, twenty-seven, a woman now, not a girl, even the way she walked was womanly; she'd gained weight in her hips; he remembered the way they'd been, thin, like a boy's hips. He watched her thin arms and the way her waist tapered, her red hair pulled back. She was better looking now, he decided. With the money he'd left her, she'd bought a pair of new jeans and a Mexican cheap gauze blouse that showed off her pretty shoulders. He remembered she was a working-class girl with working-class ideas about what was fashionable. He held the cord to the blind and wrapped it around one of his fingers. She looked his way for a moment, wondering, probably, when the fuck he would get around to her. A car started in the courtyard. Calhoun looked quickly at a family heading back out into the world. Their car was noisy. He knew he'd do it, just like that. *I went all the way to Palmdale to find out what?* He couldn't decide what was eating him, *specifically. That I would get back at her, because if I didn't . . . I might . . . What? . . . Why did it still matter?*

He watched the car leave, its broken turn signal papered over in red plastic—on and off, on and off. Celeste was looking his way again, carrying a can of Coke; coming down the arcade, looking at his room. She knew that he was back because the jeep was parked in front of his room. He wondered what she would think about the fact it was all busted up. He saw her hesitate for a moment, looking into the sun, deciding whether to come over. He told himself to get rid of her. Lust and hate gnawed at him like rats in a basement, gnawing and tearing at him. He'd tried to ignore them but couldn't, not one second more. He held the curtain open and watched her finally turn around and go back into her room.

He went to the bed and pulled on his shoes. For a moment, he wondered what he had in mind, *exactly.* He saw himself walking across the courtyard and barging in. Asking her why she'd done it. Why she hadn't told them the truth. All the anger came back, the weight of it, like something he was carrying on his back. The judge looking at him, and his father, and the reporter who had followed the story and written all the lies. *They were all there in the courtroom. And you weren't there. I prayed you'd show up . . . walk into the courtroom and tell the truth. Prayed like a little kid. Just tell them I love you. Really love you, he'd said to himself over and over that morning in court.*

The phone rang. He looked at it a moment and went to pick it up.

"I just promised Slaughter we would cross the girls by seven tonight." It was Castro.

"I should kill him . . . That's what I should do," Calhoun said.

"Amigo, you're acting very strange. How are we going to do it? We have to cross the Vascos at ten-thirty."

"We'll cross the girls at the line . . . Right here in town," Calhoun said. "It will be quick."

"No, I think it's too dangerous. Maybe we . . . "

"I'm busy right now! I'll meet you at the Arizona at six. Bring the girls down from the Cuauhtémoc." Calhoun hung up the phone. It rang almost immediately but he didn't bother to pick it up. *Fuck careful. It's Castro's fault for doing too damn much.*

Calhoun opened the door. The sun hit him in the face. He crossed the motel parking lot, felt the softness of the asphalt, knew what he was going to do to her. In his head, the judge was talking about the Marine Corps and how it was his only chance.

Calhoun glanced several times at his father behind him. The hate and shame in his father's eyes. The judge passed sentence, a sentence that wouldn't go on his record. The smile on the reporter's round white face. The reporter nodding, as if he'd written the script himself: statutory rape; the high school teacher that had banged his student and gotten away with it until now. The reporter had squeezed every dirty thing he could out of the story, day after day of lies. He'd gotten them, the family in Palmdale. Calhoun's father was principal of the high school. Disgrace spread over his father's face as the judge banged the gavel. They adjourned into the judge's chamber. Calhoun was told he could join the U.S. Marine Corps voluntarily or go to jail. Calhoun joined up the same day in San Diego. Two weeks later the School Board fired his father. They never saw each other again.

Calhoun crossed the courtyard and saw that her room door was half open, there was music coming from a radio on the maid's cart. She was doing Celeste's room now. He'd forgotten to put a shirt on. He walked through the open door of the motel room and told the maid in Spanish to get out. He'd shoved the automatic into his belt. The woman took one look at him and left without saying a word. Calhoun watched her walk past him and close the door, almost running.

Celeste was bent over, shoving her old clothes into her pack. He hadn't even tried to be quiet. He was wearing just his pants and shoes. *Guilty, guilty, guilty. Why hadn't you come to the courtroom and told them the truth? It wasn't ugly. It wasn't like it said in the paper. I was in love. You told me that you loved me. You'd cried when you said it.*

Calhoun heard the door lock click, felt the click in his hand as he locked it, leaning against it for a moment. Celeste turned around, still squatting on her haunches, her ass against the new white jeans. She stood there a moment, frozen, then straightened up.

"You bitch," was the first thing that came out of Calhoun's mouth. He came across the room, his eyes checking the bathroom. He saw a toilet brush, a pile of towels. He walked up close to her. She hadn't moved. It was as if she knew all along that it would happen; that for years she'd expected this scene to be played out, and she'd only been waiting for it, that anything else would have been impossible, that their first encounter had just been a prelude to this—the two of them alone with unfinished business.

"Why didn't you tell the truth?" He grabbed her by her new blouse, felt it rip, saw the white bra underneath. Saw the new orangeish lipstick on her face. She was saying his name, just his name.

"Vincent . . . I know. Vincent . . . I know . . . " Calhoun heard her say something else, but the sound of his father was in his ears and the sound of the sheriff and the courtroom and the way his father trotted alongside the car in the parking lot screaming obscenities at him. He'd looked for her even then, had wanted her to tell the truth about them, was expecting her to somehow stop it.

He felt the bra come off in his hands, its elastic strength, the pulling of it, then her breasts, warm white, the nipples, her throat, her eyes meeting his, the bra in his hands. The sound of his words like they were coming out of someone else's mouth. He saw her lips moving, heard his name again, her voice sweet, misunderstanding, thinking he just wanted sex. He ripped the blouse away down to her waist, the shredding sound of the material ripping off her shoulders, the thin material giving way like paper. She tried to stop him, then stopped trying, confused by what he wanted. She reached out for him.

"Why didn't you go to the courthouse? *Why not?!*" He grabbed her by the arms, shook her, asked her again, why hadn't she gone to the courtroom. She stood there, nothing in her eyes, face blank. She was looking at him as if she were waiting for him to unlock something with his questions. She tried to touch his face, he slapped her, knocking her onto the unmade bed.

"That's what you want, isn't it? That's what they all want in the end," she said. Her face had gone cold. He had his hand up and dropped it.

She tried to get up. She was talking to him but he couldn't hear anything but his own voice, voices from the trial. He put his hand over her mouth and felt for the edge of her panties with his other hand, felt her warm belly and pulled, digging down until they came apart in his hand, ripped away from her body.

"This isn't going to make it better," she said. He heard that. He cupped his hand over her mouth, and for a moment he just held her that way, her lips moving against his fingers, her nose flaring. The hot breath. She wasn't struggling. But he *wanted* her to struggle. He kept his hand over her mouth and undid his pants. All this time he had blamed her for what had happened to him later. *It's her fault, all of it. Ending up here like this.*

The car had stopped at the intersection of the courthouse. The reporter and the DA were walking across the lawn. The curious were watching his father—the fallen principal of Palmdale High. Calhoun had turned around in the squad car as best he could because of the cuff. The sheriff was saying to him that it wasn't fair, that he'd heard the real story from his daughter, how all the kids in the school knew the real story and that it wasn't fair. But Calhoun didn't pay attention, he was watching his father's face, studying the transmogrification of a man that had been destroyed. Principal of the high school to nothing in the space of a few weeks. The School Board was talking about firing him that morning, the sheriff told him.

She hadn't moved. Calhoun had her shoulders pinned to the mattress, pushed into the starched clean sheet. He saw the words "Hotel Amigo" stitched on the pillow. He didn't want to see her face. He rolled her over and pushed her face into the mattress and finished undoing his pants, felt for his cock.

Then he was suddenly there, in the room. Really there, his cock in his hand, her fleshy white ass, the torn panties, Celeste's voice muffled by the mattress, her neck red where he held it. She was coughing. The idea of killing her crossed his mind and scared him. He stopped, felt his weight on his knees, felt the bed sag. He let go, zipped his pants up and got off the bed, the anger and the hard breathing still in him. For a moment he looked at her body—the way her waist was narrow and beautifully white, her breasts pushed against the mattress. He backed up into a wall, watched her turn on the bed slowly, sick with what he'd done to her, ashamed of what

128

he'd thought. She coughed and wiped her face, looked at him, her face deep red.

"I want you to," she said, her voice hoarse from coughing. "I want you to. I want you to." She kept saying it, until it was more horrible than what he'd been about to do. "I still love you, Vince. I want you to. I understand. I want you to. Please." She was sitting up now, moving what he'd torn, holding herself on her knees, reaching for him pathetically, looking at him that way, trying to smile, a smile that he couldn't look at.

"I'm sorry. I . . . I . . . " He was breathing hard, could feel the painted back of the door against his naked back. "I'm sorry, Celeste. I'm sorry. I don't know what's wrong with me." He was crying, didn't even realize it until she got up and touched his face, kissed him.

"I'm so sorry," he said. "I'm sorry. I'm sick. I don't know why I did that. Today out there I saw . . . " He moved his hand toward the desert. He was dripping with sweat. He felt a chill from the fever.

"I don't care. I love you. I don't care." He was trying not to listen. For a moment he reached out and touched her hair. *The reporter was laughing at his father. Calhoun had seen that just as the light turned green. His father stopped his screaming and looked at the reporter who had ruined him. He was laughing at him.*

"I still love you, Vince. I never stopped. I never stopped. I want you to do this. I want it to be the way it was. I've wanted that for a long time, the way it was between us then. The way it was before . . . "

He kissed her. Brought her to him, felt her breasts on his chest. He kissed her neck and her hair. He kissed her on the mouth, put his arms around her, crushed her to him, the gun between them, cold and oily.

"Hold me, Vince . . . hold me, baby," she said. Then she brought him back to the bed, as if the years had been rolled back magically, neither one of them thinking about what they had become, just what they had been. They made love, her on top of him so he could look into her eyes, watery and sexual, and her teeth biting his lip the way he remembered and the way he loved. When it was over, he didn't want to move or think or say anything because now he was in love again and he didn't want to be. But he was. For the first time in years. They both looked up at the ceiling and the years rolled back to when they were young.

"We're going to leave tonight," Calhoun said. Celeste had her face on his chest. She pushed her hair off her face, ran her hand up his chest to his chin. "I have to go. Right now. I have to go somewhere important. I want you to wait for me here. Will you do that?" He got off the bed and started to dress.

"Yes," she said. "I'll wait."

"I'm sorry for what I did. For . . . "

"I've seen worse," she said. "Forget it."

"No past, only future." Calhoun said.

"Yeah. Vincent?" Calhoun stopped, his hand on the door knob.

"Yeah." He turned around. He was smiling at her, like they were kids again.

"If I told you that I . . . I mean if you knew about what I've been . . . would it matter?"

"I don't care. I love you. I don't care." She was going to explain. He held up his hand. "What difference could it make now?" he said.

He walked back to his room and grabbed a shirt; it was getting late. He had to get to the track. He had to place that bet. He was sure it was the bet that would change his luck. *Things were changing now*, he told himself outside, starting the jeep. He was sure of it.

FIFTEEN
Caliente Racetrack — 2:30 P.M.

The Winners' Circle at Caliente race track is as far away from God and Decency as you can get. There were bars downtown that were more frightening, but the Winners' Circle was the soft, wet pulp of greed, the hub of every human vice in the city. If the bars downtown were about unspeakable acts, then the Winners' Circle was about unspeakable obsession with fast money.

It was the kind of bar gamblers love because it sat right on top of the action. The action started at noon and went all night. Gamblers loved it; it was flashy and tawdry and reeked of cologne and cigarettes. The Circle, as it was called by the *cognoscenti,* had a great view of the Caliente dog track, windows everywhere, like a control tower. When the greyhounds went to their starting box, the hard core, the heavy money people, stood up and went to the windows with binoculars. "Girl-friends" in spandex giggled, bracelets tinkled (Why was it that gamblers liked girls with big tits? One of the seven mysteries), and men in Polo shirts did that little hopping thing while they yelled at their favorite fido running his guts out. There were a lot of fifties-style touches—wire sculptures of grey-hounds on the walls, and drinks that came in glasses decorated with black and gold diamonds. In Mexico, the fifties had never died. Marilyn Monroe had never died. Machismo had never died. There was always the slight smell of over-excited people, like walking into a room where somebody has just had sex.

131

Calhoun felt one of his chills come on. He took a drink and surveyed the once-elegant barroom. It was filled with professional gamblers and a few tourists, voices bouncing off the hot pink walls. He felt the chill pass over his big body, smiled into it, took another drink. He ordered another G and T and waited for the next chill. They had started coming in waves. *I'm not really sick,* he said to himself, raising the glass. Not sick. *After I leave here I'll get the tickets for us.* He allowed a brief, first-time fantasy to invade him. Celeste and him on the bus on their way to Mexico City in the dark, just the sound of the bus engines, and her against him, and a new life. A clean life, they would both change, maybe even have a kid.

"How'd you come out yesterday?" Calhoun said. Calhoun didn't usually talk at the bar, but he felt so good now, so alive. Part of it was the fever he was running, and part of it was because he knew he was going to win that afternoon and that he was in love. The bartender turned and looked at Calhoun. He was the kind of guy Calhoun liked having out on point when he was in the Marine Corps. The kind that can't wait to nail a bad guy. *Fucking Okies. Ninety pounds of freckled fight,* Calhoun thought. The less you fed them the better they liked it.

"I caught a show and place yesterday," the bartender said.

"So what!" There was a voice behind them; both Calhoun and the bartender turned around. The voice had come from one of the upholstered booths at the back.

"You can't beat the system—the odds. The odds are against you. You're bound to lose everything," the man said in a loud voice. The bartender gave Calhoun a murderous look. He took a book of matches out of his shirt pocket, pushed the top of the matchbook cover back and slipped a single match under his thumb and struck it one-handed. The young

American who had interrupted them got up from his booth, picked up a briefcase and walked up to the bar with his drink.

"Everybody is going to lose," the man said. "Professor Herbert C. Jones, pleased to meet you." Jones put his hand out toward the bartender, who ignored it. The bartender pulled a cigarette from the pack behind him on the CD player, put it in the corner of his mouth and lit the end, then looked at Calhoun like *one more drunk*. The bartender went back to looking at the racing film on the closed circuit TV like he'd never seen the guy's outstretched hand.

The young professor took the stool next to Calhoun. He put his plastic briefcase on the bar. His gray tweed sport coat was greasy-looking. His khaki pants were stained at the knees, like he'd knelt in an oil slick playing craps in the street. He looked haggard despite his youth.

"I can't go home," the professor told Calhoun matter-of-factly. He didn't seem drunk. *Crazy,* Calhoun figured. "What about you?" Jones asked. Calhoun didn't know what to say.

"Is that so," Calhoun said. He felt trapped. Jones sat down right next to him. He didn't feel like moving and his good mood was being suddenly tested. He would have bet even money the bartender was going to pop the guy if he said another word to him. *Well, a pop in the face might do him good,* Calhoun thought. Who could say?

"I had it. The system breaker. I did," the professor said. He was younger than Calhoun, maybe thirty. Like scores of men Calhoun had seen around the track, the professor had the tell-tale signs of the chronic losing gambler: that day's racing program from *Diario de la Sierra* shoved in the front pocket of his tweed coat, the blank look, the eyes that shoot from face to face looking for a way out of it.

"I have a Ph.D. in Mathematics . . . I do," the professor said. "I have a good job at the college in Lone Pine. I have a wife, Carol."

"Yeah? Good for you," Calhoun said.

The bartender poured himself a beer from the tap. He'd already sucked the unfiltered Camel an inch down. He made a point of knocking the ash off into that black plastic tray where the spilled beer went. It was obvious he didn't like the professor on principle, because he was an amateur.

Calhoun glanced at the television which was playing recordings of yesterday's races. The track looked almost pretty, like a park, the red dirt perfectly groomed, thick track fluff, just what the bowsers loved.

"I had it wired. I wrote a program." Jones fished out his laptop from the briefcase, flipped it open on the bar. "Now think of it this way: Chance reduced to a few variables, gentlemen. Variables you can foresee. Mathematics. Zeros and ones."

"Yeah?" *I don't need any professors because I got the fix in, baby,* Calhoun thought. He'd been having a run of real bad luck, it was true. He owed Slaughter and now El Cojo, thousands of dollars, but that would all end in about twenty minutes, Calhoun told himself. The professor's computer wouldn't turn on.

"Batteries," Jones said. "Anyway, it doesn't matter anymore. I know now I was wrong. There is no way to get your arms around the problem . . . Three days ago I thought I had the answer. I took my mutual funds, everything we had. The house. That will be hard to explain to my wife. Carol . . . She doesn't know what I did . . . I did it for us." The young professor looked down at the keyboard, touched a few of the dead keys with his long, girlish fingers. "Just three days ago. It was all in order. Organized chance. It worked in the lab—"

"Sure, buddy. You need a shower and you'll feel better," Calhoun said. He gave the guy some barroom sympathy. They were alone now. The bartender was setting up someone down at the other end of the bar.

"You don't understand! I've lost what we'd saved, everything, and I was so sure. About winning, I mean. People like you, they believe . . . You get a hunch, or whatever, about a dog, or a horse, or the jockey. But I had a Cray mainframe at the college! Science, do you understand?! Three billion calculations a second for two years. Quantification of chance. Do you understand that?" The professor's face moved closer. He smelt like piss. "What you are doing, and he is doing, is . . . is idiocy." Jones pointed to the bartender. "There are no winners. It's impossible. You see, it's impossible." The professor started to laugh. A sick, broken laugh. "Do you see, Mister? That's what I've proved. Don't you see it? There *are* no solutions. That's what I proved, after all those billions of calculations, and I finally got the answer." The professor started laughing again like a crazy man, spilling his drink. His young face was grotesque in the fluorescent light.

"Hey, pencil dick . . . give it a fucking rest." The bartender came back down the bar. "People come in here to have a nice quiet drink and think about their bets. They don't come in here for free advice from pencil necks. Okay?"

"You have a hunch about today's races, don't you?" Jones asked Calhoun. He'd been laughing so hard he'd started to cry. He had no idea the bartender hated him, the way all gamblers hate losers.

"Yeah," Calhoun said, humoring him.

"And then what?" the professor said.

"What do you mean . . . 'And then what?'"

"I mean, your system. What is it? I want to know. I collect them. I had one, too." The professor touched Calhoun's elbow.

"You want to know *my* system, pencil neck?" the bartender butted in. Calhoun was sure the Okie was going to punch him now. He'd seen it happen a thousand times. He was just looking for the excuse he needed. Then wham! The professor would get another dose of chance.

"Okay. Yeah. I want to know your system," the professor said, turning to the bartender, suddenly angry. The bartender slipped out his matchbook. Calhoun saw the tattoo on his wrist. *Semper Fi* in faded blue. He'd been right, *a fellow Marine*, Calhoun thought. He knew there was a reason he liked the guy.

"All right. I'll tell you, professor. I know something about dogs. Understand? I watch 'em. I study 'em," the bartender said. He took out a fresh cigarette and reached over the bar and stuck his index finger in the professor's chest. "I won seven hundred bucks yesterday. How about you, asshole?"

"And what is it, exactly, you know about them?" Jones asked.

"I know a good one when I see one."

"But I'm not talking about dogs," the professor said. As if that was the basis of the misunderstanding between the two men.

"Well, we're talking about dog racing, ain't we? That's a fucking dog track down there, ain't it?" the bartender shot an incredulous look at Calhoun.

"Yes. But I'm not talking about the dogs. I'm talking about *odds*," the professor said again.

"You're crazy." The bartender looked over at Calhoun for confirmation of the obvious. But he'd already gone.

136

• • •

The men were standing in the track's crowded shape-up area. The track's loud speakers crackled on a pole above them. The shape-up area smelled of greyhounds and hay. It was covered by a huge aluminum roof that amplified the loud speakers. The track announcer's voice was calling a race. There was yelling from the crowd . . . *"We got the Torres dog in the Winners' Circle."*

They'd passed a bottle around before they did it. A pint bottle of Southern Comfort went to the trainer, then the vet, then the Mexican handlers, then Calhoun. Calhoun took a swig and held the bottle. He watched the veterinarian open his bag and get down to it. The vet, a Texan with dirty fingernails, had come from El Paso. He had one of those black string bolo ties with a big piece of Indian turquoise jewelry for the clasp. The doctor ordered the dog pinned The trainer and his men grabbed 99, his racing number that day, and pinned the greyhound against the vet's old white station wagon. Calhoun bent down and put his knees into the dog's ribs.

"Would you fucking pussies *press* for Christ sakes!" The veterinarian had the syringe pointed up in the air. He looked at them angrily. Six sets of knees smashed down harder on the slender, whimpering greyhound, driving him into the doctor's car door. Calhoun could feel the animal's shaking fear through his own knees, saw the look in the dog's black eyes–confusion, almost human. Calhoun wanted to stop it but couldn't. He needed the win, nothing else was important now. *Win, then get the fuck out of Tijuana forever.*

The vet reached inside his bag, got out the vial, his big white hand holding the illegal drug, shaking it, taking a look around, syringe ready. He poked the needle through the rubber top, trying to hide the works with his body. Calhoun

137

could hear the squeaky sound of the syringe against the rubber seal. The greyhound, sensing something bad was about to happen to his skinny ass, started to move with desperate, hopping shoves. One of the Mexican handlers clamped a beefy hand down on the dog's mottled rear. Someone else got him by his leather collar.

Judging from the men's faces you could have fit all the sympathy for the animal onto the head of a pin. The vet sunk the needle in the greyhound's ass, dirty fingernails toward Calhoun. He watched the syringe's clear contents empty, the vet's big white fingers and wrist, the way they held the works. Then it was over. The vet threw the syringe back in the old-style doctor bag. The dog looked behind him and then at the conspirators as the knees stopped hurting him. In a moment the men were standing up straight, looking down at the greyhound. The medical bag disappeared into the back of the vet's car with a slam. The vet got hurriedly behind the wheel. Calhoun looked up just in time to see Cienfuegos, the trainer, pass a wad of bills through the car's window. The doctor grabbed the money and started his car at the same time. The station wagon started up, tires popping gravel underneath, throwing hay-filled dirt. Calhoun watched the vet's car wind its way around the myriad of shiny dog trailers and drive off the curb onto a side street that followed the back of the dog track and disappear into Tijuana's evening traffic.

The trainer gave some orders to the Mexicans, then hustled the dog toward the check in, where he would be weighed and where his blood test would, for another payoff, be "confused."

"Hey, Miguel," Calhoun yelled over the sound of the track's loud speaker that was announcing the winners of the last race. "Hey, thanks!" The man raised his right arm, keeping the greyhound close to him, not bothering to turn around. Calhoun watched them disappear into the crowd of owners and handlers checking their dogs in. Then he trotted off toward the track entrance.

Caliente's betting windows were crowded. Calhoun went to the hundred-dollar-and-up window. The line was considerably shorter. There was a Mexican dowager in front of him in a white pants suit that was thirty years too young for her big, fat, cracker-barrel ass. He watched the old broad put down forty thousand pesos on three different dogs, take her tickets, then turn around and give him the eye. He got around her with some trouble.

Calhoun pulled out his envelope. This was all the money he'd gotten from El Cojo. Even if it was a sure thing, it wasn't easy to part with it. The dark-skinned man behind the cage looked at him blankly. Calhoun opened the big manila envelope. It was wet with sweat. He counted out a hundred thousand pesos.

"Put it all on ninety-nine," Calhoun told the man. The guy inside the cage looked at him like it was the stupidest bet he'd ever heard. Calhoun watched him count the dirty bills a second time.

He finally stamped Calhoun's ticket and handed it to him. Calhoun checked the odds board as soon as he got out of line. His dog was paying six to one.

When 99 went into the starting box, Calhoun felt a chill run up his back. This was it. Luck, the lady he'd been waiting for all day, would start smiling at him. Things were going to smooth out, come up roses. Good-bye to Tijuana. Everybody had to have their luck change sometime. *Even a fucked-up no good son of a bitch low-life like me,* he thought. He raced up the stairs to the gallery.

The buzzer sounded and the dogs broke from the starting boxes, all chests and throats and long snouts. The mechanical rabbit they were chasing was just in front of them, running down the rail at thirty-five miles an hour. They were taking it on. Calhoun looked for 99 and saw that *his dog was in front* . . . 99 in front. He grabbed the big iron bar that kept the top tier of spectators from falling off the stand and gave a big cowboy whoop.

Another greyhound, thinner and white, like a cloud, was digging in, edging 99, trying to wedge in from the outside, almost even, its back legs pumping for all it was worth. Then his dog got some drugged-up, crazy, buggy surge that just wasted *all* competition and 99 was about to come down on that mechanical rabbit that Calhoun and 99 had been chasing their whole lives. Then it happened, quick and complete and terrible: kidneys burst, stumbling front legs, trying to keep going. Head down. Gut-broke, 99 caved in, 99 yapped kidney-exploded-hell and the other dogs passed him, passed him, passed him. The white dog latched onto the mechanical rabbit, prancing, never looking back at his brother animal, 99 halfway in the stretch, crying like dogs cry, dragging his useless back legs in the thick dirt of the track.

For a long time Calhoun just watched: first, the crippled, dying dog, then the proud white dog running with that bit of tail they tie on the mechanical rabbit between his teeth. Calhoun watched the white dog prancing down the rest of the straightaway. Happy owners rushed onto the track. Calhoun's mind emptied, got so empty that he could hear the yapping of the dying dog in his ears as if he were standing right next to him, watching him die confused and betrayed, pissing blood.

SIXTEEN
Downtown — 3:20 P.M.

Selena's "Tú Solo Tú" was on the juke box. *We're all finished off in the war of life—some just take more killing than others,* Calhoun thought, looking at his beer. He thought of running to a theater and hiding from himself. He saw Celeste waiting for him back at the motel. He was stone broke. He smirked at himself in the brown tint of the Dos XX's bottle. He looked up at the yellow barroom wall in front of him.

No se puede vivir sin amar, a sign said. There was a collection of Mexican homilies in Victorian script on the wall. "You can not live without love," this one said.

He wiped his face. He didn't know what to do. It was the first time in his life he'd felt this way. He needed money and didn't know what to do. He was sweating again and felt light-headed. Scared. He remembered the professor. *He* was there now. Broke. He owed El Cojo money he couldn't pay. In Mexico City maybe he could find something to do . . . a job. Celeste would go with him, money or no money. He would take care of her. He would stop gambling. *Never again,* he told himself.

"They got a new donkey at the Coco Loco," the bartender said. Calhoun looked up from the bottle. The bartender had put his hands apart to show how well endowed the donkey was. "He's coming down the street now," the bartender said, nodding toward the window. Calhoun saw the boy leading the donkey. It made him sick. The bar was empty. This wasn't one of his regular haunts. But he'd wanted a quiet place where people didn't know him. He knew he had to be more careful now. He knew El Cojo would hear soon enough about his big loss and come looking for him.

"I stay away from the Coco Loco," Calhoun said. "I don't go any place that has the condom machine by the bar . . . that's a rule of mine."

"You miss the show, amigo. They got a new girl, you know, with the donkey. A Yugoslavian. She . . . " Calhoun didn't listen. It was too disgusting. The man made the international fucking sign men use, clenching his fists, moving his arms toward his body. "Fuck the donkey twice . . . She fuck the donkey at nine and eleven, man."

"There's a lot of things I don't do in Tijuana. That's one of them," Calhoun said, wiping his mouth, tasting beer. He wasn't listening.

"She got big tits. The donkey likes it. I think he like it when they have big tits."

"I'm sure *she* does," Calhoun said. "I don't go to the Coco Loco. Do I look like a fucking college boy?!"

"Amigo, she's very pretty. They never had one like that . . . You know, not with the donkey. Look . . . look, the boy takes the donkey now," the bartender said. He pointed out the window of the bar. A boy was leading the animal down the Avenida Revolución. It was black, his legs shorter than a horse's. He brought it down every afternoon from La Cumbre. It was the boy's job to bring the donkey down to the Coco Loco bar and get him ready for the show, comb him down, put his straw hat on. Sometimes he washed him out in the street on the sidewalk with a bucket and a brush, all part of the show.

"Not right . . . Everyone gets a turn with the donkey, I guess," Calhoun said.

"Hey, the donkey is lucky," the bartender said, wiping the bar in front of him. "He shits outside and he fucks inside. It don't get any better than that."

"Yeah, but they don't pay him," Calhoun said. The bartender burst out laughing.

"Hey, that's funny," the bartender said. " . . . but it's an imperfect world, you know."

"Yeah, I know," Calhoun said. "Full of jokes . . . Full of them. Now bring me another beer and leave me alone."

"Sure, amigo. Sure, I leave you alone." The bartender walked down to the cooler, uncapped another beer and sent the bottle sliding down the wet, empty bar. Calhoun stopped it. He got up and went to the juke box by the door and played Selena's "I Could Fall In Love." Two men walked into the bar and sat at the end near the door. They had the PFN uniform—cowboy hats and boots—and were wearing their arm bands. Since the devaluation of the peso, there were more and more of them. The bartender came down the bar and got their order.

"Hey, where'd you guys get those hats," Calhoun said, turning around, all the hate from the day coming up into his throat. He wanted a fight. "Versace or what?" he said in English. The bartender looked at him, frightened.

"¿Qué dice el gringo?" one of them asked the bartender.

"He wants to know where you get those hats," the bartender said.

"Dígale que coma mierda . . . tell him to eat shit," one of them said.

"Amigo, he says he thinks you should leave. He says the bar is for pure Mexicans," The bartender said.

"He does?" Calhoun said. "How come? Somebody that fucking ugly is lucky to get any kind of company at all."

"*¿Qué dijó el gringo?*" the bigger of the two said, looking down the bar. He'd made out the word *fucking*.

"The gringo says he's a fascist, too," the bartender told him. The big one smiled back down the bar. He stuck his hand out in the fascist salute and lifted his beer, very *übermensch.*

Calhoun stuck his hand out halfway, then stopped and scratched his ear. "He ain't used to being with human beings and he appreciates us when we give him the chance," Calhoun said.

The bartender came back down the bar and wiped the spot in front of Calhoun. "*Señor.* Please leave before there is any trouble." Calhoun looked the bartender in the face.

"Fuck Hitler," Calhoun said. The two men looked down the bar at him. The first one closest to him got off his stool and broke the beer bottle in one easy motion. Calhoun saw the bits land on the bar. The guy had a grin on his face from asshole to earlobe.

"Did you know Hitler was a faggot?" Calhoun said, speaking loudly. He tried to sound like one of the Englishmen in *Sense and Sensibility.* "He used to fuck Göering in the ass every Saturday night. He'd get Himmler to watch and suck his dick when he was finished." The man was walking toward him hefting the broken bottle.

Calhoun let him get close. He stood up smiling, opened his coat and pulled out his forty-five. The man tried to run toward him. Calhoun saw the fear on the man's face. He fired into the man's shoulder at half a yard. The bullet tore through him and hit the other man in the leg, knocking him off the stool onto the floor. Calhoun walked toward the man on the floor. He stood over him. He stepped on the man's hat and crushed it.

"What is it you motherfuckers *want,* anyway?" Calhoun wiped his face with his palm, then looked back at the bartender, who'd turned white. "He'll live," Calhoun said, walking out. "And we'll all regret it, I bet."

There was marimba music on the plaza. A troupe of dancers from Patzcuaro, in those big wide straw hats and sandals, white baggy cotton pants, had come up to play for the holiday. The plaza was crowded with tourists. Calhoun pushed through the crowd. He had a strange look on his face as he crossed the plaza. The music was dark and forlorn—country music. Music from another world. A world that didn't belong in Tijuana, a music from the jungles much farther south, complex and melancholy. He grabbed a red-capped college boy from the back and spun him around.

"Give me your wallet." The American boy looked at him in panic. Calhoun brought the forty-five up and put it against his temple. *"Give me your fucking money!"*

He got across the plaza, stepped out into the traffic and went across the street into the *Tres Estrellas* office.

"I'll take two tickets for the express to Mexico City," Calhoun said. The ticket agent looked out from the black bars of his booth. He wore a cap with the company's logo, three gold stars. The office smelled of car exhaust from the plaza. It had a few chairs, the counter, and a map of Mexico with red lines showing the company's routes.

"It leaves at one o'clock in the morning," the agent said. He was a short, squat Indian, his skin red-colored. He said it as if that fact would put anyone off from making the trip; Mexicans always phlegmatic about travel.

"That's okay," Calhoun said.

"How many?" the agent asked.

"Two . . . two tickets. Two tickets—one for me and one for my . . . one for my wife." He put his hands through his hair. "Yeah, one for me and one for my wife," he said again.

The man stamped two tickets for the express. Calhoun unfolded the college boy's billfold and took out forty-three hundred pesos and paid. He tucked the tickets into the pocket of his coat.

"You got the last tickets," the agent said. "That's always good luck."

"How long does it take?" Calhoun asked. "To get to the capital?" He was holding the kid's billfold open, looking at it. The room started to get small, his whole body started to shake. He put his hand on the counter.

"Oh, that depends. This is Mexico. You could have bad weather in Durango," the man said. He turned to look at a map on the dirty wall behind him showing Mexico and all its states in primary colors, a big red star where the capital was in the center. "And the holiday . . . two days," he said, contemplating it, *"más o menos.* Two days, *si Díos quiere.* If God wills it. But Mexico City, she's always there, no?"

The two looked at each other for the first time. Calhoun didn't look like the type to leave Tijuana by bus, the ticket agent thought. The young gringo looked odd, his face flushed; he was sweating. He was very handsome, well-dressed, clean shaven. Not like some of the gringo students who came in.

"The plane is quicker," the man said, watching him. Calhoun didn't answer him. He took his gun out and dropped the empty clip on the floor of the office. The man looked suddenly horrified. Calhoun jammed a fresh clip into his weapon and turned around and walked back out into the street. He went down the sidewalk. Women and children, tourists, filled the sidewalk. He heard the music from the plaza. Faces seemed bigger. He saw a woman grab her child and pull him out of Calhoun's way. He saw the man he'd wounded stumbling out of the bar into the traffic, trying to cross over to the plaza. Someone screamed. The man turned around and froze, spotting Calhoun. He started to trot, thinking Calhoun was coming back for him. A taxi slammed on its breaks, hit the wounded man, sent him in the air into the intersection. His body hit several people, knocking them down like bowling pins. Calhoun kept walking. A young white couple jumped into a doorway. Calhoun kept walking, retracing his steps into the bar. The bartender was on the phone. The police still hadn't answered. There was a long red scum on the floor. The man he'd shot was lying on the floor, his eyes open. Calhoun reached down and turned him over. He took out his billfold, grabbed the cash, a big wad of dollar bills, and threw the wallet into the bloody spore and went back outside. There was the sound of ambulances now. He stopped on the street. His knees were wobbly. There was a crowd of people looking at him. His hands were red with blood, the bills falling as he stood there. He focused on the sidewalk, looked at the lines, heard someone crying in the intersection. He watched a red-stained dollar bill float gently in the hot air toward the dirty sidewalk, like a leaf from a tree. Things were moving. He sagged to his knees suddenly, then fell flat out, face down. He put one elbow on the sidewalk. He tried to focus on the feet in front of him. All he saw was shoes and socks and a woman's legs, fat ones, someone running out of the corner of his eye. *Not sick. Get up. Get up. Not sick! Tickets. Going to get married. Get up.* He heard a siren. Then another scream. The wounded man was dead in the intersection. Calhoun tried to stand but couldn't. He was lying almost face down. He saw his red hand stretched out on the sidewalk, clutching a handful of blood-wet dollar bills. He felt the sun on his face but he couldn't move.

"Don Vincente." He heard the kid's voice. Police car doors. He felt himself being dragged to his feet. The boy had him trotting toward the plaza. It made a strange sight, the small boy holding him by the waist, running with him into the crowd.

SEVENTEEN
Downtown — 5:30 P.M.

Calhoun was lying on a bed in one of the hotel rooms they kept around the city. This one had a view of the bullring and a technical college from the window in front of him. When he'd woken up he could hear the students outside on the street getting ready for evening classes. He wasn't sure what had happened or how he'd gotten there. He didn't know that the kid from the Escondido had called Miguel and they'd brought him there. He'd listened to Castro's voice and now tried to pull himself upright on the bed.

"Slaughter expects the cargo in San Diego . . . by seven tonight. No excuses, amigo . . . And he wants to see you on the plaza when we're finished," Castro said. "I just hope you stop shooting people and then collapsing." Calhoun rolled on his side. The bed was very soft. He looked on the night-stand and saw his cell phone and cigarettes.

"There's just one little problem. How the fuck do we do that now? I just shot two men in the middle of the fucking day in downtown Tijuana," Calhoun said. Castro was sitting in the shadows across from the bed. Calhoun reached for his cigarettes.

"I took care of your problem. The police matter is closed," Castro said. His voice was relaxed, quiet. "It was very queer, but I got the case and determined the two individuals at La

149

Cantina Machete shot each other. Police work is always a challenge," Castro said. "I do my best."

Calhoun got up on his elbow and looked at his friend. He saw Castro's harness, two forty-fives and the extra clips on the shoulder holster hung over the chair in the corner.

"Good."

"Don't thank me right now. Because soon you are going to be angry with me."

"Yeah, how come?"

"I can't say just yet. But I had to do it. As your friend. You have to believe me."

"Okay . . . well, I guess I won't worry about it."

"That's the spirit. Just remember it is for your own good. I don't want to talk about it anymore because I think maybe I made a mistake but it's done now . . . Someone called," Castro said, changing the subject. " . . . your cell phone while you were sleeping. They hung up." Calhoun shrugged his shoulders. "Slaughter is waiting. He wants to know how we propose to do it now. It's too late to take them through Palmdale. He has to have them in San Diego tonight by nine o'clock."

"Maybe I won't do it at all. Maybe I changed my mind." Calhoun sank back on the soft bed, holding his cigarettes. He knew what he said was the wrong thing. "Not today, anyway." He heard Castro laugh.

"Hijo de la gran puta. I don't know about you, but I plan on living to see my thirtieth birthday," Castro said. Students' voices came up through the open window. They were happy, youthful voices, carefree and in stark contrast to the mood in the room. Calhoun knew that his illness had made things worse, that it would be almost impossible to get the girls across in time.

"Miguel. I'm . . . "

"You're scared, amigo?"

"Maybe I am. Or maybe I'm just sick of it all." His cell phone began ringing. Calhoun let it ring. Castro looked at him the way he'd been looking since the morning. As if he knew something but didn't want to talk about it.

"Don't you answer your phone anymore? I think someone is very interested in talking to you."

Calhoun picked it up. "This is Breen . . . They've decided to come for you here. Here in Tijuana." Calhoun heard his partner's voice. He rang off, folding the phone up, and fell back on the bed.

"Who was it, amigo?"

"If you call me amigo again . . . I think I'll shoot you," Calhoun said. "I'm serious." Calhoun felt something flop on the bed at his feet. He pulled himself up on his elbow and looked on the bed by his foot. It was one of Castro's automatics. The policeman was smiling at him. It was that smile Castro had that was all nerve and balls and mayhem in a light brown package.

"Go ahead, amigo. Go ahead and shoot me. But you still have the cargo at the Arizona, and Slaughter expecting them in . . . " Castro looked down at his watch. " . . . in less than two hours."

Calhoun lit a cigarette, finally, going through the ritual with a new package, trying to think of a plan.

Calhoun sat up on the bed. "I should kill Slaughter," he said. He heard Castro laugh.

"Not a good idea. You don't have the *pelotas* for that." Calhoun could hear Castro move in his chair. Heard his cowboy boots drag across the floor. He grabbed his rig and strapped it on. He fastened the Velcro strap around his narrow chest and cocked his cowboy hat forward.

"I've got *pelotas*," Calhoun said. He swung his feet over the bed.

"I think you'll stop for a beer and forget all about it." Castro got up out of his chair and picked his gun off the bed. "But I like you anyway."

"Miguel, what did you agree to, why am I going to be mad at you?"

"I can't tell you right now . . . anyway we have this very big problem," Castro said. "We have to have the girls across the border in San Ysidro in less than two hours." Castro picked up the cell phone.

"Yes. Okay. Fine," Calhoun said.

"Amigo, are you listening to me? I have to call them back with a plan." Castro pointed to his watch again. Calhoun just looked at him. "I've got to call Slaughter back," Castro repeated.

"Fuck . . . all right. All right! We'll do it here . . . right in town. Right at the wire. That's the best I can come up with."

Castro picked up the cell phone and, pissed off, began to dial. "Let me talk to Slaughter . . . " He looked at Calhoun, who had gotten up and gone into the bathroom. He covered the phone. "Okay. You haven't told me what we are going to do."

"God damn you, I just did. I'll take them across here . . . use my DEA credentials." Calhoun looked at his face in the mirror above the sink as he spoke. He was pale. He ran the tap, splashed himself with water.

"That won't work," Castro said. Miguel spoke to Slaughter, told him to hold on a moment. Castro held the cell phone against his chest.

"What the fuck do you want me to do . . . ?" Calhoun said.

"We have to think of something else."

"Guess what, I don't give a fuck." Calhoun came back into the room wiping his face with a towel.

"You're going to be caught. It's stupid. It's amateurish. We aren't . . . "

"Just meet me at the fucking Arizona in an hour," Calhoun said. Castro got back on the horn and told Slaughter they were taking them across right at the line. Calhoun could hear Slaughter swearing at them on the other end of the phone. Castro folded up the phone. There was a knock on the door. The vet from the track stepped into the room. He had his doctor bag in his hand. Miguel turned around.

"I promised Slaughter you wouldn't pass out." Calhoun looked at the vet and then at Castro. He didn't understand at first. He put the towel down. "I had to promise him or he was going to get someone else to do it and then he was going to kill you," Castro said. "I had to agree."

"What the fuck are you talking about?" The vet looked at Calhoun and nodded. The vet was drunk. He teetered a little. He took something out of his coat pocket. Calhoun started to turn around and was struck from behind. Calhoun fell to his knees, stunned, halfway on the bed. Castro picked him up and rolled him onto the bed, then pinned his shoulders down with his knees. They looked at each other for a moment. The vet came over and looked over Castro's shoulder.

"Hey, I know you." The vet moved to the other end of the bed.

"Miguel . . . no . . . get the fuck *off* me!"

"Amigo, I can't. I promised and I don't think you'll make it through the night if we don't do this."

"Miguel, you don't understand, this guy isn't even a fucking doctor. He'll kill me."

"Yeah? What are *you?*" the vet said from the foot of the bed. Calhoun heard the needle-rubber sound and tried to fight, kicking his feet out violently, but he felt the doctor climb onto the bed and pin his knees. He felt the weight of both men on him. He looked up into his friend's face.

"Miguel, god damn it, you don't understand, this guy is going to kill me. I saw . . . " He felt the icy cold needle slip into his thigh.

"I may not be a doctor," the vet said, getting off the bed, "but I promise you one thing . . . this motherfucker here won't pass out *now.*" The vet popped his face over Miguel's shoulder again and looked down at Calhoun.

"That shot might make you a little horny, son, but otherwise you're going to feel, well . . . special," the vet said. He started to laugh one of those deep West Texas laughs. Miguel climbed off him. For a moment the two men looked at him. The horse medicine they'd just injected him with started to come on. Calhoun could feel it. It was as if his heart had just been expanded in his chest. Then he felt icy cold.

I'm a dead man, he thought. Then, for some reason, he started to laugh. The vet looked at Miguel and made the *he's crazy* motion with his finger and went out the door.

"Amigo, look at me. I'm sorry." Castro was shaking him by the shoulders. Calhoun's eyes had rolled to the back of his head and he was still laughing. It was the strangest thing Castro had ever seen. The veins on Calhoun's neck looked like rubber hoses. Castro looked back toward the vet for help. But he was gone.

EIGHTEEN
Hotel Arizona — 6:00 P.M.

Calhoun made a call from the Hotel Arizona's front desk up to their room. The lobby was crowded with American men in for the weekend. Middle manager types with girlfriends. It was that kind of hotel. For some reason, the sight of them made Calhoun nervous. He put the phone down and walked back outside to the street. The vet's shot was working; he felt better.

The evening was warm and close-feeling. He crossed the street to the hotel parking lot and got into the jeep. He took stock, checked the back seat, made sure it was orderly. The customs police would notice things like that. Something felt wrong. He saw the greyhound dying on the track, closed his eyes and grabbed the wheel. *Soon I'll be finished with all this.* He started the engine.

He pulled the jeep out of the lot and pulled into the hotel's loading zone. *Be nice. Be nice to the girls.* Be nice to them. *It's important they relax.* Calhoun watched Castro lead the girls down to the street from the hotel lobby. The Chinese girls lined up by the car door on the sidewalk. Calhoun nodded to the pretty one. The rest of the girls stood stoop-shouldered, like they were about to disappear. Not her. There was something different about her. "How are you doing this evening, ladies?" he said. He opened the back door of the jeep for them and waved them in. The pretty one went in last. Miguel had bought her a Coke in the lobby. She had it

155

in her hand. Calhoun could see the cheap fabric of her worn dirty pants hugging her ass when she bent over. He slammed the car door behind her.

He waited for a moment and looked down the street. Nothing special, just a busy Tijuana street in the evening. He had a feeling then that it wasn't going to go right. It was just a feeling. He felt the sweat suddenly roll down his arm. He almost had them get out of the car right then but stopped himself. It was ridiculous, he told himself. He'd been doing this for months and nothing untoward had ever happened, but he'd never done it like this. Never tried to use his credentials at the line. He looked at Castro on the stairs of the hotel. They looked at each other. They had never been forced to go on blind chance before. Calhoun nodded and Castro turned around and disappeared back into the lobby. *This time everything has gone wrong. Everything.*

Calhoun could feel the sweat start up like he had a radiator under his shirt. He felt it start to trickle down his arms before he got into the jeep. He took his coat off at the last minute. It was better if he wore it. But it was too hot. He glanced at the front of the Hotel Arizona through the open doors of the lobby. He had a feeling, something . . . today. He looked at the girls. *Get in the car,* he told himself. *Get in the fucking car . . . No time now. They're waiting.* He saw Castro watching, waiting for him to leave.

Calhoun threw his coat onto the seat and slid in. He could smell the girls, the city, the jeep's interior. He adjusted the rearview mirror, brought it down for a moment to look at the girls. They were all looking at him. They didn't know what the hell was going on. He adjusted the mirror back, forced himself to move the shifter into first gear.

156

The jeep's plates said U.S. Government. Calhoun had stolen them from the motor pool at the consulate. He'd been saving them for this kind of emergency.

It got crowded as they approached the crossing. They had to queue up like everybody else and wait in the broad sixteen lanes of traffic under the halogen lights. The street hawkers worked the stopped cars waiting to cross into the U.S. Calhoun inched the jeep forward. He fished for his DEA credentials and laid them on the dash. He was a wanted man, the credentials might not even work, now. *You have no choice,* he thought. He glanced back at the girls. He caught the pretty one's eye.

The hawkers worked the lines of stopped cars with piñatas and cowboy hats, plaster Madonna dolls and plaster SS helmets, shoving the stuff up against the windows of the jeep. An old woman lifted one of the Madonna dolls with silver painted conical tits up to Calhoun's window. He shook his head, mouthed 'No thanks.' Another vendor was holding up a donkey piñata, the colored bunting raggedy and soiled-looking. The man held up their progress, walking across the front of the jeep, stopping Calhoun from moving up in line. *Better ones in town,* Calhoun thought. Other vendors took advantage and suddenly the jeep was surrounded—piñatas, newspapers, puppets, Madonna dolls, everybody's mouth moving. He couldn't see the car in front of him anymore. Calhoun honked his horn.

"Get the fuck out of the way. U.S. government business." He nudged the jeep against Mr. Piñata. *Out of the way, Mr. Piñata.* The man slammed the hood of the jeep with his open palm. *BANG.* Pissed. *Fuck you.* Calhoun rolled down his window, tried to wave them out of the way. The vendors, angry now because he'd run into Mr. Piñata, didn't want to move. All

their faces had turned ugly. He leaned on the horn, gunning the engine, popped the clutch and the jeep pushed through the mob.

Calhoun heard a loud cough. He glanced into the mirror. The pretty one held her hand to her mouth. She coughed again. From somewhere deep in her, a guttural rip. *Not normal, too short.* It stopped just as suddenly. Calhoun, surprised, glanced in the rearview . . . *the pretty one.* He nudged the brake, his eyes fixed on the girl, now. Her face was waiting for something bad—she had gone ash-colored. She was staring at nothing, her eyes big in her pretty face.

The sound came again, out of nowhere, deep retching. Guts loosed suddenly. Liquid blasted out of her mouth. The pretty one heaved a stream of vomit, glutinous-white, like bad milk. She grabbed the head rest in front of her with both hands, tried to stand up, spilling and spraying hard enough to hit the dashboard across the front seat.

Calhoun had to grab his DEA credentials as she sat up and shot more vomit onto the dashboard, like some kind of machine gone haywire. He looked in the rearview mirror, saw the girl's tongue, the way it was hanging over her teeth, the color of the tip.

He looked up in time to slam on the brakes, knocking the girl back into the other girls. The horrible sound went with her. There was no way he could back up out of the traffic now. He was caught. The line was straight up ahead. He saw the green lights of the customs booth. *We'll be caught now.*

"Ahhhhhh yhaaa . . . Ahhhhhhh yhaaaa!" The girl screamed something.

"Hey! Can't you get her to . . . Jesus . . . Shut up. Jesus." Calhoun let go of the wheel. People from the other cars were looking in at the girl. She stopped screaming, was coughing, asking for help. The other girls tried to move away from her.

Then she stopped; there was quiet in the car suddenly. She said something to the others, scared, waiting for the coughing to come back. One of the other girls opened the back door for her, started to help her out of the car.

"No . . . no . . . lock the fucking door!" Calhoun tried to reach over the seat, his seat belt stopping him. Two girls, somehow understanding him, began to hold her back. Calhoun hit the seat belt button, felt it pop. The car behind him began to honk, wanting him to pull up. *Honking now, honking at me. Can't let her out.*

"Keep her in the fucking car!"

She was going for the open door, the horrible coughing sound scaring the other girls, making them back away. The coughing girl put her hands up to her throat, tried to stop it, tried to control the coughing.

Calhoun hung over the front seat, grabbed her by the pants. He felt her fleshy soft ass. He managed to get a hand on her ponytail and yanked her backwards all the way back into the car. The girl turned on him, threw the Coke in his eyes. A horn honking, the traffic behind him somewhere, honking. Suddenly everything had gone dark, the Coke in his eyes making it impossible to see, burning him.

He could hear her moving out of the door. Calhoun lunged over the seat again, tried to grab her again, blind, unable to see her, trying to keep driving, too. He got hold of her shirt tail in his hand. His hand slipped down to her kicking knees, his eyes stinging. The traffic in front of him came back into view. He began to see again.

"God damn it. Grab her, for fuck's sake! What the fuck is wrong with her?"

He let go of the wheel and turned around completely. The other girls screamed, seeing the jeep go slowly out of control. Calhoun tried to grab her ankles with both hands. She was getting away. She pulled herself through the open door, almost free. For one more second he held her by an ankle. His shoe slipped off the brake pedal. He managed to keep hold of the ankle. The jeep headed for the car in front of them. She broke for it, out the door, falling first on the pavement, shoes in the air, kicking one of the other girls in the eye.

Free. Calhoun watched her in disbelief. He pushed an hysterical girl back from him so he could watch where she went. He could feel the jeep free-wheeling then. They crashed into something. HONKING HONKING HONKING. He continued to watch the girl. His vision was still clouded. He rubbed his eyes with his fingers. *"Grab her!"*

The girl was kneeling by the jeep, holding her throat, trying to breath. She staggered off, moving between the cars, crying out in Chinese, heading toward the customs booths.

Calhoun twisted back around. The jeep had stalled against the rear end of a van. He stared at the girl as she stumbled toward the line. The van's driver got out, a white guy with a beard. Calhoun ignored the man yelling at him, watched the girl, wiped his eyes. Calhoun heard a horn again, LOUD. Stunned, he watched the girl walking between the lanes of traffic, wiping her mouth, stumbling toward the customs booths, shoulders forward, hands slapping her chest between gags.

He threw the jeep into park and opened his door all at once. Outside, hundreds of people stared at him across lanes of stopped traffic. He moved around the back of the jeep. He heard the van's driver yelling at him. He started to run after her.

For a moment Calhoun wondered if he were dreaming, if it was some kind of nightmare. In the red blur from his burning eyes he saw the girl zigzagging between stopped cars— someone reached out and pushed her away from their

160

window. She stumbled, got up, the cars closed up. Calhoun couldn't reach her. He jumped up on the hood of a station wagon, over that, then over a VW. He fell, a woman, not the girl, screaming somewhere close to him. He tried to focus, his eyes coming back now, better, but burning. Everything behind a red-gray film. The next car over, a fat Mexican lady, mouth open, yelling at him. He wiped his eyes. He could see normally again.

They still weren't in the same lane. The girl was trying to run, hands at her sides, pathetic. She was trotting toward the border in front of her, slowing. She was one more lane over to his right. Calhoun jumped on the hood of a truck and realized there were dozens of people getting out of their cars to look now. He jumped down, slipped, got up. He was in her lane now, a few yards away. She turned around and looked at him. She was saying something to him in Chinese. She stopped. She was trying to say something, holding her throat, coughing quietly, as if she were just someone at a restaurant that suddenly had swallowed something too big and needed help. He stepped toward her, hands out in the *I'll help you* sign.

"Stop, please stop. Let me help you. For Christ sake, let me help you . . . We have to get back in . . . " She started walking backwards away from him, stopped, tried to catch her breath. A women nearby screamed at Calhoun to help the girl.

He tried to get her to stop walking, made a stop motion with palms held out. Then she just stopped, like a switch had been thrown. She crumpled onto her knees. She was turning blue.

Surprised, she looked up at him, then collapsed completely. Calhoun rushed her. She was kicking on the ground, supine. He looked up. The U.S. Customs people were coming out of their booths. She turned over, began crawling toward the

U.S. One of the U.S. Customs men stepped into Mexico toward her.

"Don't touch her," Calhoun ordered. The customs guy stopped in mid-stride, confused. "I'm a doctor, don't touch her," he screamed.

Calhoun knelt down, pinned her with his knee, tried to clean her air passage with his finger, but it kept being blocked.

"Hey, buddy, you better do something quick." The customs guard was looking down at them.

Calhoun reached into her mouth. His fingers touched something plastic, there was something plastic in her throat. He poked it with his fingers. Her air stopped. He tore at the object with his index finger, the capsule thing broke apart. The girl immediately started breathing again, then just stopped in mid-breath. People were crowding around them now, watching. He looked up, holding the girl down at the same time, afraid she would stand up and run.

"I'm a doctor . . . she's sick," he said. "I'm a doctor." He bent down and blew into her mouth, the taste of vomit on his lips. She was still trying to crawl toward the U.S. side. He had to put a knee on her chest to keep her from struggling. A chunk of something blew into his mouth. He spit it away, tried again to blow air into her lungs, but there was too much in the way.

He lifted his head up. It was doing no good, she was going purple from lack of air. She was dying. They were only a few yards from the border. She seemed to understand that she was close to the U.S. She put her head down on the black asphalt and closed her eyes. One of her hands reached frantically up toward the border guard.

Don't die . . . please don't die on me. Calhoun picked her up and tried the Heimlich maneuver twice, his fist deep into her gut. It popped. A balloon of heroin rolled out of her mouth and fell onto the street, and then another. He felt her chest expand against his fist and let go. She sucked air frantically. He stepped back, waited. He saw her do it again. Calhoun bent down and picked up the balloons. She was breathing normally, standing there looking at the crowd. He walked her back all the way to the jeep. He crushed the balloons on the asphalt before he got in. When they drove up to the booth she was fine.

"What's the story with the girl?" the man said.

Calhoun flashed his DEA credential and didn't answer. The man looked at him for a moment, hesitated, then waved them through.

• • •

Calhoun stepped out of the shower. Castro had brought him in the jeep back to the Arizona. Castro, smoking, waited in the bedroom. Calhoun looked at his watch. It was only seven o'clock. He wiped the steam off the mirror. The mirror had some kind of black chips on it. He saw his face. He looked tired. He heard a knock on the bathroom door.

"Amigo? *¿Qué dices?* Bad day. Just like the movies. Like *Asphalt Jungle.* You saved the girl's life. You should be proud of yourself." Calhoun opened the door to the bathroom.

He walked into the room, a towel around his hips. He saw his suit on the bed, stained with vomit and asphalt. He didn't want to look at it. Castro followed him into the room.

"What happened, amigo?" Castro sat down in one of the chairs by the bed and lit a cigarette.

"I can't wear this shit. Look at it. Look at this shit. How the fuck do I know what happened? She nearly died." Calhoun heard his own petulant voice. It sounded strange to him. Not the same now, something changed. The hot shower had just

163

made him feel sick, not clean. Calhoun threw his suit pants on the floor; they were splattered with vomit, still wet. Castro just looked at him.

"Amigo. He still wants to see you tonight. I think you better get dressed." Calhoun looked at Castro a moment.

"Here," Castro extended his big brown hand. "Take this. It will calm you down. You saved a life. It's a good thing." He handed him a new pint of *Presidente* brandy.

Calhoun closed his eyes, saw the way she'd struggled, sucked for air, eyes open big.

"Take it, amigo." Castro was dressed in a blue silk shirt and jeans. He had his service auto stuck in the belt of his pants in one of those hand-tooled holsters the Mexican police used, a spare clip next to it.

"Fuck Slaughter," Calhoun said. He meant it now. He'd had enough. "Fuck him."

"I have to get back to the station," Castro said. "I'll meet you at ten on the plaza. Drink this. I promise you it will make you feel better." Castro pushed the bottle at him. Calhoun pushed it away.

"Take it, Vincente." Miguel went to the bathroom and unwrapped a paper-covered glass and poured him a drink.

"I want to know why he doesn't leave me the fuck alone," Calhoun said.

"There are so many things people want to find out in this town ... You know, it's like they tell Nicholson in that movie: 'It's Chinatown, Jake,' you know."

Calhoun picked his pants up off the floor. "You go tell Slaughter I'm through. All right?"

"I tell him that and you're a dead man, amigo. Do you want to be a dead man?"

"Yeah, I do. Tell him I'll try to pay him somehow."

"Vincente, I like you, okay?" Castro came up behind him and gave him the glass. "You are my amigo. I think you should reconsider. He'll tell me to come back and kill you. That's a *predicamento*," Castro said.

Calhoun opened his dirty pants and put them on. "That's a *predicamento*," he said, agreeing. "How would you do it?" Castro walked to the door and turned around.

"I'll see you later then . . . I'll leave this." He put the bottle on a table.

"I asked you a fucking question. How you going to do it?" Calhoun said.

Castro stopped and thought about it. "That's not funny," he said.

NINETEEN
La Avenida Revolución — 7:15 P.M.

For some reason, Calhoun had a hallucination/dream that he was a rat and that he was running down the street on four legs. It was very bizarre, but since he'd gotten the shot he'd had interludes that weren't right. He saw things that just weren't right.

"Pussy, pot or pills?" a kid whispered his offer in a doorway. Calhoun ignored him and kept walking down the brightly lit Avenida Revolución, part of the multitude on Tijuana's main drag where the action never stopped. Tonight, because of the big holiday, the street was packed with tourists. The wide boulevard was full of car headlights, lit shop windows and all manner of human beings looking for entertainment, victims, or escape to America. Calhoun climbed one of the shoeshine stands that lined the sidewalk. He'd undone his tie. His hands were moving all the time now, and it felt like the skin on his fingers and toes was too tight. He could hear his heart pounding against his chest like he was running a race. He gave orders to the shoeshine man in Spanish and tried to settle back to wait for Slaughter to show. He tried to relax but it was impossible. His foot started to shake and he started to sing softly to himself in a kind of whispered monotone.

"I'm gonna to tell you how it's a-gonna be . . . " He beat out the rhythm on his knees. "One of my professors at UCLA told me rats from the same colony won't attack each other," Calhoun said to the shoeshine man. He spit, leaning out over

the stand. "He claimed there was a kind of group solidarity. Human beings on the other hand—we're an entirely different story. *Aren't we?"* Calhoun told the shoeshine man. "Put two of us in the same room, drop in the money and the biggest ass-kicking rat comes out on top . . . Fuck everybody and get out of my way is our motto. It should be written on all currencies," he said, looking down at the shoeshine man. People on the street were looking at him as they passed.

Hustlers on the street measured Calhoun as they passed, their faces pale, colored from the ugly electric lights of the Avenida. Their eyes said: in a week where will you be? In a week you'll be lower still. And a week after that? You'll be our bitch, our bidding, ours to feed on. *Not yet,* he thought, glaring back at them. *Not quite yet. I'm still strong, I'm still strong—can fight if I have to. God damn right.* He watched the other rats pass from his perch on the shoeshine stand. A pop song was playing in a bar down the street . . . loud. *"You're so pretty the way you are. You're so pretty the way you are."*

I got rat insides. Most of me has turned to rat. That's what I am, you know. A rat, hairy and greasy and afraid of the daylight. I'd do anything, anything, for money now. They're coming, coming with the rat poison and putting it out for me, he told himself. Then he realized that he was talking to himself and stopped it. He took his cell phone out and dialed the Amigo Motel; he asked for Celeste's room.

"It's me, it's Vincent."

"I wondered when you were getting back to me," she said.

"I'll be there in an hour. Sorry. We're leaving tonight. I love you. I love you. Did you hear me? I'm better now. I had some medicine. Better now," he said into the phone, looking out into the street.

"Vincent?"

"Yeah."

168

"Vincent, no matter what happens . . . I want you to know
. . ."

"Don't talk like that, we're leaving tonight for Mexico City.
Okay?"

"Sure . . . " she said.

"I'll see you in an hour. I have the tickets. I have two tickets
for Mexico City. Tomorrow morning we'll be gone," he said.
"Did you hear me?"

"I heard you."

"I love you. Nothing matters but that." He closed the phone
and looked down the Avenida and then at his shaking feet.

The assortment of lights on Tijuana's main strip created
more shadows, hiding more than it illuminated. Calhoun
watched the crowds stream past. There was a heat to them. It
was a gross collection of eyes and mouths gaping and wanting
and being in harsh electric light. *Ghastly isn't the word for it.
Dead frightening, when you got a good look at it,* he thought. *At
them, at this awful collision of humanity. It makes you want to
take drugs. They might as well be walking around naked. Liberté
Égalité, Fraternité,* amigos!

Calhoun watched the nameless faces pass, big gringos,
Guatemalans, Serbs, whores of all colors, sexes, catamites.
Asians in cheap suits, gang-bangers in Hush Puppies, all of
them glistening, inhuman, in the harsh electric light like some
bad science fiction movie. *Night Of The Living Fuck-ups,* he
told himself. Every pock mark and dimple, crease, panty-
line and tattoo caught in the light seemed to dwell on the
obvious and the garish in full black and white hysteria. It was
peoples' desperate faces that had begun to bother him—having
to see them like this—raw human faces, a stream of face
sewage. *"Well, it ain't opening night at the opera,"* Calhoun
reminded himself, saying it out loud. *"It's Tijuana at seven
o'clock. Pussy, pot or pills is the order of the day!"* He felt a chill

go through him and grabbed the arm of the stand and smiled at no one.

He tried to remember what it had been like before all this, before it went bad. Before he'd started losing. In April he'd been on top of the game. It seemed he couldn't lose. It had been a Sunday at the Winners' Circle at Caliente, the beginning of April. That was the first gate he'd run through that he shouldn't have.

"There's money in wogs, Serbs, you just have to choose," Slaughter had told him. Money was the word Calhoun remembered hearing *so* well. He'd been looking down at the familiar scene: trainers and their greyhounds on the track, a plastic cup of Dos XX's in his hand. "You could get some of that. Good money in cargo right now," Slaughter had said. Slaughter used the slang expression that was popular: People had become cargo, merchandise.

"It sounds illegal," Calhoun had said. But the M-word had been used and he was all ears.

"I'm in it up to my ass," Slaughter had told him. He had a beautiful English accent. It made everything Slaughter said sound righteous and clean despite his trendy grunge look. He could have said corn-hole the Pope to a priest and made it sound good. "Could get you wogs, for example. If you wanted to do wogs . . . " he offered again. Slaughter turned around and faced him. "The wogs trust white people. And they are splendid about paying. Believe me. Like clockwork, old man . . . Money in the bank. My service is different. First Class. Only people with money. We bring them from the capital ourselves," Slaughter said.

"How much?" Calhoun had asked.

"Five thousand dollars per head on the U.S. side. And I'll pay in any currency you'd like: guilders, deutschemarks, whatever you want. You just get them across. However you like. I've heard about you," Slaughter said. "You grew up around here. You know the desert." His girl, a petite Mexican girl, came from the bar and put her hands around Slaughter's waist.

"Fuck!" Calhoun had said, looking at her ass wrapped in a leather mini skirt, and not the cheap kind. This was beautiful black leather that fit. *If he can afford that kind of pussy looking the way he does, I'm in.*

"Yes, well, as I said. I can get you the work if you want it. I've heard that you could use it." Slaughter turned back around and faced the track, full of himself.

That's where it started. Calhoun had called Slaughter the following day from his office. They'd had lunch at the Hotel Coronado in San Diego in the old wood-paneled dining room and it was on. He'd been doing cargo since. After Slaughter, he'd found others. He'd grown up on the border, knew the hundreds of desert arroyos to the east intimately. And then there was his ace in the hole, as he called Castro. That had been six months ago. Now it had all changed. He was just one of the rats now waiting for them to put out the poison. *It's just a question of which plate I eat from.* He felt the sick feeling in his stomach. He touched his face; it was warm and wet. The shoeshine man was looking at him. It was obvious now. People could see he was sick.

Calhoun searched the faces in the crowd. He was scared and pretended that he wasn't. *Of course I'm scared.*

Calhoun looked down the street and saw Castro. He pretended to be waiting for a bus, his foot on the bench, smoking, watching the women pass. Calhoun looked away toward the bright lights of the jai alai palace, headlights stared back at him, metal animals, moving in through the warm, greasy night.

"¿Señor?" The shoeshine guy was staring up at Calhoun, finished. His shoes were clean. Calhoun handed the shoeshine guy five dollars and looked down the street, watching for Slaughter.

"Otra vez," Calhoun said. "Clean 'em up again." He rubbed his hands together. The shoeshine man went back to work, got out his jar and carefully daubed shoe polish over Calhoun's left shoe. Calhoun bent over and admired them, a two hundred dollar pair of Kenneth Coles. *Mighty fine.* A drop of sweat hit one of the shoes.

You've got . . . He did a quick calculation. *Almost a thousand in cash left for emergencies. That's enough to break for it, isn't it?* Calhoun spit on the ground. The problem was he owed thirty grand to Slaughter. And more to El Cojo. And where could they go on a thousand dollars? *I want to leave with her. I want to be in love with her.*

A cockroach skittered out from under the shoeshine stand onto the sidewalk. The thing's shell was big and glossy-dark. It skittered up the stand, then changed direction and dashed back to its hiding place.

If he tried to leave town and El Cojo or Slaughter found him? They'd cut everything but the bottom of his feet. He'd be one of those corpses they find in the Tijuana dump with radio antennas sticking out of his asshole and eye balls. The message received by everyone loud and clear: Don't fuck with the boys.

The shoeshine man looked up at him—his face blurred, then reformed as the sepia visage of Pancho Villa. *"Cucaracha,"* he said, grinning, nodding at the big one that had climbed all the way up the stand and stood on the tip of Calhoun's left shoe, almost the same color. The shoeshine man tried to brush it off. The bug raced up his arm and sat on the man's shoulder. Calhoun could see its antennae moving, the fever intensifying it. Calhoun reached over and got the shell between his ring finger and thumb and pressed until the shell caved in and the bug danced-died, scratching him softly, staining his hand.

"Don't encourage them," Calhoun said. "They'll take over. I know. They're like Nazis."

Slaughter stood out. Maybe it was the whiteness of his skin. Calhoun watched him go into the cafe across the street. The place had no front doors, all open air so you could see all the way through to the back. Calhoun watched Castro come up through the crowd, the Mexican's face anonymous at night. Castro climbed up in the chair next to him.

"He's not alone . . . he's got two people with him in a car down the street. How are you feeling?"

"Better. I feel better."

"Good."

"Can anything else go wrong today?" Calhoun asked. He looked at Castro. The man's eyes glowed at night, or at least looked that way. He seemed like some kind of nocturnal animal. "I don't think I'd do very well in jail," Calhoun said for some reason.

"Amigo. You have to be like Paul Newman in *Hud*," Castro joked. "You go in there and you act like you are the biggest cock in this town. Just like Paul Newman in *Hud*."

"He wants his money." Calhoun said. "And I don't have it."

Calhoun climbed down from the shoeshine stand and crossed the street to the cafe. Calhoun saw Slaughter sitting in the back corner of the place. He'd never seen Slaughter completely sober. Not once. He sat down across from him. He fished into his pocket for a cigarette. Slaughter had a coffee and brandy in front of him. He looked very young. You could have mistaken him for a fraternity kid.

173

Calhoun ordered from the waiter, who looked like he'd rather be any place else in the world.

"Do you know why I like Mexico, old man?" Slaughter said, leaning close.

"No, why?"

"Because everyone is crazy and they know it. They expect you to be crazy, too. And *you* are crazy for trying what you managed tonight. I admire that in a man." Slaughter had a square jaw and a flat nose. His hair was covered with the same blue do-rag from the afternoon. His lips were moist as he watched the passersby. He glanced at Calhoun for a moment then back out onto the street. A good-looking whore went by and gave Slaughter the eye.

"You lied to us . . . I said no drugs, ever," Calhoun said. "She was full of them."

"I didn't lie in the beginning. Things change. That's capitalism. It's fluid, dynamic. People in China wanted to maximize their ROI. It was their idea. We had to accept. Return on investment. I try to be on the cutting edge, old man."

"Fuck you. What do you want?" Calhoun said. He started to sweat. He took the paper napkin off the table and ran it around his face. The drinks came. Slaughter waited for the waiter to leave. "I say, you don't look well, old man."

"No past, only future," Calhoun said.

Slaughter eyed him and smiled. "How did the shot work for you?"

"Yeah, thanks. I appreciate your concern for my health."

"If I didn't know better, I'd say you had dengue fever."

"Fuck you. Now, what is it?"

The waiter came to the table with Calhoun's mescal. "Time to pay up."

"I have a problem," Calhoun said.

174

"Everybody in Casablanca has problems." Slaughter smiled. "Frank Guzman, cross him and we're even. He's here in Tijuana; I told him you could get him out."

"No," Calhoun said. "He's too big. He's wanted for being behind the assassination of Asturias. I read the papers. His picture's everywhere. No way. The police will shoot him on sight and anyone with him when they catch him. And they'll catch him. He went against his pals in the PRI. They don't like that," Calhoun said.

"You owe me a great deal of money, isn't that correct?"

"Yes, I owe you money. But I'm not dying for you."

"How much?"

"I forget."

"Two hundred thousand pesos. You owe El Cojo a hundred thousand pesos now, plus interest. He's looking for you already. I could take you to him right now. I have people outside."

"So do I," Calhoun said. "I'll have it for you tomorrow,"

"You're lying. I doubt you have a thousand. I know. I've heard. You owe everybody in town . . . You're finished . . . Do this and I'll take care of El Cojo, too. You don't want to end up with an irreversible medical problem." Calhoun took a drink and thought about it.

"Tonight, you said."

"Yes. It has to be tonight."

"Okay, I'll do it," he said. "Then it's over. You and me canceled out. And you pay Cojo, too."

"Fine," Slaughter said. "It's over then. Here's his number." He slid a paper over to him. "He's at the Empresa in a penthouse. He's waiting for your call. Get him to Palmdale. My people will pick him up on the other side. You get him to Palmdale and you don't owe me anything," Slaughter said.

175

"Do you know what it is, Calhoun? What the Mexicans are getting so excited about out there on the streets tonight?"

"Yeah . . . *Día de Los Muertos.*" Calhoun wiped his face with the paper napkin again and it started to come apart.

"That's correct, Day of the Dead. A celebration of death. Thanatos . . . as my Classics teacher at Eaton used to call it. They're celebrating Thanatos." Slaughter put his elbows on the table and reached for Calhoun's collar. He touched it gingerly. "If you don't do this for us . . . I suggest you put on your very best suit and start celebrating, too." He let go of his collar and smiled. "You know the best thing about an English public school education, Calhoun?"

"No."

"It builds character. And it's character that allows us to succeed in this miserable life. We public school boys built an empire . . . people forget that now. As far as I'm concerned, you're just another bloody wog who might be standing in my way. Have I made myself clear?"

"Perfectly."

"Excellent . . . I've heard that dengue fever makes you fuck like a rhino," Slaughter said. "Is it true?"

"Yeah. Ask your girlfriend. She knows," Calhoun said.

"You manage to make everyone hate you. You're good at that. That's a talent," Slaughter said. "Very good at it. Why weren't we friends?"

"Well, amigo . . . " Calhoun said, getting up, "I ain't running for mayor. So I don't have to be nice to assholes."

TWENTY
Amigo Motel — 8:00 P.M.

Calhoun walked down the dark court of the Amigo Motel to his room on the end, furthest away from the street. He had two tickets to Mexico City in his pocket; he'd gone over his plan a dozen times on the way from his meeting with Slaughter. He got his room key out and unlocked the door. The phone started to ring in the darkness—the room's phone old-fashioned, sounding with a bell. His heart began to pound involuntarily, almost painfully. For a moment he stood in the dark and listened to the bell-hammer. Frozen. Since the shot from the vet, his whole nervous system could go ballistic. He stared at nothing. The ringing suddenly stopped and he felt himself start to breath normally again. *Can't cave in now. Work the plan. Work the plan.* He went to the window and closed the blinds. He walked through the dark to the closet and slipped off his jacket. He found a hanger and hung up his coat. He took a suitcase off the shelf and walked it to the bed and opened it. The phone started up again. He took his jeep keys and put them on the nightstand. It didn't matter, he told himself. *Nothing mattered anymore except leaving Tijuana. Nothing but leaving with her mattered.* He would deliver this last cargo and then leave Tijuana for good. Forever.

Calhoun turned around and walked toward the ringing. The phone stopped just as suddenly as it started, then started

177

again. Over and over. He faced the telephone, afraid that it was El Cojo or the police checking to see if he was here. He wanted to tear the phone from the wall. He grabbed it with both hands, felt the hand set come off the cradle. He heard a voice.

"It's me. It's Breen . . . Vincent . . . ? They're here . . . in Tijuana at the office right now. They're looking for you right now. I've got to go. Did you hear me?" Calhoun brought the phone to his ear.

"Yes."

"They have a list of places," Breen said.

"I understand."

"I'll do what I can to . . . " the phone went dead. Calhoun sat down on the bed. He knocked the suitcase off angrily, then got up and walked across the courtyard to Celeste's room. There was no time to pack now. They would take nothing.

He knocked and waited. There was a strange light on behind the curtains, a flickering light. There was no answer. He knocked again, nothing. He turned and looked through the courtyard to the street. He'd parked the jeep in the courtyard and wished he hadn't. The police would be looking for it. He turned and faced her door, backed up and kicked it open. The lights were off. He switched the light on and looked for her.

"Hey, baby."

For a long moment he was caught immobile, held by what he saw. He saw the candle, a small white one on top of a beer can, flickering. It gave the room its miserable light. There were big shadows on the wall behind them that acted out the nightmare. Paloma Vasco behind her with the thing on humping so she was big on the wall and Celeste, her face turned toward him, all of it on her face, every thrust in her eyes that caught the light of the candle. A car drove by behind

178

him, the headlights shining into the room, and they didn't stop.

"Stop it." Calhoun heard the sound of his own enervated voice. Paloma Vasco turned and looked at him, her beautiful face darker in the shadows, smiling, thrusting her hips, quickening, as if to taunt him.

"Do you want me to stop, *mi amor?*" she said. Vasco was looking Calhoun dead in the face, not caring about the door being open or any of it. The thing was moving between them, Celeste reaching her hands up, climbing the wall slowly as she was fucked, trembling, climbing up the wall, green shadows on the wall and a yellow brightness that caught the expression of her face.

"I said, stop it." Calhoun's voice sounded strange and pathetic. He took his gun out and walked across the room. He could smell them. Paloma Vasco looked at him and kept humping, not afraid.

"She belongs to me. Not you," Vasco said.

Calhoun raised the gun. He thought of shooting Vasco. He put the gun up against Vasco's jaw. He could smell them even more strongly now. He could see Celeste's face and the long line of her body and her hips in the candlelight. She was looking at him.

"Tell him . . . who you want," Vasco said. Her hips saying it with her. Calhoun didn't want to look down at her. He heard Celeste's voice.

"I want you," she said. "I want you. Oh god, I want you . . . Paloma, fuck me," she said. Calhoun felt the gun pulled, Celeste had grabbed it and pointed it toward her own face.

"Please, don't. Please . . . Vince. I need her." He felt himself sink to his knees. Calhoun looked up again and for a moment he thought he was dreaming, that it was the vet's shot, that it was a nightmare. Celeste was holding the gun, barely. Paloma

179

Vasco was fucking her again. It wasn't a dream because he heard Celeste and felt her clinging to the gun barrel, pulling it slowly to the rhythm of the fucking.

"Get out," Vasco said. "Get out." She reached down and made Celeste let go of the gun. Calhoun let go at the same time. It fell heavily on the floor at his feet. Vasco started laughing at him, laughing and fucking her with that thing on. He picked the gun up and walked out into the night.

Celeste came into the room while he tore up the tickets. It felt cold in the room. They were at his feet. He'd torn them and torn them into small pieces until they were too small to tear. She was wearing jeans and was barefoot, one of his shirts on.

"I'm sorry," she said.

"How long?"

"What does it matter?" He didn't know. He couldn't answer. She touched his hair, pushed it back on his forehead. Sat on the bed next to him.

"I want you both," she said. He looked at her, the idea that it wasn't over between them suddenly possible.

"Then come away with me," he said.

"I don't know what to do." He turned and looked at her. She was flushed from the love making. She looked more beautiful now than she ever had. "I thought you were going to shoot her," she said.

"I almost did."

"I want you both," she said. "Is that wrong? I want you both. I'd like to make love to you both. Right now. That's why I came here. She's waiting for us. She says she . . . Vincent she said you . . . "

"You're crazy."

"No. I want to make love to you both at the same time. That's what I want. I want you both. Why can't we? Why? Why?" She was speaking very softly. She touched his face, kissed him.

"Because. I can't, that's why. You're sick."

"Why, because I want two people?"

"No. I don't know." He didn't know what to say. It was as if he were drowning. "I want you with me," he said, as if that was somehow an explanation. "We'll go away. I'll take care of you. That's what I want," he said. "I want you for myself."

"You mean like a car. I'm not a car, Vincent, or a bank account."

"Don't you understand, I love you, it's not about all *that.*" He pointed to the outside. "I love you." He turned around and put his hand on her leg. "I loved you all this time."

"What about Paloma?" she said. He shook his head.

"I don't know."

"Come back with me." She stood up. Her shirt was open. She grabbed him by the hand. "I'm this way. I want you both. If you want me, you have to have me this way or not at all," she said. "Give me the gun." She pulled his jacket back and lifted his automatic out of the holster under his arm. She took it and slid it in the front of her jeans. He looked at it. The door was pushed open; they both looked up. Vasco was standing in the door. She was wearing a robe, black satin. Her black hair fell on it.

Celeste took off her shirt. Vasco moved across the room. She had it in her hand, dangling. The dildo and belt it was on.

"He's beautiful. I told you, look at him," Celeste said.

"Not like a woman," Vasco said. She stepped closer into the room. For some reason Calhoun was afraid of her in a way he'd never been afraid of any man. She slid her robe off

181

her shoulders and let it fall to the floor. He saw how tall Vasco was. She looked like a brown Amazon.

"Well? Who's more beautiful?" Vasco said. They both looked at Celeste. Celeste had climbed to the center of the bed.

"She doesn't care," Vasco said. The phone started to ring again.

"You nodded off," she said. Celeste was looking down at him. Calhoun tried to sit up. He tried to swing his legs over the bed. He got one leg over and stopped trying. It was as if he suddenly weighed a thousand pounds. The fever was back and different now. He looked at Celeste's face. It turned into a pattern, like cards. There were seven or eight Celestes looking down at him. Her mouths moved. He closed his eyes.

"Where is she . . . Vasco?"

"She's gone," Celeste said.

"What time is it?" he asked. It felt hot in the room. He touched his face. It was burning up. He lifted up his head and looked at the clock on the table but couldn't make out the blurred digital image. He was naked, just a sheet over him. He felt the warm touch of her along the length of his body. She climbed up on him.

"Almost nine o'clock," she said.

He looked into her eyes. He waited for his vision to be normal again, then reached out for her. Held her. He felt his arms circling her naked waist. Celeste looked at him. Kissed his face. He pulled her closer to him in the dark.

"I want you to leave here with me," he said. "We'll go to Mexico City."

"What about Paloma? I can't change who I am," she said.

"I'm taking her and her parents across tonight. Did she tell you that?" Calhoun said. Celeste nodded her head. "She's going to America."

"Yes . . . I know."

"Then it will be over between you."

"Yes." Celeste rolled over away from him. He looked at her back. He put his face against it, felt her backbone, ran his finger along it.

"Then it will just be you and me?"

"All right." He got out of bed slowly. Turned the light on, put his pants on.

"We have to leave here. The police are looking for me. I want you to go to the central police station, ask for Miguel Castro. I want you to wait there with him until you hear from me." Calhoun turned her around.

"Celeste, do you love me?" She nodded her head.

"Yes . . . that's the problem. I do," she said.

"Okay."

"Vincent . . . You promise you'll still take her tonight. Paloma and her parents, for me."

"I promise," he said. He got dressed. There were a thousand things they didn't say to each other.

"You promise me," she said again while she dressed.

"I promise you."

"You liked it, didn't you?" she said. He was putting his shoes on. He thought back to the moments of passion. Of watching her come.

"No. I tried, but I didn't," he said. "It's different when you love someone," he said.

TWENTY-ONE
Hotel Empresa — 9:30 P.M.

After Calhoun had been patted down by Frank Guzman's bodyguards, a shouting match started about his weapons. Calhoun had been made to leave them in the living room. A young woman took Calhoun through the suite to the huge bedroom. Guzman was still in the bed, elephantine and naked under the sheets, watching television, his corpulent body like a monstrous human slug. Stunned by the sight, Calhoun stood in the doorway. He could see the ripples and puddles of fat. Guzman had a fan on him that pressed the sheet down on the whole fucking jellied mess of his body so you could see it. *How the fuck am I going to cross that? He must weigh five hundred pounds,* Calhoun thought to himself.

"Slaughter sent me," Calhoun said finally from the doorway.

"Buenas noches," Guzman said. His voice was raspy from all the weight on his chest. He grabbed the TV control and turned down the volume. Calhoun noticed how short his arms were.

"What's so good about it?" Calhoun said. He came into the room. He hadn't expected a morbidly obese billionaire.

"Muy Américano. You are the crazy gringo . . . I heard about you. Slaughter says you do anything for money. All you have to do is get me to Los Angeles," Guzman said. He didn't bother to sit up. "You get me there and I'll be okay . . . I have friends in the Congress."

185

"Good for you," Calhoun said. Calhoun saw a row of matching new black suitcases lined up under the window. There were at least ten of them. It was cool inside the bedroom with the AC on. The fan went back and forth across the fat man. Calhoun had heard from the newspapers that the PRI had been raiding Guzman's bank accounts. He assumed that the bank accounts were now sitting on the floor in the suitcases.

"Get ready. I'm taking you to the other side—Palmdale, not Los Angeles. You can't take much. Not all those, anyway," he said.

"Los Angeles," Guzman said. "Los Angeles. Take me to Los Angeles. You can do that."

"Then you can die here for all I care," Calhoun said. "Because that's what's going to happen . . . It's my way or nothing." Calhoun lit a cigarette and looked at the fat man. He wasn't in the mood to argue. Guzman tilted his head up. He hadn't shaved. His blubbery cheeks were covered with a scruffy day's worth of black beard. Guzman looked at him from the bed.

"Well, maybe. Okay, maybe . . . Okay, I'll go to this Palmdale, then. Just get me to the other side. I tell you what, you let me take my woman and this money and I let you have a suitcase. That's a good deal *muy bueno para el gringo.* Huh . . . go on . . . open one. Go on . . . open one. I got more in Europe these *cabrones* don't know about," Guzman said.

Calhoun went to one of the suitcases. They were all new plastic jobs. He picked one up and put it on the foot of the bed.

"$100,000 weighs, huh?" Guzman said. Calhoun hit the levers and opened the top. It was full of American money.

"So, what you say, gringo? You let me take my money and the woman." Calhoun had seen the girl. She looked like a New York runway model. Guzman was too fat to fuck her. He guessed he had her around to look the part, even if he was too fat to get out of bed without help.

The girlfriend came into the room while they were talking. She had a fresh brandy on a tray. She put it down on the table at Guzman's side, then asked him if he wanted anything else. She was only about twenty.

"I'll have some dinner," Guzman said. She'd been smoking weed with the security people when Calhoun came in. Her eyes were red and she had that high half-smile like she had a secret.

"You want to stay for dinner, *señor?*" she asked Calhoun. She wasn't looking Calhoun in the face.

"No thanks."

"She comes with me," Guzman said.

Calhoun looked at the girl. "Nobody comes with you and you can't take that money either," Calhoun said. "There's no room for it."

"She does. Or I don't go. Monica comes, too. And the money," Guzman said.

"Then Monica here can cross your fat ass herself." Guzman looked at the girl, then at the suitcases full of money sitting around the bed.

"All right . . . Monica, you understand. You have to meet me in Los Angeles. Okay? You take the money with you. I'll meet you later."

"Okay, Frank." The girl looked at the suitcases. Calhoun watched her. If she kept that date, he would be very surprised, he thought.

"You go to the Beverly Wilshire where we always stay and you wait for me."

"*Sí, como no,* Frank. I wait for you at the Beverly Wilshire." Guzman smiled at the girl and picked up the drink on the table.

"She's *muy guapa,* no?" Guzman said. "Go on, honey, and get me something to eat." Calhoun watched the girl walk out of the room and close the door.

"Why'd you do it?" Calhoun asked.

"Do what?"

Calhoun laughed; it was in all the papers. "Have the president of the republic's brother killed in broad fucking daylight."

"I don't know who did it," Guzman said. He smiled. "But I know *why* they did it. You don't understand Mexico. Look out the window. What do you see?" Calhoun turned around and looked at the skyline.

"One very fucked-up city."

"No. That's property, amigo. Twelve people own this country. Twelve. Sometimes we don't get along, and there's a misunderstanding and then something like this happens," Guzman said.

"You're saying twelve people own Mexico?"

"Yes . . . and I have their phone numbers. Now one of them wants to own it all."

"That wouldn't be you, would it? Or are you just an innocent billionaire?"

Guzman laughed. "It's the same in your country. Look at the headlines . . . Forbes, Perot. What's the difference?"

"Yeah—what about democracy, asshole . . . it isn't the same at all."

"That's very funny. Tell me something, gringo, how many political killings has your country had in the last twenty years?"

"What do you mean?"

"We've had many in Mexico; how many have you had?"

Calhoun looked at him, suspicious. "What are you getting at?"

"Look at the streets in Los Angeles. What difference is there between any of your big cities and Mexico City, now? People living in the streets, billionaires running things. Why do you think you're so different . . . because everyone has television? Go to the poorest parts of Mexico City or Tijuana, what do you see? TV antennas. You're just like us now; but you don't want to admit it. You walk through a ghetto and see a street-light and call *that* democracy. The greatest country on earth. Isn't that what your anchor people call it? Look out that window, amigo, the view is the same everywhere now. Jakarta to New Jersey . . . It's over."

"Shut up," Calhoun said. "We *are* different. We aren't anything like this stinking country. We have rules and laws and you can drink the fucking water.

"How much do you weigh?" Calhoun lit a fresh cigarette. The room smelled like patchouli oil and fat man, and he didn't like it.

"Why do you want to know? Nobody asks me questions like that. Who the fuck are you? Nobody." Guzman was a little drunk. He moved his hand in the air. "Do you know who I am? I got more money than Bill Gates. You see . . . look." Guzman threw a *Fortune* magazine he had on the night-stand. *The World's Richest Men.* Calhoun looked at the picture of Guzman and then Bill Gates; they were both stone ugly.

"Look. See, more money than Bill Gates. See?" Calhoun threw the magazine back at him. It landed on his chest and stunned him.

"I don't give a fuck. *How much do you weigh* is what I want to fucking know."

"What difference does it make?"

"Let's just say that the trip, with our service, is a little like flying. Can you walk?"

"Of course I can walk."

"Why are you in bed then?"

"I'm tired." Calhoun looked at his legs. They looked like they were each about two hundred pounds worth of pure lard, the hard kind.

"Prove it. Get up then and walk around the room for me," Calhoun said.

Guzman looked at him. Then at the ceiling like it was his friend. He took his hands and tried to push his body toward the headboard. His hands looked like two small flesh paddles on some kind of weird amphibious animal. Guzman struggled to get his chest up off the bed. He tried to sit up, pounds of tit-flesh avalanched toward his right side. Guzman started to breathe hard. His small dark hands pushed against the mattress and disappeared. It was pathetic and sickening.

"Call some of the boys . . . that's how I do it," he finally said.

"You can't walk, can you?" Calhoun said.

"I can walk . . . !"

"No, you can't . . . You're lying. Well, get up then. Fucking walk then . . . "

"I can . . . walk. I tell you!" Guzman started cursing, wheezing, all at once, trying to sit up in the bed, wheezing and sucking air like he were running a marathon instead of trying to shift his big fat ass three inches off dead center.

"Great. Now what?" Calhoun said. He went to the window. He rolled it open and threw his cigarette out into the night, watched its orange light fall twelve stories to the parking lot. He could smell the stench of the city, the acridness of the *maquiladoras* out along the line. You could see the giant spotlights they used to light up their perimeter fences like forts.

190

He thought about what the fat man had said. He remembered what America was like when he was a child, what it was now. He got mad suddenly. It wasn't Mexico yet, but it wasn't America anymore either; it was on the way to being something he didn't want to think about. Calhoun turned around.

"Stop it." Guzman was still pawing the sheets. "Stop it. You're making me sick." Calhoun went to the phone and picked it up, then realized that he shouldn't and got out his cellular phone, which was safer.

A room service kid pushed a cart through the door. Guzman's girl took the cart and paid him off at the door. The living room was empty when Calhoun came out.

"Where're his guards?"

"They left," she said. She went to a table and picked up Calhoun's handguns and brought them to him. Calhoun looked around the suite. There'd been three professional body guards. He had been counting on them to help him get Guzman to the Cuauhtémoc.

"They don't want to die. They think he's lost his *cuello,*" the girl said. It was the saying Mexicans used to mean influence. "They know that when they come, they will kill them. They think you are a spy and the police will come here soon."

"Why didn't you leave, too?"

"I got no place to go," she said. "I have nothing but him."

"You could take some of the money and just go. Is that what they did?" She nodded her head.

"Can he walk?"

"No, not really."

"How the hell did they get him up here?" He looked at the girl. She pointed to something leaning up in the corner of the room. It was a kind of dolly leaning up against the wall at the front of the suite.

"In that," she said.

191

"That's a refrigerator dolly," Calhoun said. He started to laugh. "It's a fucking appliance dolly."

She smiled at him. "That's how they have to move him. It took two men before to get him up here," she said.

"I'm sorry I can't let you come with us," Calhoun said.

"I understand."

"There's no room."

"I understand, *señor*." Calhoun looked at the girl. She looked decent, like she didn't belong with Guzman.

"Can you help me get him dressed?" Calhoun asked. The girl nodded.

"What about the money?" she said. "There's so much."

"I called someone. Someone to help us get you across."

They went into the bedroom and started to dress him. The girl went over to Guzman and ripped the sheet off his body. It was the ugliest thing Calhoun had ever seen in his life. It was funny, the way the girl wasn't bothered by it. Guzman didn't say a word. He couldn't. He knew he was running out of time.

"Where are the boys?"

"They're gone, Frank. They left," she said.

"Are you going to leave me, too?" He was scared now.

"No, Frank, I'm not going to leave you," she said in Spanish. She pulled a huge fat arm through his shirt like he was a little baby.

"You will meet me in Los Angeles?"

"Yes," she said. She was kneeling up on the bed. Calhoun looked at her rear in a mini-skirt. It was hard to believe she was in love with the fat man.

"You promise . . . I need you . . . I love you," Guzman said. It was pathetic. He looked at Calhoun while he said it. "The gringo here is crazy," he said.

"I promise you, Frank."

192

Watching her, Calhoun got the feeling that the girl actually cared about him. All Guzman's clothes were special, no zippers, just buttons. To put his pants on, they had to lift his legs one at a time. His ass was unbelievable. Guzman stayed expressionless the whole time they worked on him.

"I'm hungry," Guzman said while they were putting his shirt on. It was like a regular shirt, except giant size, and went over his big belly and down to his knees, a kind of giant *guayabera.*

"Shut up," Calhoun said. "We don't have time to eat."

"No!" Monica said angrily. She put down his arm. There were small red sores where the skin had worn off from spending so much time in bed. "If he doesn't eat he gets sick," she said. "He has to eat every few hours."

"All right. But make it fast," Calhoun said. He looked down at Guzman, and let go of his arm. Guzman's hair was a mess, matted and greasy and long, and his big fat cheeks were puffed out from moving him around.

The girl went into the other room and rolled in the cart with the dinner she'd ordered. There were a couple of covered pans. She took a cover off of one. It was a potato dish, the way the Mexicans cook up potatoes, boiled with cilantro and swimming in butter. She took the dish over to Guzman and sat on the bed next to him. Guzman couldn't wait to get his hands on it. Calhoun had to go out to the other room, he couldn't watch him eat. It was the sickest thing he'd ever seen: that beautiful girl standing there in a red mini-skirt holding the plate for him while the fat man ate, clear lines of butter running out of the corners of his small mouth and down those fat unshaven cheeks.

TWENTY-TWO
Hotel Empresa - 9:45 P.M.

They stood waiting in an alcove at the back of the hotel. Calhoun had rolled the refrigerator dolly with Guzman strapped to it to the elevator and then through the hotel's empty kitchen. It took every bit of Calhoun's considerable strength to handle Guzman. The girl had put several of the suitcases on the room-service cart. They had to leave the rest of them up in the hotel room. The trio came out at the back of the hotel to the service dock. Hotel workers watched the three of them go down the concrete ramp to the parking lot.

"I'm going to roll him up to the Cuauhtémoc," Calhoun said. He didn't know what else to do. It was too dangerous to call a taxi. He'd hidden his jeep at the Cuauhtémoc because he was afraid to use it. The police, he knew, used the cab drivers of Tijuana as informants. There was a complex web of police eyes and ears on the streets, fruit vendors, store owners, plainclothes men, something gringos didn't understand about Mexico with their naïveté. But it had been that way since the revolution. If the Mexican Federal Police were corrupt, they were not, contrary to American accounts, fools or Keystone Cops.

The girl had changed clothes in an attempt to look more ordinary. She'd put a scarf on and some ordinary pants and a T-shirt that was several sizes too big for her. Calhoun was looking at the street that passed in front of the hotel. The

195

idea of wheeling Guzman all the way to the Cuauhtémoc by hand seemed impossible.

"How far is it?" she asked.

"On foot . . . I don't know. He'll meet you in Los Angeles," Calhoun said. The girl looked at Guzman. He was strapped to the dolly. Several dirty white canvas straps wound around his girth. Guzman couldn't see her because Calhoun had put the dolly down, leaving Guzman supine.

"Monica, I love you," Guzman said. He tried to turn his head and see her.

"Frank, I don't know what to do. I mean, if you don't show up." A four-door white Ford pulled up at the loading dock. Breen got out from behind the wheel of his government car.

"What the hell is going on?"

"I want you to take this girl to L.A.," Calhoun said. "She's going to give you a suitcase when you're finished. The Beverly Wilshire hotel. Right now . . . You'll be a lot richer for it. Don't say I never did you any favors," Calhoun said.

"Vincent, they've been to the Amigo. There's a bulletin out for your arrest on both sides of the border. You better come with me," Breen said. He looked at the girl for a moment. Then at Guzman, finally realizing it was a man on the dolly.

"Max, do me a favor and shut up. Put the girl in the fucking car and get her across the line." Breen looked at Guzman, trying to take in the strange scene.

" . . . That's Frank Guzman, Vince." Breen turned white, like he'd been hit with something cold. "It's Guzman, isn't it? The guy everyone is looking for."

"Yeah, the fat man himself," Calhoun said.

"You aren't going to make it, Vincent. It's completely crazy. They'll kill you."

"Maybe, maybe not."

"Don't listen to him, gringo, we'll be all right," Guzman said, trying to see who was talking.

"Vince. It's not worth it. Just leave them. I'll get you out of here. Leave them here. For Christ sakes. Guzman's *death,* Vince."

"Yeah, so am I. Max, take the girl to L.A. Do yourself a favor."

Breen took his gun out. "No. I'm not going to let him get you killed." Breen lifted his gun and pointed it at Guzman. "You'll get him killed . . . For what . . . " There was a shot. Breen fell backwards. No one had been watching the girl. There was silence for a moment, just the report of the pistol shot against the concrete walls of the loading dock. Calhoun walked over to Breen, then looked back at the girl. She was still holding the little gun. The bullet had torn a hole in Breen's throat. Breen scrambled up on one knee, tried to say something. He looked at Calhoun and tried to stand up. The girl shot him again.

Calhoun turned, he had his gun pointed at the girl but couldn't pull the trigger. He tried to pull it. He wanted to pull it but couldn't. She looked at him. He walked up to her and ripped the gun out of her hand and punched her. The fat man was yelling. Calhoun walked over to Breen and knelt down. Breen was trying to talk. Calhoun put his ear near his lips.

"I . . . I . . . I . . . " He reached up and tried to touch Calhoun's face. Calhoun tried to push the throat wound closed. He looked at the girl. She was crawling toward Guzman, her mouth bleeding. The suitcases had rolled down the ramp and turned over in the parking lot. One of them was open, the money thrown out.

"Stupid . . . I . . . " Breen said.

"What?"

"I love you," Breen said.

"My friend," Calhoun said, standing up. He looked at the suitcases in the halogen light and the way the money drifted across the parking lot in the wind. The girl had crawled over to Guzman and was holding him, wiping the blood from her face.

"He was going to hurt Frank," she said, looking up at him. "Nobody hurts Frank." Calhoun looked back at Breen's body, the blood running down the little ramp. His body seemed pathetically small.

"He was my friend," Calhoun said again. The girl got up, walked over to the body and took out his wallet.

"I need his papers," she said. "Which ones are they? His papers! So I can cross." Calhoun looked down at the body, then at the pretty, bloody face of the girl fishing through his friend's wallet. "The papers," she said. "The money. We have to think about the money. Now."

• • •

"Where are you going with that man, *señor?*" Calhoun wiped what he thought was sweat out of his eyes. He stopped and propped the dolly up in the dirt road so that Guzman faced the traffic like a fat Jesus on the cross. He'd struggled with the fat man up the Avenida Maria De Leon that led up to La Cumbre and the Hotel Cuauhtémoc. It had taken everything he had left, physically. He'd had to stay out in the street like the donkey carts, wheeling Guzman along over the chuck holes and through the pools of dirty piss-water. His arms were burning. He heard the sounds of the cantiñas along the way in his ears. He was exhausted. The crowds on the side-walks coming down the hill toward town stared at him, at the strange scene of a white man in a white suit pushing the

198

dolly up the dirt road in the miserable electric street light of Tijuana's worst neighborhood. They couldn't see what he was pushing exactly until they got right on top of him.

Calhoun had moved around the parked cars. Guzman got heavier by the minute, making him sweat. Calhoun's cotton jacket was drenched, the material sticking to him. Every step with the fat man hurt. Calhoun had to carry him almost supine, his biceps burning, his feet sometimes slipping in the dirt and donkey shit, so that they both fell more than once. Guzman was telling him to be careful each time, almost hysterical.

There were moments when Calhoun couldn't see, something he thought was sweat dripping into his eyes and rolling down his cheeks. The evening became a watery nightmare of car headlights and the sharp stares of people on the street as they rolled by. The fat man was talking sometimes, asking to be stood up, asking for a drink. Guzman could hear the music from the bars and wanted to go inside for a beer. Calhoun kept moving, the pain and the agony in his joints blotting out what Breen had said to him before he died. "I love you." That's what he'd said. And what had his love got him? A bullet in the throat, Calhoun thought.

By the time he heard the boy ask him what he was doing, Calhoun was breathless and exhausted. Calhoun stood Guzman up. A donkey passed, almost knocking Guzman over. Calhoun smelled the animal. It was the donkey going downtown for the show at the Coco Loco. His sunglasses smeared with sweat, Calhoun halfway heard Guzman asking for water. They were in La Cumbre now, only a few blocks from the Cuauhtémoc.

"Where you go, *señor* . . . with that man?" The kid was tall and skinny and there were four other kids with him, sixteen or seventeen years old. The kid talking to him had on a hairnet, the kind that comes to a point just above the nose. They were wearing plain white T-shirts and over-sized blue jeans and standing in front of one of the scores of small cantiñas that blared *ranchera* music. Even at night the dust from the road was thick and you could taste it. A truck passed and blew dust into Calhoun's face.

"You mean my uncle Billy?" Calhoun said in English. The fat man tried to look at the kids.

"Dice que es su tío," one of them translated.

"I don' think that your uncle," the one with the hairnet said in broken English.

"Sure it is. That's my Uncle Billy," Calhoun said. He tried to spit but he had no liquid left.

"You look like shit, *señor,*" Hairnet said.

"So do you," Calhoun said. He noticed that his jacket sleeve was streaked with blood. He touched his face; it was warm and sticky.

The other kids came down the steps into the street. Pedestrians passing gave quick sideways glances at the group in the street. Calhoun had put his havelock on Guzman's head. It had done the trick, hidden his face enough so that you had to get very close to see who he was. Calhoun reached over and pulled the hat straight.

"I think, *señor,* you have a big problem here." Hairnet held up a copy of the photo El Cojo's man had taken that morning showing Calhoun standing next to the priest.

"I think you come with us," the kid said. "El Cojo is look for you." Hairnet reached over and ripped the hat from Guzman's head and put it on. Guzman was scared. One of the other kids turned the dolly around so that Guzman was facing the sidewalk. Calhoun looked at Hairnet through his dark glasses that reflected all the lights of the shops.

200

"Hey, *muchachos,* how about some beer?" Guzman said. He tried to lift his hand but it was strapped down. He'd started complaining of thirst almost immediately. Calhoun looked down on the mountains of wet flesh. The fat man picked up his hand as best he could, looking up at the night sky, the fat face unsure of what was happening around him.

"Muchachos, I buy you the whole cantiña for a big *cerveza* now," Guzman said.

"Me va a comprar la cantiña," Hairnet told his friends. They all laughed. More people passed them. There was a shift change at ten in the *maquiladoras* and the streets in La Cumbre were full of workers coming and going to and from the factories, some of them in their white uniforms.

"Fuck you." Hairnet spit on Guzman's face. A big yellow glob stuck on his forehead.

"Hey, you spit on my Uncle Billy," Calhoun said. "Why did you do that?"

" 'Cause I felt like it, asshole."

"I need the hat back," Calhoun said.

Calhoun laid the dolly down in the street so that Guzman was supine. The kid pretended to adjust the hat. It shaded his whole mean face. The others hadn't said anything, watching Calhoun. The one with the hairnet took a knife out of his pocket while Calhoun leaned over the fat man. He opened it up. People on the street hurried past and pretended they didn't see anything.

"Hey *muchachos.* I buy you the cantiña for a *cerveza.* Get me a *cerveza,* huh?" There was a disgusting whining quality in Guzman's voice. He was squinting into the headlights. People in the passing cars were looking at the boys, knowing what was going on, but not doing anything about it. Not in La Cumbre.

"Give me the hat, kid, before somebody gets hurt." Calhoun said it in Spanish this time so that there wouldn't be any confusion. Calhoun stood up. He looked at the boy and saw him in double vision. He blinked, hoping it would change. He suddenly felt cold. He tried to open his coat but something was happening to him, something strange, the sudden dyskinesia. He tasted something running into his mouth. Calhoun blinked again. The boys blurred. He didn't see the knife. The fat man said something. It became a nightmare vision, the fat man was trying to get up off the dolly, fighting the straps. Calhoun bent down to pick up the dolly again and stumbled, dizzy. He heard the laughter from the boys.

"This motherfucker is bleeding from his fucking eyeballs man, check it out. Motherfucker is bleeding out of his *pinche* eyeballs man, check it out," one of the boys said. Calhoun saw a face move down close to him. He tried to reach for his gun but something was standing on his arm. The face looked strange, double, then triple, so there were six eyeballs staring at him, a bandanna on the forehead. He flexed his hand and felt the pain race through it.

"You one fucked-up motherfucker, pal." Then the face pulled away. Calhoun brought his chest up off the ground. He willed himself to stand, slowly. All the time cars were moving past him trying to avoid him, honking. The fat man asking for help. He felt something sharp in his shoulder and saw another face again pushed up against him. Hairnet's. Calhoun looked at his shoulder and saw the buck knife stuck into it, the kid's hand planted around the black handle, his head turned, laughing with his friends, like they'd just played pin the tail on the donkey.

He's going to kill me. The thought suddenly penetrated through the effort Calhoun was willing into his body. He watched the hand grasp the black handle of the knife and

202

pull the blade out, all of it in triplicate. He saw in slow motion the clean silver of the knife coming out of his shoulder, the sound of pain. A guttural sound from Calhoun's throat that you might have heard from an animal.

"I'm going to kill you." Calhoun heard himself say it. The kid was in front of him. He'd stepped back but there were three kids, three knives. A car horn sounded, the world was shrinking away. Calhoun turned to the right and saw the faces of the crowd in the street, the squares of white *maquiladora* uniforms. The giant headlights of a bus. Calhoun realized suddenly that he was kneeling and not standing. That he was looking at Hairnet's knees.

"What are you going to do to me, motherfucker, bleed on me?"

"I buy you the whole cantiña." The fat man was digging in his pocket. He held up a wad of money. The kid looked at it like he'd never seen money before, surprised.

"Here. Take it," Guzman said, trying to see them. He struggled to turn in the dolly, his big fat arm in the dirt like a ham.

Calhoun got to his feet while the kid was taking the money. With everything he had left in him, he pulled his forty-five out of its harness. The effort was almost too much. He stumbled into the kid. He blew his hand off at the wrist. Blood splattered Guzman's face. The kid turned and looked at him, surprised, the bills blown into the air.

"I told you to leave my uncle the fuck alone." Calhoun had the barrel of the forty-five tucked under three chins. He looked into the big set of eyes in pain, confused by the sudden burning explosion. Calhoun wasn't sure what would happen when he pulled the trigger. The kid was talking when the bullet went out the top of his head, blowing gray matter all over Calhoun's face. Calhoun held the dead body for a moment, then threw it into the traffic. The others scattered, some back up the stairs into the cantiña, one of them ran into the street, another two across the street. People on the sidewalk ducked. Calhoun turned on two of them on the stairs. *Pick him up. Go on. Pick up the fucking dolly.* He had the gun out and was pointing it at them. His eyes were cloudy. He wiped the mess on his face with his sleeve.

They went that way down the street to the hotel, Calhoun, the gun out at his side, the *pachucos* holding the fat man. They rolled him up into the lobby of the Cuauhtémoc. *"Call Miguel,"* Calhoun said from the door. He looked at the night man who thought Calhoun was some kind of monster. *"Call him right fucking now!"*

They had Guzman leaned up against the bathroom door in room twelve, still strapped to the dolly.

"Well, Vincente?" Calhoun was sitting in the chair across from Castro. He was trying to explain. His jacket was crimson and gray on the right side. Every time Castro tried to get him to take the jacket off, Calhoun waved him away and said it would be all right. Castro could see the wound, could see it drizzle blood while they spoke.

"Amigo, if you don't stop the bleeding, you are going to die. Is that what you want?" Castro said.

"Who is this man?" Guzman said. "Who is this man?" Calhoun turned and looked at the fat man.

"I haven't introduced you two. Mr. Guzman, I want you to meet my good amigo, Mr. Castro." Castro turned around and looked at the man in the dolly.

"Frank Guzman, I suspect," Castro said.

"That's right, all five hundred fucking pounds worth. King-size billionaire. What movie does this remind you of? Come on! How about *King Kong?*" Calhoun said. Castro smiled, but he was scared. It was the first time Calhoun had ever seen him scared.

"How about Orson Wells in *Touch of Evil,* huh? 'Lay off the candy bars' . . . huh? Well, amigo, you don't seem so happy to see me," Calhoun said.

"I'm very glad to see you . . . definitely," Castro said. *"Touch of Evil.* Why didn't I think of that . . . You've fucked up this time, amigo. That's *Frank Guzman."*

"I know, and we've got to get him to Palmdale. Right, fat man?"

"Yes," Guzman said. "You get me to the American side. I give you lots of money. I promise . . . "

"Shut up," Castro said. "Amigo, you've gone too far. You can't get Guzman across. Every policeman in Tijuana is looking for him. Do you understand that? *Judiciales* from other states. Everyone. They are to kill him on sight and anyone with him. You can't pay me enough money to cross him."

"I pay you more fucking money than you ever seen," the fat man said from the wall.

"I said shut up, you disgusting ton of shit. If we turn him over to the people that want him, we will have it made. I promise you. We can go on doing what we've been doing," Castro said.

"Amigo, I don't think you understand. I have to get the fat man over to Palmdale. I'm asking you to help me. There's a broad waiting for the fat man in L.A. She's got money . . . lots of it. I know where she is. You can have the money. She's alone. Suitcases full of the shit. Just help me get the fat man to Palmdale and keep a little of the money for me, and I'll tell you where she is."

"Look at you, you're sick," Castro said, shaking his head. Calhoun raised his hand and waved him away. "Full-blown dengue fever. I called the doctor. And what about your shoulder?"

"That's just a scratch. The broad, she's fine . . . Your type, too. And I'm sure she hasn't gotten laid in a long time."

"I pay you both more money than you ever seen . . . More money than you could imagine." Castro and Calhoun turned and looked at the ridiculous figure, the grotesque quality of his fat that hung between the straps, the way his chest heaved as he spoke, the short beard that had grown on his unctuous face. They both burst out laughing simultaneously.

"No!" Castro said. "Not *Touch of Evil.*"

"Then what?"

"I can't think of anything I've ever seen that looks like that tub of shit, Vincente. You know something–you *are* crazy. Look at you. You're bleeding to death . . . you have dengue fever, and you want me to die with you for some money supposedly in Los Angeles, held in trust by a pretty girl."

"That's right."

"You know, if I didn't know better, I'd say you're part Mexican."

"I said I pay you more money than you've ever seen." Guzman said.

"Yeah, yeah," Calhoun said. "We got the picture, fat man. You're going to make us rich."

"He's bleeding from his eyes," the fat man said. "I saw him. Your friend is bleeding out of his damn eyes!"

"Dengue hemorhaggic fever," Calhoun said out loud. "And I've been using a condom, too."

"Very funny, amigo, very funny."

"Well, are you going to help me or not? I haven't got all day," Calhoun said.

"I can see that," Castro said. It was the fat man's time to laugh.

"When did you leave Guzman's hotel?" Castro asked.

"Less than an hour ago."

"Fat man, if I help my amigo, here, I expect to be compensated."

"You'll be shitting hundred dollar bills. Both of you. Shitting them," Guzman said.

"Did you hear that, amigo? We are going to be shitting hundred dollar bills," Castro said.

"Yeah, he's some kind of poet," Calhoun said. "Well, Miguel, are you in or out?" Castro ran his fingers around his narrow waist, tucking in his shirt carefully. He looked at the fat man, then at Calhoun.

"Where is this girl?"

"Well, if I tell you that, you might just decide to go to L.A. without me," Calhoun said.

"Amigo, I'm your friend, but I'm not stupid. Where is she?"

" . . . The Beverly Wilshire, in one of the cabanas."

"How much does she have? Tell the truth," Castro said.

"I think maybe three, four million at least."

"He's going to leave you, stupid. You're stupid," the fat man yelled. He began gesticulating, the straps on the dolly holding him back. "Asshole. He won't help you." He flailed his arms, the straps of the dolly squeezing the fat into balloons.

"All right, but we get her to bring the money to Palmdale." Castro went across the room and picked up the phone.

"Get me an American operator," he said.

Calhoun was in the toilet throwing up. He was on his hands and knees. It was a horrible sound. Castro closed the cell phone and shot it into his holster.

"They have road blocks at every exit of Tijuana, amigo. They're expecting me at headquarters." Calhoun couldn't hear him. Castro went over to the fat man. He was drinking a glass of water. The straps on the dolly had bled into his suit so that there was a slight pinkish run from the sweat and the straps. His fat hung around in bulges, looking like peas in a bag. Calhoun walked back into the room from the bathroom.

"If he dies, I'll kill you myself and still get the money. Do you understand that?" Castro said.

Guzman nodded. "He isn't going to die," Guzman said. He kept drinking, pouring the water into his open little mouth. "I need something to eat. I'm very hungry," Guzman said. "Could we somehow . . . "

"You should be in a fucking zoo," Castro said.

"Amigo, if you get me a sandwich, I'll pay you a thousand dollars; no, ten thousand dollars." Castro stepped back and shook his head. He had a bad feeling about it all. A very bad feeling. He turned around. Calhoun was standing in the doorway of the bathroom trying to hold himself up. He was sweating like he'd run a marathon. His mouth was dirty.

"What does Bette Davis say in that movie?" He wiped his mouth with a towel and looked at his friend. His eyes were bleeding. Castro had heard it described, but he'd never seen full-blown dengue hemorrhagic fever before. There was a fine red sweat on Calhoun's face.

" . . . *fasten your seat belts . . . it's going to be a bumpy ride',"* Castro said in a monotone, quietly. "I called headquarters, they've brought in people from Baja Sur, more *judiciales*. The roads are all blocked. They raided Guzman's hotel."

"Good, we don't want to make it too easy on them, do we? I mean, you'd think he was a great big fat guy that stuck out like a sore thumb . . . What are you looking at, fat man?"

"Nothing, it's just that I thought maybe, I was wondering if I could get something to eat. Before we go," he said.

TWENTY-THREE
The Escondido Bar — 10:00 P.M.

No one knew where the riot started, exactly. By the time Calhoun drove down from El Cumbre, the streets around the city center were in chaos, bands of men smashing windows, people running out of businesses with television sets and pieces of furniture and boxes of sodas and Pampers. As in the Los Angeles riots, the police had retreated from the streets. Calhoun drove on, one hand on the horn, swerving, driving fast, the jeep with its big black bumper intimidating, the horn loud. The fat man lying in the back asked what was going on. You could hear the sirens and the fire alarms on individual businesses blaring as they drove down the hill toward downtown, toward the Plaza Tijuana with its holiday lights shooting up into the night sky.

Miguel had called the station. Celeste wasn't there. She hadn't answered his calls at the Amigo either.

"What do you mean she's gone?" Calhoun said.

"I checked, *señor*. I went to the room myself." The kid was standing in front of him at the bar. There were tourists in the back of the Escondido staring at the way Calhoun looked.

Calhoun had come at the busiest time through the front door and stood there for a moment, bleeding from the shoulder, his clothes dirty, the jeep parked out in front on the street, the music from the celebration on the plaza behind him. He'd stood there and looked for the kid. One of the waiters had rushed up to him and Calhoun had pushed him away.

209

"Get me the kid," he'd said.

"*Señor* Vincente, you're . . . "

"Get me the fucking kid." He'd said it loud and people in the bar had turned around and stopped talking.

"I need the kid, that's all . . . I'll be in the bar." He concentrated on the bar for a moment, its wood-paneled reddish hues, and the sound of people's voices. He'd walked in amongst the whispers and walked up to the bar and leaned on it, his shoulder bleeding through the bandage Castro had made for him.

"Tecate," Calhoun said. The bartender looked at him.

"*Señor* Vincent, good evening."

"Good evening, Fernando." Calhoun reached for his lighter but it wasn't there. He took out his cigarettes and looked around the bar as he put one in his mouth. The bartender lit it for him.

"Tecate, Fernando. *Por Favor*. There's a riot . . . uptown in the hills," Calhoun said matter-of-factly, exhaling. "They'll be down here before too long, I imagine . . . Kick some tourist booty."

"*Sí señor. ¿Cómo no?* Tecate." The bartender had missed what he'd said. He was looking at the wound, at the way the blood had stained Calhoun's white jacket. Calhoun picked tobacco out of his teeth and saw himself in the mirror. He hadn't shaved; he noticed the red stain on the white coat, the dark brown of his beard and his eyes. The pupils were dilated from the vet's injection. It made him look frightening. He smiled at himself. The bartender brought the Tecate and a glass. It was quiet now. People started talking again but were watching him.

"How are you this evening, *Señor* Vincente?" the bartender said carefully.

"Not bad, Fernando. How about you?" The bartender put both hands on the bar.

"Did you get in a fight, *Señor* Vincente?"

"You should see the other guy," Calhoun said. He said it loudly and several people around him started to laugh. It was the kind of humor Mexicans liked.

"You are most definitely bleeding, *señor.*"

"I realize that, Fernando."

"Would you like something for that, *señor?*" He was about to say yes when they brought in the kid. Calhoun told him he wanted him to take a taxi and go to the Amigo, to room twelve, and bring back the girl he found there. He gave the boy money for the cab ride. Then he turned around and waited. Someone came in and said that the riot had moved closer into town, that maybe it was getting dangerous.

"She's not there, *señor,*" the kid said again. Calhoun looked at his watch. It was ten-fifteen. He had to meet Castro on the plaza in twenty minutes to pick up the Vascos.

"They said she checked out, *señor.*" Calhoun knelt down and looked into the boy's eyes. He was scared of the way Calhoun looked at him.

"Boy, you're lying."

"No, *señor.* I'm not lying."

"Yes, you are. You didn't go to the hotel!"

"*Señor,* they don't know where she is." Calhoun held the boy by the shoulders and looked into his eyes. "What else?"

"The police were there, *señor*–gringos looking for you, *señor.* I heard them talking." Calhoun started to shake him slowly at first and then hard, then suddenly stopped.

"I'm sorry, kid."

"*Señor,* you are hurt." The kid reached up and wiped the red sweat that was collecting on Calhoun's face, wiped it on his own shirt, leaving a streak on the front of it. Calhoun looked at it, then stood up and walked toward the door. The Yaqui girl from the night before was standing on the sidewalk looking at him, caught in the light of the street, her hair shimmering. She was selling roses, had a bundle in her hand.

"See! You were wrong after all, I'm still alive." He pushed past her out into the street. The jeep was parked on the plaza side where the taxis parked. He looked over at the *Tres Estrellas* office and saw a gang of PFN men smash the windows out of one of the big tourist bars. They were dragging American college boys out into the street. The dancers came out onto the sidewalk half-naked. Calhoun walked by them in the chaos. He had his forty-five out at his side; no one bothered him. A dancer grabbed him by the arm and he pushed her away; kept on walking up the sidewalk. Two old men came by. They were trying to move a new washing machine. They had it perched on a tricycle and were guiding it up the street. Cars honked at them to get out of the way. Calhoun stopped in front of the ticket office. The door was locked. He shook it. One of the old-fashioned blinds pulled over the door came up by itself. The ticket agent was standing behind the counter. Calhoun knocked on the door with the butt of his pistol, rapping the glass.

He held his finger up and made the "2" sign. "I need two tickets to Mexico City." His face was bleeding. The ticket agent had never seen anything like it. The whole city had exploded and now people were bleeding from their eyes and ears, the man thought.

Calhoun turned around and leaned against the door. He was crying now. He screamed into the night. *PLEASE OPEN THE DOOR. PLEASE OPEN THE DOOR. MY WIFE AND I NEED TWO TICKETS TO MEXICO CITY. PLEASE OPEN THE DOOR . . . FOR GOD'S SAKE HELP ME.*

212

TWENTY-FOUR
Banco Popular — 10:00 P.M.

anks in Mexico close late. The Vascos had counted on
that to make the difference, but, being foreigners, they
hadn't counted on the holiday. Customers, who had
come in to cash their checks before the weekend, were queued
up at the counters. The bank was packed when they walked
in the doors.

Now, five minutes later, the guard at the Banco Popular
was dead. He was lying in the middle of the bank's brightly
lit lobby, his entire face cratered from the impact of the M
16 bullet. Paloma Vasco had shot him. The guard, in
plainclothes, had shot her mother as soon as they walked
into the bank. He'd shot her mother in the stomach, and she
was halfway in the bank and halfway outside, her body
holding the doors open. Everything that could have gone
wrong had gone wrong. The general alarm had been pulled
and was ringing loudly. Paloma was in charge, her father no
longer able to cope. He was trying to pull his wife out of the
door by her feet. He had worn a gray suit and he was on his
knees crying and pulling her. He'd thrown down his gun and
was oblivious.

"Get the money, Celeste," Paloma screamed. "Get the
fucking money!" Paloma reached over and slapped her in
the face. *"Get it now!"* She could hear her father trying to get
his wife out of the doorway. Paloma let go a burst of fire over
his head. The glass in the doors exploded and they swung
open, and her father dragged her mother back into the bank.
She was bleeding from the stomach, the blood pouring out

213

of her, spilling onto the clean white marble floor, oozing toward the customers who'd been made to lie down with their hands on their heads.

Celeste stepped over the red ropes of the queue and went from teller to teller with the bag they'd brought. The frightened young women looked at her.

"Just dollars," Celeste said. She found her voice again and felt better now that Vasco had stopped screaming. "Just the dollars," she said. "Quickly." She lifted the M-16 up and brought the muzzle down on the marble counter at the first teller's chest line. The alarm was so loud that she had to say it again. The teller hadn't heard and was picking up peso notes and throwing them into the bag. Paloma came over the ropes and took the pesos out of the bag and threw them in the air and screamed.

"Sólamente dólares!" The teller, shaking, picked out the packages of dollars they had in the till and dropped them in the bag.

"You have to leave her, *papá*, she's dead." Vasco looked at his daughter, then at his wife leaning against the marble desk in the middle of the bank.

"The police are coming, *papá*, we have to go. You have to leave her." Paloma was pulling him by the coat. He looked at his daughter as if she were a stranger. Paloma Vasco had her M-16 slung in a fighting position so that she could maneuver it and at the same time pick up the valise she had dragged from the safe. They heard the sirens in the street. A crowd had gathered across the street and was looking at them. One of the red streetcars that came from downtown San Diego had come to a stop just across the street on the American side.

"Pick up the other bag, *papá! Please!* Pick up the bag! *Papá*, the police." Paloma Vasco looked for a moment at her mother.

She reached down and double-checked that there was no pulse. It was as if she had been born to be a soldier.

Paloma opened up on the police before they could get out of their car, the M-16 cutting through the windshield, shattering it. The bullets pocked the doors of the Mexican squad car, rocking the occupants. There was no going back now. One of the policemen crawled toward the streetcar. They ran out of the bank, Paloma in the lead, Celeste behind her and Vasco dragging his dead wife by the sleeve of her dress, her body bumping over the tracks.

• • •

"I want to thank you for opening the door," Calhoun said.
"Yes, *señor.*"
"I need two tickets for the one o'clock to Mexico City," Calhoun said.
"Señor, I'm afraid that is impossible, the bus is full."
"No, you don't understand . . . I need two tickets for that bus tonight!" Someone threw a rock through the window next door. They heard the crash and the laughter from the crowd.
"I'll give you a thousand dollars for two tickets," Calhoun said. He took a wad of bills he'd taken from Guzman and put them on the counter. "Two thousand." The man watched Calhoun count out the money, his face tarnished by a terrible sweat. "Three thousand then . . . you see, it's my girlfriend. We're going to get married in Mexico City," Calhoun said. "And I can't disappoint her. We're in love and we're running away together," he said. Calhoun stopped counting and looked at the man.

There were big white spotlights in the plaza. The city had moved them in for the festival. The big bars of light cut through the olive trees and shot light on the dark offices above the plaza. Calhoun walked through the revelers who hadn't noticed the riot yet. He headed for Hughes' office. He crossed the street, looked up and saw a light in the window and went up the stairs. A few men in cowboy hats ran down the stairs toward him. One of them looked at Calhoun's face. For a moment they looked at each other. He was one of the waiters at the Escondido, and they recognized each other.

"Ignacio," Calhoun said.

The man said nothing.

"¿Ignacio, qué pasa aquí?"

"El Facismo happens here, *señor* Vincente." Calhoun put his hand on the man's shoulder.

"I *know* you. What are you doing, Ignacio?"

"We've had enough," he said. "For once in our lives we are going to have a voice. For once in our lives, all the people that your kind spit on everyday, are going to spit back." The two looked at each other. It was an odd look, something passing between them as if they'd both understood each other in some way that wasn't normal, yet profound.

"What are you talking about?"

"Tonight we take back what people like you have stolen from us. Tonight all over the country we are taking Mexico back from the gringos and the homosexuals and the Jews." The other men had stopped on the stairs above them.

"Ignacio, shoot him. What are you fucking with him for? He's a foreigner." One of the men took a gun out from the small of his back.

"No. He's all right. Leave him alone. I know this man. The police came to the restaurant. They're looking for him. He's one of us." Ignacio said.

"Fuck him. He's a foreigner, a Yankee. Let's kill him," the other one said. Calhoun looked up, could see that there was blood on the man's hands who wanted to kill him. He was pointing a gun at him.

"I said leave him alone. I know this man. He's one of us," Ignacio said.

"Fuck you," Calhoun said. "No, I'm not. Fuck all of you."

"Ah, he's fucking crazy, Ignacio." The one at the top of the stairs put his gun back into his belt and they started off.

"Can't you see the gringo's crazy? Look at him," another one of them said. "He's fucking bleeding out of his ears."

Calhoun grabbed the last man by the arm. The one that wanted to shoot him.

"I'm looking for Dr. Hughes. Is he here?" The others went on, their boots loud on the stairs. Someone laughed.

"Viva la muerte," the one he stopped said. He tried to push him aside. But Calhoun was too strong. Calhoun let him go.

"The doctor, is he here?" There was more laughter in the stairwell and then they were gone back out onto the street. Calhoun turned and looked at the steps again; they seemed steeper than a moment ago.

Calhoun looked up at the top of the stairs. He heard voices, whispering voices. His mind was playing tricks on him. He was sure of it. He turned back toward the street, saw a group of men run by, wraiths of light and noise. He held the handrail and spoke to himself. He patted his pocket. He had the tickets now. He lit a match and looked at his watch. It was 10:30 exactly. In fifteen minutes he would have to be back on the plaza, ready to leave. He needed the doctor to fix his shoulder so he could drive.

Calhoun climbed the stairs, grabbing the balustrade as he went. He pulled himself up the dark passage. At the top there was a watery yellow light at the end of the hall in front of him. The doors were yellowish shapes and something else, impres-sions of darkness. Calhoun turned and felt his shoulder and walked toward where he knew the office was. It was late but he'd seen a light in the window and took a chance that maybe Hughes would be in, that he could fix his shoulder well enough for him to drive.

"It's Vincent Calhoun." Calhoun knocked on the door. There was no answer. "It's Vincent Calhoun!" It was quiet in the hall, just the watery yellow light and the feel of the thick glass on the door. Calhoun put his head on the door and ran his fingers over the bumpy, cold, obscured glass.

He tried the doorknob, it opened. He swung the door in. The waiting room had been ransacked, all its furniture over-turned. Something was scrawled on the wall in spray paint. The door to the consulting room swung open. Hughes looked at him. He was bleeding between his legs, the blood like satin in the half darkness. Hughes' face was white.

"I need your help. I was stabbed and . . . " Calhoun said looking at him.

"Help?" Hughes said vacantly.

"Yes. I . . . "

"Help?" Hughes said again. Calhoun looked behind Hughes. The consulting room was dark, and then suddenly painted bright by the light from the plaza.

"What happened?" Calhoun said.

"They did something to me. I took a shot. I can't feel anything, now," Hughes said. He hadn't moved. "I took a shot," he said again.

Hughes was sitting on one of the couches in the dark. He could see the blood falling in waves over Hughes' shoes. Calhoun reached for the light switch.

"No! Don't!" Hughes screamed. "Please don't. I'm going to die soon. I don't want to see what they did." Calhoun felt his hand on the switch.

"I could get someone."

218

"No."

"What happened?" Calhoun said. He came across the room. He saw Hughes sitting clearly now. The spotlights from the plaza swept by the window again, giving the room an eerie white dim glow.

"I'll be dead in a few minutes," Hughes said. "I can't feel anything now. Nothing. Maybe . . . four minutes." Calhoun walked close to where the doctor was sitting. His lap was full of blood. He looked up at him. "Why? . . . I didn't even know them . . . There's some alcohol in a blue bottle . . . in there . . . clean the wound with that . . . " Calhoun looked into the destroyed consulting room. "In the drawer . . . there's a butterfly bandage in the drawer . . . inside, fourth down. On the left I think . . . clasp the wound together, pinch it." Hughes was talking like a textbook now, his lips moving but not opening much. Calhoun looked at his lap. "Pinch the edges of the wound together, then apply the dressing so that . . . " Calhoun saw the razor slit in the pants, through to the white underwear, as the light from the plaza got brighter.

"Jesus Christ . . . They've . . . They've . . . Jesus Christ." Hughes stopped talking. Calhoun waited for him as if he had simply had a lapse for a moment. Calhoun reached over and touched him. He was dead. Calhoun walked into the consulting room and switched on the light. They had smashed everything. The table and drawers were pulled open, gauze and blue paper strewn all over the floor. He went to the bottle Hughes had described but it was broken, smashed. He saw something on the floor and stopped, he'd nearly stepped in it. He looked down on the floor and saw it. Saw what they'd cut from Hughes. He backed away, terrified by it. The bright spotlight flooded the room again, moved across the wall, across a crude yoke and arrows spray-painted on the wall.

Calhoun went to the window. He could see the lights below on the plaza swirling helter-skelter, touching the four corners of the plaza. In the lights he saw the rioters and the band still on the bandstand and revelers who didn't realize what was happening and the little lights in the olive trees. He saw Castro's car pull up in front of the Escondido, then make a U turn on the street and park in front of the old clock on the plaza. His cell phone rang.

"Where are you?" Castro said.

"Above you. In Hughes' office."

"Could he help you?"

"No. He's dead."

"Can you drive?"

"I don't know."

"Well, you better get down here, amigo."

"Do you see them . . . the Vascos?"

" . . . No, not yet. We have no protection from my people. No one will help. The fat man is too hot. We go alone tonight."

"I want you to do something," Calhoun said.

"What?"

"Miguel, I want you to drive to the Amigo motel and check room twelve for a girl. Please. I'll come down there and wait for the Vascos. It will only take you ten minutes, maybe fifteen. Please. If she's in the room bring her here to me."

"No."

"Miguel, I'm in love with her. I'm leaving tonight for Mexico City with her. I'll give you all the money if you just go look for her. I can't go, the border patrol is looking for me."

"God damn you son of a bitch." The telephone was cut off. Calhoun watched Miguel's car swerve out into the traffic. He heard the tires and the horn blare. It disappeared up the Avenida. Calhoun's face was suddenly painted by the lights as they swept over the room.

TWENTY-FIVE
The Plaza Tijuana — 10:25 P.M.

The boy had followed Calhoun across the street from the Escondido. Calhoun had sent him away twice. But the boy wouldn't go. He'd wandered off into the plaza as if he were watching out for him. The plaza was still full of people and music. The mariachi band still played on the bandstand. It was pure Mexico for the musicians to ignore the riot. The holiday was reaching its drunken crescendo and no riot was going to stop it.

Calhoun looked at the boy and waved him away. He kept scanning the street, expecting a taxi to pull up with the Vascos. They were late. It was 10:25 and they were supposed to be there already. He knew Miguel would be back with Celeste in a few moments and they would have to leave. It was too dangerous to stay any longer.

A car stopped. Calhoun watched Slaughter get out. His driver took off. He trotted across the street.

"I have to go with you," Slaughter said.

"What?"

"The fucking PFN are looking for me. They came to the Coco Loco looking for me." Calhoun smiled. "They're killing foreigners, Calhoun. Murdering them in the streets," Slaughter said. "They have a list." The Englishman looked scared. He looked at Calhoun, then out into the Avenida. The traffic had slowed, the rioters scaring the usual army of taxis away.

"There's no room," Calhoun said.

"What do you mean?"

"I mean there's no room in the jeep."

"We'll make room," Slaughter said.

"I don't feel like it," Calhoun said.

"You can leave Guzman."

"No. He paid for his ticket," Calhoun said.

"I'll pay you," Slaughter said. "You can't bloody well leave me here to die." Slaughter looked down the street. He could see a band of *milicias*. They were cleaning out another tourist bar.

"Looks like you got a problem," Calhoun said. The music started up on the bandstand. The solitary voice of the singer came over the loudspeakers in the trees. Slaughter looked down the street toward the men.

"Look, Vincente, we're both white men. This is a city of—"

"Of what . . . ? You helped make it, didn't you? You and me. People like us."

"I promise you. We'll come back. As soon as this is over, we'll be partners. I have money in San Diego. Just get me over the wire," Slaughter said. The brassy sound of the mariachis came up over the loudspeakers above them.

"It doesn't matter. You and I are finished. Part of the past. Something new is coming. We're part of the past," Calhoun said.

"What are you talking about? You're crazy."

"Am I? Look around you. Listen to the music. They're not going to take it anymore. It's changing. They've had enough of people like you and me," Calhoun said. The spotlight from the plaza raced over his face.

"Fuck you. You *have* to take me," Slaughter said.

They were coming up behind him and he hadn't even seen them. Twelve or more men crossing the Avenida. They'd

222

spotted the two foreigners and come running. Calhoun could see their brassards.

"Hey, it's the crazy one." It was the man from earlier on the stairs. The one with the bloody hands. He was the leader. Calhoun spit on the ground. Slaughter turned around.

"El Inglés," the man said. "You son of a whore."

"Calhoun, use your gun," Slaughter said. The men laughed. One of them swung a club in the air for emphasis. The other men made a semicircle around Slaughter. The boy ran up and held Calhoun by the jacket, standing between him and the gang.

"He is one of us," the boy said. The band began to play, the rhythm of the music speeding up.

"The gringo has many friends," Bloody Hands said. The other men looked at the boy and smiled and made jokes.

"What friends do you have, *Inglés?*" Slaughter looked at the men surrounding him.

"I got money. I can pay you," Slaughter said.

"Your money's no good tonight," Bloody Hands said. "Everything isn't money." He turned around. *"El Inglés* wants to pay us."

"You're all a bunch of niggers," Slaughter said. The music rose up louder through the speakers. The men dragged Slaughter off toward the fountain at the center of the plaza. The boy hung onto Calhoun's jacket while they did it. They beat the Englishman down in front of the fountain. When they were finished, Bloody Hands climbed in with him and held him under the water.

The jeep pulled up. Miguel was sweating. "She's not there. She left hours ago." Calhoun bent down and held the boy. He gave him a hug.

"I want you to be my father," the boy said.

223

"Okay," Calhoun said. "Relatives do things for each other, don't they?"

"Yes," the boy said. Calhoun pulled him back and looked at him. "I want you to go across the street now. I want you to go into the Escondido and I want you to stay there. Do that for me now."

"No, you need me," the boy said. "You need me to protect you."

"I'm going to be all right. If you want me to be your father, do what I ask." The boy looked at him, then down at the ground and nodded. "I'll come back for you tonight. I promise. You and me and my friend will go to Mexico City together," Calhoun said. "I promise you. Now go wait for me in the bar."

"You promise me?" the boy said.

"I promise you. We leave tonight. Here are the tickets." Calhoun took the tickets out of his pocket and handed them to the boy. The boy took the envelope.

"Okay, I'll get ready. I don't like Tijuana anyway," the boy said.

"Me, either," Calhoun said.

"Will you be my father?"

"Yes. I'll be your father. Now go."

"Amigo, you'll be the worst father in the world," Castro said. He had gotten out of his car and come and stood by the clock. "We'll give them five minutes and then we have to go. The border patrol and DEA were at the motel. They are waiting for you," Castro said. "Hey, amigo, I think this day, I scheduled too much. You were right."

"I told you," Calhoun said. "You always do too much."

"We should have done just half of what we did," Miguel said. He'd sat down on the bench, playing with his cowboy hat as he spoke. A cab pulled up. Calhoun saw Celeste's red

224

hair and ran toward the door. He was happy like he'd never been. In those few seconds, Calhoun felt as if all the bad luck had finally been changed. She looked at him from the back seat. He turned to Miguel.

"That's her," he said. "I knew she'd come." And then Calhoun saw that Paloma Vasco was driving the cab, and it all changed.

TWENTY-SIX
Sonoran Desert — 11:35 P.M.

Which way are we going?"

"What difference does it make?" Calhoun said. He was looking into the jeep's mirror. They'd moved Guzman all the way to the back. The girls were holding hands, Celeste comforting Vasco. They'd left Vasco's father on the plaza. He wouldn't come. He'd gone mad and wouldn't leave his wife's body.

"What's in the bags?" Calhoun asked.

"None of your business," Vasco said. "Just drive."

"It was all bullshit. The whole story about Chile and the bank . . . all of it was bullshit." Calhoun said, looking into the mirror.

"Life is strange and then you die," Paloma said from the back seat.

"Life is strange and then you die. Did you hear what she said?" Calhoun asked Castro. "Did you hear that, amigo?"

"I heard it," Castro said. "Which way are we going?"

"We're going a new way," Calhoun said. "A way we've never been before. Los Tecates."

"Does he know what he's doing?" Vasco said.

"He knows," Celeste said. "I'm sorry, Vincent. I couldn't tell you about . . ."

"Shut up," Paloma said. "Shut up . . . don't talk to him."

"What difference does it make?" Celeste said. "We robbed a bank, Vince. That's why we came to town. We were in jail together, she and I . . . I couldn't tell you. I promised."

227

They went further east on Mex. 2, then turned off suddenly. They were in one of the score of canyons that ran toward the Tecate Mountains. The lights of Tijuana were to the left, a gentle yellow blur. There was a full moon so that you could see cliffs and barrel cacti, a forest of them straight off into the night, sharp and clear. The evil-looking Tecate range beyond that was in front of them.

"I need water," Guzman said from the back. "Water."

"Who is that?" Vasco said. "He smells."

"That, ladies, is the guest of honor," Castro said. Calhoun stopped the jeep and got out and went to the back. They were in a very wide canyon. It was muddy from the rain. They were following a track that Calhoun knew ran back toward the border, then came out just east of Palmdale. He opened the rear door and looked at Guzman.

"Water. I can't stand it anymore," Guzman said. Calhoun got the water they kept strapped to the radiator and came back around to the back and poured a stream into the fat man's mouth. The moonlight glinted on Guzman's face.

"Get out of the jeep. I want to talk to you," Calhoun said to Celeste. He closed the back and went and reattached the canvas water bag to the grill and came around to her door and pulled her out. Paloma grabbed her hand and Calhoun pulled out the forty-five and put it against Vasco's forehead. For the second time, he wanted to kill her.

"Vincent, okay . . . put the gun down." Celeste made Vasco let go. She stepped down from the jeep.

"You see this big Amazon bitch, Miguel? If she even looks at me funny, I want you to shoot her." He put his gun down. Miguel pulled his own gun out and pointed it at Vasco.

"I think you are practicing bad manners, *señorita.* I can correct that. I'm a very immoral man. I'll shoot you," Miguel said. "It makes no difference to me that you are very pretty."

The two of them walked away from the taillights. They could see the yellow play on the spots of water in the canyon from the moonlight, even see that the sand they walked in was red.

"I wish this hadn't happened," Celeste said. Calhoun walked on for a moment. He wanted to stop everything and be alone with her. He glanced back at the jeep, then at her. Her hair was pulled back into a pony tail. He reached for it and held it with his hand.

"For a moment, let's pretend it hasn't . . . Do you remember how I used to come get you . . . We'd walk out there by your old man's ranch." She nodded her head. "Just like this," he said.

He let go of her hair. Celeste bent down and scooped up water from a rill at their feet and cleaned her face. "It was so different then," she said.

He stood above her. His fever had waned. He felt like himself for the first time since the vet had injected him. "I want you to come back with me tonight. Will you do that? I have tickets for the one o'clock bus to Mexico City. I'll have money. Give her what you stole. We won't need it." He helped her up. Celeste shook him away and started to cry. Calhoun looked back at the taillights, red chinks in the night. He noticed there were big clouds forming in the sky.

"It's too late now," she said.

"No. It's never too late. It's not too late for us." Celeste looked up at him, the moonlight in her face, more beautiful than ever.

229

" . . . Paloma protected me in the jail, her father and mother. I wouldn't have survived if she hadn't looked out for me those first few weeks. She's very strong."

"Just tell me if you love me, that's all I want to know," Calhoun said. "Just tell me that." They'd walked far enough away from the jeep that they could hear the sounds of the desert.

"I didn't think there would be water out here," she said. Celeste looked back toward the jeep. He knew that she cared about Paloma and it didn't matter to him.

"You'll still take her to Palmdale like you promised?" she said.

"Yes."

"She won't want to leave me."

"It's up to you."

"When I saw you this morning . . . I got frightened because I felt it right away, what we had, and I didn't want to feel it," she said.

"Me, too, right away." He grabbed her and kissed her. They sank down into the sand on their knees. He knew now without having to say anymore that his bad luck was over. He felt the water soak his knees and fill his shoes, and the softness of the sand, and he knew that it was over.

"This time it will be different," he whispered. "Nothing will come between us again. Nothing." She kissed him and washed his face off with the water and the moon glittered on its surface. He took his jacket off and she washed his shoulder wound, tore the sleeve off his shirt and tied it up fresh. All the time he was telling her where they'd be going, about the boy that he wanted to help, about a place he knew in Cuernavaca that a Frenchman had, cottages near the train station.

"Amigo, we have to go. I saw something." Castro had gotten out of the jeep and walked toward them. Calhoun looked up. He hadn't felt like this in so long. His trousers were soaked. He was stripped to his T-shirt and Mylar vest.

"I'm okay now, Miguel," Calhoun said. They both stood up. "We're going to Mexico City. Tonight." Castro looked at the girl, at her long red hair and beautiful face; he saw that Calhoun looked different somehow.

"I'm happy for you, amigo. But it's time we go. I saw headlights east of us. Just for a moment, but I saw them."

"All right. We'll be in Palmdale in an hour or less," Calhoun said. He took Celeste's hand and walked her back toward the dark red taillights of the jeep.

TWENTY-SEVEN
Base of the Tecate Range — 11:45 P.M.

The full moon hung west of them like a headlight itself. Calhoun had taken a jeep track that ran east toward the Tecate range. The desert had opened to a flat pan that was free of even cactus. He was able to get the jeep up to a good speed, seventy miles an hour. He'd moved Celeste into the passenger seat next to him and put Castro on Vasco, afraid she would try something.

"You don't love him," Vasco said. "Look at him. He's getting old. Look at him. He's finished. I'm young." Celeste turned around and looked at her. She did look young and strong, like nothing could stop her. Calhoun watched her for a moment, afraid to take his eyes off the track too long at those speeds.

"Slow down," Castro said. "It's too fast. We hit a rock and we're fucked." Calhoun had turned off his head and taillights so they could run undetected by the rat patrols that were more frequent near the Tecates. He slowed down, caught Vasco looking at him.

"Coward," Vasco said. "You're a coward . . . you're going to get us all killed."

"Who *is* this bitch that does all the talking?" Guzman said. Calhoun had almost forgotten the fat man was with them.

"It's Mary Magdalene," Calhoun said. The jeep sailed off a dune and then landed. Guzman groaned. Vasco hung onto

233

the strap at her side, her eyes bright with hate in the moon-light. The jeep's speed seemed to be animating her.

"He's sick. I've watched him . . . Do you want a sick man? An old, sick man." She reached over and touched Celeste's shoulder.

"Don't touch her," Calhoun said. He heard Vasco spit. She'd spit on him, on the back of his neck.

"Jesus Christ," Castro said. "She spit on you. She just spit on the back of your head." Calhoun felt Celeste's hand clean the back of his neck, wipe the spit off.

"Why won't you talk to me, Celeste . . . *querida*? You're mine. I'm not sick and I'm not old, and we have money now," Vasco said, leaning with both hands on the strap now, like she wanted to tear it off.

"Stop it," Celeste said. "Just stop it. I'm not what you want." Vasco nearly tore the strap off. She picked herself off the seat. The black T-shirt she'd worn for the robbery sprung to life around her biceps. They were as big as a man's.

"I'm going to kill you," she screamed. "I'll kill you both."

"Woman, I'll pay you five thousand dollars to shut up," Guzman said. He put his hand on the back of the seat, tried to lift himself, enough to see who the girl was, but they were airborne again and the jeep slammed and glissaded to the left. They plowed through two barrel cactuses. The mirror on Calhoun's side was torn off, left hanging. There was silence for a moment as Calhoun fought for control of the jeep. They were on the edge, and he brought it back before they plowed into more cactus.

" . . . I have to turn the lights on," he said.

"You mean we've had no lights?" Guzman said. "Mother of God." Castro laughed. Then he reach over and slapped Calhoun on the back and they both started to laugh. Celeste looked into the back at Castro and the smile on his face.

"I'm going to kill you all," Vasco said.

"Hey, Jesus, don't you have a sense of humor? What's wrong with you?" Castro said. "That was funny. I don't like people without a sense of humor. You can't trust them," Castro said.

"Fuck you," Vasco said. She let go of the strap. They started laughing again, Castro and Calhoun.

"Hey, amigo, I think this is the best ride we've ever had. Don't you think? I mean, you have managed to fill the jeep up with arguing lesbians and a billionaire, a renegade Mexican cop, driven by a lunatic. This is better than *Stagecoach,*" he said.

"I liked the movie," Guzman said quietly. "I liked the picture very much. I like John Wayne very much."

"It's a classic," Castro said. "Of course you like it."

"You know, fat man, you're all right," Calhoun said. "I mean for a billionaire. You're okay." He looked up into the mirror and saw Vasco.

"I think so, too," Castro said. "I like him. *Es simpático.*" The headlights appeared then for just a moment about a mile behind them. They'd hit the same patch of cactus and for the same reasons had been forced to turn on their lights. Miguel saw it in the mirror.

"Vincente, did you see that?"

"Yes."

"How far do you think they are?"

"Four miles, maybe less," Calhoun said.

"I think you better turn off the headlights," Miguel said. The barrel cactus were thick here, and Calhoun knew it was too dangerous to run without light. He waited a moment, looked at Celeste. She was scared. He cared now whether he lived or died. His fingers tightened down on the steering wheel. Love had changed him. It made him calculate.

"It's a gamble . . . bet black, it might come up red," Calhoun said.

"No choice now," Castro said. Calhoun's fingers moved from the steering wheel and depressed the light button. The way in front of him went dark and then slowly, too slowly, the moonlight came back. He hit something and panicked but it was just a rock kicked up against the undercarriage with two loud bumps.

"Who are they?" Guzman said.

"You could say they're businessmen. Like you," Castro said.

"What do they want?" Guzman said.

"Shut up," Calhoun said "What the fuck do you think they want?"

"Give me my gun back," Vasco said. Calhoun looked at Miguel in the mirror. He slowed down, looked at his watch. The luminescent dial said eleven-forty five. If they could get up into the Tecates, he could lose them.

"Give her the gun back," Calhoun said.

"Amigo?"

"I said give her the gun." He heard Castro laugh.

"I'm sorry, I didn't hear you. I thought you said give her the gun back so she could shoot you."

"I said give her the gun," Calhoun said.

"That's a very nice idea, but I'm afraid she'll shoot us."

"She might. But I don't think so. Listen to me." Calhoun downshifted. The jeep slowed so the cactus that had been indistinguishable suddenly looked larger and you could see how thick they were, could make out the white fuzz they had near the needles.

"If you kill us, those men behind us will kill you both. But not right away. Do you understand me? And if you think you can drive out of here, you can't. You'll get lost. Now if you love her, you'll do as I say," he said.

"Give me my gun," Vasco said again. Miguel pulled the automatic he'd taken from her and handed it back. She dropped the clip out and examined it, then reinserted it. She put the barrel at the back of Calhoun's neck. He felt it immediately, cold and heavy.

"Now listen to *me,* you piece of shit." Vasco leaned over the seat, close to his ear. "The girl is mine. You get us out of here and I will let you live." Then she picked the gun up. Calhoun speeded up again, the cactus starting to blur and darken, the Tecate range closer now in front of them, steel blue in the moonlight.

"I told you," Castro said. "People without a sense of humor, don't trust them." He turned around and looked behind them. He saw the headlights again. Then a second pair. "Anyone for ammunition?"

"What's going on?" Guzman said. "Give me a gun, too."

"My hat. I lost my hat," Calhoun said. He tried to remember where he'd left it and couldn't.

Calhoun looked out at the desert; he knew then but he didn't want to think it. He looked at his watch. Five to twelve. He down-shifted and gunned the engine. *There was nothing now but to try to make it into the Tecates,* he told himself. He looked out at the mountains. *Twenty minutes away,* he thought, *only twenty minutes away.* The Tecates had a thick chaparral they could hide in. The sand was changing here. He felt the added strain on the engine suddenly. He was afraid to look into the mirror now but forced himself to. There were two pairs of headlights now. *Two jeeps.* They didn't care about trying to play it coy. They kept their headlights on. It was a race, now.

He looked for any kind of canyon, any depression where he might be able to hide, throw them off. There was nothing, just flat plain endless desert. He tried again, searching to his left, turning his head. Twice he almost hit patches of barrel cactus. Then he saw something, a low spot, to his right. Calhoun slammed on the brakes; the jeep skidded through a long slide to the right like a boat in water.

"We're going to die," Guzman said.

"Shut up, don't say that," Calhoun said. He up-shifted. "No one is going to die," he said. "You understand? No one is going to die." The jeep torqued through the sand and sped up again. Calhoun could feel the frame twisting, the flexing of steel against sand.

Calhoun headed for the depression three hundred yards away. It was a narrow canyon. They were lucky, he'd almost missed it. The jeep sped down the slope into the canyon. Calhoun heard the reassuring sound of water slapping the jeep's undercarriage. Ribbons of liquid silver spun off the tires.

"It's okay," he said, "they won't see us." The walls of the canyon started to grow to six feet, then higher.

"It could dead-end," Castro said calmly from the back. The water started to pool up deeper. They could hear the splashing of it against the frame.

"You should turn up, go west again," Castro said. Calhoun looked for a break in the canyon, the water was getting deeper. He went to the right to ride the sand bank. The creek was quickly turning to something else. He looked at the speedometer—67 miles per hour. He began to slow, not wanting to, too afraid of what he would see behind them. Afraid that he would hear their engines.

Calhoun made a run across the creek, heading for a jeep track that ran up the canyon wall on the other side of a narrow beach. He'd seen it quickly out of the corner of his eye and drove for it instinctively. The engine screamed, torquing out. There was not enough power to pull them forward. *Silica sand,* Calhoun thought. The back tires were still in the creek, the front tires deep in the silica sand in front. It was as if they'd suddenly lost all traction. He down-shifted quickly, let the weight of the jeep carry them backwards into the water. Then stepped on it, the engine roaring again. *"Fuck! Fuck!"*

"What's wrong?" Vasco said.

"Shut up."

Calhoun looked at Miguel. He saw a look on his friend's face he'd never seen before, a distant look, as if for a moment he wasn't there.

"Roll back again. Get in the water. Try again," Castro said. Calhoun put the jeep in reverse, hoping he could back away. They rolled back a foot. He took his foot off the gas for a moment, then stepped on it again. There was a terrible sound of water and mud but no traction either way.

"Fuck . . . "

"What's wrong, Vince?" Celeste asked. Calhoun looked at her.

"Nothing. We have to get out and push, that's all," Calhoun said.

He looked at Castro again. They were both afraid to say it. So neither one did. "You get behind the wheel. Me and Vasco will push." Miguel nodded and slid out of the seat. Calhoun opened the door and stepped down into the sand. He looked at Celeste. She held out her hand and he took it. Their eyes met and he tried to look confident, then let go and walked quickly up the beach. He could feel his shoes sinking in the slick sand. He turned, saw two sets of headlights going past above them on the desert. They'd missed the ravine. He got across the beach and saw the track start up into the mountains. It was only twenty-five or thirty yards away across the beach.

Get across the beach. That's all we have to do, he thought. He turned around and looked to his left. It was a box canyon. The creek slipped into a cave. He could see the moon on the canyon wall fifty feet in front of them. They were trapped. They *had* to cross the beach. He jogged back to the jeep. Miguel was behind the wheel, pale.

"We can try," Calhoun said. "There's a track, just cross the beach."

"All right, we'll try," Castro said.

"Just ease it over, whatever you do. You can't stop once you get going," Calhoun said.

"I know."

"We'll jump in while you're going. Just don't stop if we get you going." Castro nodded, looking back up the canyon.

Vasco dropped out of the car. She'd been listening. "What's wrong?"

"What the fuck do you think is wrong? We're stuck. You have to help me push," Calhoun said.

"What about her?" Vasco said, nodding towards Celeste.

"What *about* her?" Calhoun said. "Come on." He walked back into the creek. He could hear Vasco behind him. He faced the creek and got his hands on the bumper, told Vasco to do the same. They were both facing out towards the water.

"Use your legs on three. Push up. All right?"

"Fuck you," Vasco said. She knelt into position.

"Miguel!"

"On three." Calhoun counted then . . . "*one . . . two . . . three!*" Calhoun felt the tires suddenly spinning, water was thrown across the creek in two rooster tails. He lifted with his legs with every bit of strength he had. Nothing. He heard Vasco grunting just like a man.

"Stop it . . . Stop it!" Calhoun yelled. Calhoun stumbled to Miguel's window.

"It's the fat man," he said. "Too much weight." Castro looked at him. There were lights in the canyon now. Headlights a mile or two back. They'd found them.

"We could stand and fight," Castro said.

"No." Calhoun looked at Celeste. "No. The fat man goes." Calhoun went to the back and pushed Vasco away. She fell into the water backwards. He pulled up the back door. Guzman looked at him horrified.

"I'm sorry," Calhoun said.

"No . . . Please!" Calhoun grabbed Guzman by the shirt and rolled him out like you would a sack of flour. He fell into the water face down. Calhoun bent down and rolled him out into the creek face up and pushed him out of the way. He looked down into the fat man's face, dirt and water on it and moon light.

"I don't want to die," Guzman said. Calhoun let go. The fat man started to float away. He ran back to the rear of the jeep and pulled down the hatch. He heard Guzman yelling and ignored it.

"Again. Come on." Vasco was swearing, hunched down. He heard the sound of engines now. Saw the rat patrols' headlights on the canyon walls. "If you want her to live you'd better fucking push!" he said, then counted. The rooster tails sprung out from each tire again. He heard the grinding water sound. This time the jeep started to move.

"Don't stop pushing," he yelled. They were both backpedalling out of the water. The big tires were moving now, grabbing the silica sand. He looked at Vasco, told her to turn and keep pushing. They fell backwards, both of them, then crawled together toward the moving rear of the jeep, got a hold and started pushing again, sand thrown out at them by the tires. They kept crawling and pushing, the sound of the engine drowning everything else out.

241

Calhoun felt the blow on the side of his head. He fell face first into the sand. Castro had seen Vasco stand up in the rearview mirror and tried to warn him but he hadn't heard. Vasco hit him again with the shovel. Calhoun rolled, saw the spade smack the sand where his head had been. He saw her above him in the moonlight. Vasco had the shovel raised again behind her. The look in her eyes was cold murder and moonlight. Calhoun threw a handful of sand into her eyes and rolled. He heard the shovel come down. Vasco was rubbing her eyes, lifting the spade again, looking for him. He stood up. She turned, wiping her eyes, spitting. Calhoun hit her in the face and she crumpled. He took the shovel out of her hand. She was spitting now, blood and teeth and sand. The jeep kept moving down the beach.

"I can't see," Vasco screamed. She tried to crawl toward the water. He swung once and hit her in the back of the head, smacking her face into the sand. Vasco dropped like she'd been shot. He turned around and ran for the jeep and pushed. It was still struggling. Miguel waved his hand for him to get in. Calhoun heard the engines in the canyon behind him. He saw their headlights a hundred yards away, saw the tops of the jeeps in the moonlight. They had turned on their big search lights and were flooding the canyon with light. He kept pushing.

"Get in," Miguel yelled. "Get in, for god sakes." Calhoun kept pushing, watching the tires roll, the sand shooting out. The rat patrols were nearly on them, their spotlights making a kind of daylight on the beach. Calhoun trotted along to Miguel's side of the car and jumped on the running board. Calhoun looked at the two of them.

"Amigo, what are you doing?" Castro said.

"I want you to keep driving. You can't stop."

"Vincent, get in!" Celeste was reaching for him.

"Miguel . . . You can't stop."

"Hang on!" Castro said.

"I can't. Give me your gun." Miguel handed him his gun, trying to get the speed up so that they wouldn't stall. Calhoun dropped off the running board. He started pushing, trotting alongside them.

"Vincent!" Celeste was screaming now. "Vincent, please get in!"

"I'll try . . . the other door. Miguel. You know you can't stop for me."

"Amigo . . . I . . . " Castro nodded. He understood that Calhoun had no intention of trying to get in, now.

"Miguel, please don't stop," Calhoun said. He was pushing the jeep, looking up at them, trotting alongside. They were only a few yards from the track.

"You're always asking me favors," Miguel said. It was his way of saying good-bye.

"You have to get up in the Tecates. Fifteen minutes and you'll be there." He looked at Celeste. She was trying to get out of the car. Calhoun reached inside and locked the doors automatically. He was trotting more quickly now. Miguel started to speed up.

Calhoun ran along. He wanted to see her face for the last time. Suddenly the jeep was free of the sand. He tried to keep up but couldn't. He saw Miguel looking into the mirror. Calhoun fell on his knees. He followed the jeep up the track. He saw Celeste's face looking back at him. Then they were gone.

Calhoun stood up. He saw the fat man floating in the moonlight. He trotted down toward the water, walked out into the middle of the creek and watched the headlights grow. He heard the roar of two engines. He pulled the hammer back on his automatics and waited. For a moment, he thought he

243

saw the Yaqui girl next to him. And then he was blinded by the spotlights.

• • •

In the morning a buzzard walked across the beach and then another and another. The first picked at the head of the dead girl and then flew slowly over the creek and landed on the hood of a jeep and paused for a moment and sat. There was a big white man in the water face up, two men next to him. There was another jeep abandoned in the sand with bodies inside it. Calhoun had stood in the night and killed many of them. It was late in the afternoon now of the following day, and the canyon was quiet. There was only the sound of the water lapping against the dead and, above all of it, the sky went on clean and blue. Under it, somewhere to the south, a bus pushed on to Mexico City.

saw the Yaqui girl next to him. And then he was blinded by the spotlights.

• • •

In the morning a buzzard walked across the beach and then another and another. The first picked at the head of the dead girl and then flew slowly over the creek and landed on the hood of a jeep and paused for a moment and sat. There was a big white man in the water face up, two men next to him. There was another jeep abandoned in the sand with bodies inside it. Calhoun had stood in the night and killed many of them. It was late in the afternoon now of the following day, and the canyon was quiet. There was only the sound of the water lapping against the dead and, above all of it, the sky went on clean and blue. Under it, somewhere to the south, a bus pushed on to Mexico City.

"Miguel . . . You can't stop."

"Hang on!" Castro said.

"I can't. Give me your gun." Miguel handed him his gun, trying to get the speed up so that they wouldn't stall. Calhoun dropped off the running board. He started pushing, trotting alongside them.

"Vincent!" Celeste was screaming now. "Vincent, please get in!"

"I'll try . . . the other door. Miguel. You know you can't stop for me."

"Amigo . . . I . . . " Castro nodded. He understood that Calhoun had no intention of trying to get in, now.

"Miguel, please don't stop," Calhoun said. He was pushing the jeep, looking up at them, trotting alongside. They were only a few yards from the track.

"You're always asking me favors," Miguel said. It was his way of saying good-bye.

"You have to get up in the Tecates. Fifteen minutes and you'll be there." He looked at Celeste. She was trying to get out of the car. Calhoun reached inside and locked the doors automatically. He was trotting more quickly now. Miguel started to speed up.

Calhoun ran along. He wanted to see her face for the last time. Suddenly the jeep was free of the sand. He tried to keep up but couldn't. He saw Miguel looking into the mirror. Calhoun fell on his knees. He followed the jeep up the track. He saw Celeste's face looking back at him. Then they were gone.

Calhoun stood up. He saw the fat man floating in the moonlight. He trotted down toward the water, walked out into the middle of the creek and watched the headlights grow. He heard the roar of two engines. He pulled the hammer back on his automatics and waited. For a moment, he thought he